NEGATION FORCE

OBSIDIAR FLEET BOOK 1

ANTHONY JAMES

REBELLION

The *Juniper* was a massive, infinitely-complex cylinder of alloy, which remained in stationary orbit a few thousand kilometres above the surface of the cold moon Nesta-T3 and far from any of the twenty-six populated worlds which made up the human Confederation.

While not quite ancient, the orbital had operated as an off-world command and control facility for more than four decades. Such was its strategic importance it had seen three extensive overhauls, during which additional housing, weapons and research modules had been added. The vessel had grown to a length of twenty-one kilometres, with a diameter of two thousand metres. It had reached what the Space Corps' high command referred to as *critical mass,* where it was too costly and too vital to be decommissioned.

The interior was mostly cold, spartan and impersonal. Metal-walled corridors lit in cool blue-white went from laboratories to analysis rooms, or from intel departments to logistics areas. Silent shuttle lifts carried personnel between the many hundreds of floors. Strangers, dressed in uniforms of drab cloths, would speak to each other only to pay lip service to the dictates of civility. The *Juniper* was not an unfriendly place, it was simply home to many people who lived and breathed their work in the Corps.

Captain Charlie Blake walked along one of the corridors, doing his best to weave through the press of humanity. There was a problem somewhere – a big one – and even a fool could pick up the undertones of panic. Everyone was going somewhere. A brisk walking pace was evidently not enough for some of the space station's occupants and a few of them ran, shoving their way through the crowds.

Blake was heading towards the office of a man known for his lack of patience towards incompetents and career ladder-climbers. Lieutenant Caz Pointer strode at Blake's side, uninvited and unwanted. Pointer was short, slim and exceptionally pretty, with long blonde hair and wide, blue eyes that spoke of sweet innocence. It hadn't taken Blake long to learn she was ambitious and sharp as a razor.

"What's going on, sir?" she asked. There was a hint of demand in her tone which Blake found grating.

There was a lot of noise and a distant siren whined in an adjacent area of the orbital. Blake had to raise his voice to make himself heard. "I'm damned if I have any idea, Lieutenant."

"A friend told me they've called up every senior officer, whether on leave or not."

"You heard that?" he asked.

"It's true. The shit must have really hit the fan somewhere. I can't believe nobody's told you what it is, sir."

Pointer was always trying to stir up crap. That was her game – play people off against each other. Blake didn't know if it was something she did for fun, or if she thought it would benefit her career. If it was the latter, it wasn't working out too well for her.

"I'm sure I'm about to hear in precise detail what's going on," he said, increasing his pace so that Pointer struggled to keep by his side in the throng.

"I'd love to hear, sir," she said, trying out the charm.

"No doubt you will, Lieutenant. In due course."

"I can't wait!"

Blake gritted his teeth and kept on walking. He wasn't long past his thirtieth birthday – a good-looking guy and a rising star in the Space Corps. It made him the perfect target for someone like Caz Pointer to latch onto. The flirting might have been an interesting diversion, even knowing what she was like beneath the undeniably attractive surface. However, there was something distinctly off-putting about the ambition in her face which she was too poor an actor to hide.

He stopped at a door – it was a metal slab in the wall of a main corridor somewhere on the 78th level. There were no markings on the door. If you didn't have specific business here, there was no need for you to take an interest in what lay beyond, though the *Juniper*'s security system wouldn't let unexpected visitors through anyway. Blake took a deep breath and stepped forwards. The door opened for him at once, making the familiar whooshing sound as it slid to one side.

"I'll stay out here, sir," said Pointer.

Blake stepped across the threshold, fervently hoping she'd be called elsewhere while he was within. He found himself in a short passage leading to another door. When the outer door closed, the inner door moved aside, allowing Blake into the office beyond.

This office was a large, square room, panelled in wood and with a holographic window on the back wall which showed an image of a warm day on a hillside somewhere a trillion miles away. There were carpets and plants as reminders of home. One wall was covered in banks of screens and there was a compact console on the floor in front of it. A man sat behind a desk. Like seemingly every other Admiral in the Space Corps, he was grey-haired and with a fixed scowl.

"Captain Blake, take a seat," said Admiral Carl Murray.

Blake had met Admiral Murray a couple of times before, though not enough that he could claim to know him well. It didn't take a genius to see Murray was pissed at something. Not just pissed, but absolutely, completely and utterly royally pissed.

"Sir," said Blake, pulling out a chair and keeping his expression neutral.

Murray growled, the noise an indication of his frustration and anger. His deep-set eyes glowered across the table and the furrows on his forehead looked like lines drawn in marker pen. He slapped both palms down hard onto the top of his desk.

"We're screwed," he said. "It's damn well happened! What those idiots said would never happen has come and kicked us where it hurts the most!"

Blake wasn't lacking in confidence, but he wasn't sure if he was expected to say anything. Experience told him that when he was facing a superior officer in a situation where he didn't have any idea what the hell was going on, it was best to keep his mouth shut. It was the right choice.

"There's been a rebellion, Captain. A damned rebellion within the Confederation! Every single metric, every single poll tells us humanity has never been happier, but there's always someone who wants a little bit more."

Blake was aware of the rumours, but to be confronted by the truth came as a shock.

"Roban?"

"Roban *and* Liventor. The two newest planets in the Confederation and the pair of them have gone ahead and set up what they call the Frontier League."

"Which we haven't accepted, I assume?"

"That's for the Confederation Council to decide. I very much doubt they'll accept the secession, but it's a bad situation. A very bad situation."

"What do you want from me, sir?"

Admiral Murray calmed himself with an obvious effort. "You come highly recommended, Captain. You're not the most senior captain we have here on the *Juniper*, but the reports I've received are glowing. You've been selected to lead an important mission."

Blake nodded at the words, sat back and prepared to listen.

CHAPTER ONE

HIGH ABOVE THE Confederation world Atlantis, there was a sudden build-up of energy – a huge cloud of it was forced into local space by the imminent arrival of something forging a way through high lightspeed.

On the planet's surface, a monitoring station situated on the Tillos military base detected the fission cloud through its network of satellites. In a split second, the installation's cluster of processing cores checked the flight plans for every single warship in the Space Corps and determined there was nothing expected. Obeying its programming, the mainframe sent off a series of Priority 1 warnings to numerous personnel, including the base commander and the *Juniper* orbital.

It was early evening and the base was on wind-down. Nevertheless, the warnings reached their intended recipients, spurring several dozen people into activity. The base commander opened a channel to the monitoring station to ask what the hell was going on.

Before the alarm could produce a meaningful response, a number of spaceships exited lightspeed, emerging thirty thousand kilometres above the planet's surface. To a seasoned observer of known warship types, these vessels would have appeared unusual – dark-metal, tapering cylinders with a series of forward-pointing arrays. The alien craft shimmered in an unexpected way, winking in and out of sight like a faulty viewscreen and making their exact locations hard to pin down.

The largest spaceship was something different again. Even when compared to the battleships in the Space Corps' fleet, this one was massive. At eighteen thousand metres from nose to tail, it dwarfed everything humanity had put into the skies, bar the *Juniper* orbital.

It wasn't only the size of the spaceship which made it unusual. This vessel was clad in metal so dark it was almost black. Across its surface, sparks of white and blue crackled irregularly as though the energy generated within the ship was far more than it was able to contain, leaving it to discharge the excess through its outer armour.

There were Space Corps warships stationed in orbit above Atlantis. Once the threat was identified, they moved to intercept.

Meanwhile, on the surface of Atlantis, the lights went out.

———

CAPTAIN HANZO SMITH was sitting in his seat on the bridge of the Resolve class light cruiser *ES Termination*, dealing with the mundane task of checking his personal messages. With a press of one finger, he deleted the most recent arrivals in his mailbox and watched impassively as five more appeared.

News of Roban and Liventor's declarations of independence was an open secret now and it was quite obvious many people amongst both the Confederation Council and the Space Corps had been caught off-guard by the suddenness. So far this evening, Smith had come across at least a dozen different opinions on how best to deal with it and these were only the ones he'd heard about. He'd even received a message from an old acquaintance, now based on Liventor, asking if he wanted to bring the *ES Termination* out to join the rebellion.

"How long are they going to keep us here at Atlantis, sir?" asked Comms Lieutenant Fi Rydale. She made a play of indicating over one shoulder with her thumb. "The rebel scum are that way."

"Lieutenant," he warned her firmly. "This is not a situation that requires humour. These are our people we're talking about."

"Yeah well, they shouldn't steal our planets and our warships then, should they?"

Rydale had a rebellious streak of her own, though it could manifest itself in numerous, often conflicting ways.

"Just be quiet for a moment," said Smith. "I need to think."

"You're the boss, sir."

"Something you would do well to remember, Lieutenant."

Smith was as worried as most people about the news. The Confederation had been settled for decades – ever since the war with the Ghasts was brought to a close. Now there was this. It didn't take a genius to figure out that if the talking failed to bring the breakaway planets back into the fold, there was a chance matters could take a nasty turn. Neither Roban nor Liventor had the warships to repel a determined effort to retake the planets by force, but who within the Confederation wanted to deal with the long-term results of keeping a suppressed population in line? It was unthinkable.

"There's just us, the *ES Stinger* and the *ES Craster* up here," said Lieutenant Lars Jansson, evidently not comprehending his captain's desire for quiet. "They won't send us somewhere else, will they?"

"I don't see why not," said Rydale, pouncing on the opportunity to stick her oar in again. "There's absolutely no need to keep a permanent patrol around Atlantis. Not these days. Who's going to attack? Not the Ghasts, that's for sure. Plus, we've got seven more ships on the ground undergoing routine maintenance. I'll bet they could be up in the air in minutes."

"Six of them, for sure," said Smith, finding himself drawn back into the conversation he'd already tried to put an end to.

"We're about a hundred days from Roban, I reckon," said Jansson. "Whatever's going to happen, it'll be done by the time we get there."

Jansson's statement was wrong on so many levels but Smith couldn't bring himself to open up a new avenue for the discussion to continue, so he pretended he hadn't heard. Smith closed out of his mailbox, which now contained seventeen unread messages. It seemed best to let things settle down a bit and then read the important ones once there was some sort of consensus.

The ES *Termination* was about halfway through its scheduled month-long patrol orbit of Atlantis. When it was over, another vessel would arrive to take its place. It was only within the last year Fleet Admiral Duggan had allowed the numbers of warships in a combat-ready orbit to be reduced from eight to three and that was on the condition of having more of the fleet's light repairs done on the planet's shipyards. It was as though the Admiral feared Atlantis was somehow more vulnerable than all the other worlds in the Confederation.

Personally, Smith thought keeping three or four warships here in total was more than sufficient, especially given the cutbacks within the Space Corps. Atlantis was a beautiful place, for sure, but its economic contribution to the whole was modest. Most people only came here for a holiday on one of its countless beaches, or on the shores of its idyllic lakes.

"We're going nowhere," Smith stated with certainty. "The Fleet Admiral likes to know he's keeping Atlantis safe."

"At least we've got nothing to worry about," said Rydale. "Two more weeks of boredom."

"Which you'll spend planning your holidays," said Smith, aware his lieutenant was due a month's worth of accrued leave as soon as the patrol time was done.

"Already sorted, sir," she stated, unabashed. "The first week will be in one of the resorts on the planet right below us. I got a last-minute deal."

"Sir?"

It was Larsson, his eyes focused on something on his console. Smith detected a note in the man's voice – fear and uncertainty in equal measures.

"What is it?" asked Smith. It was easy to be lulled into complacency on these long patrol assignments and he struggled to bring his mind to the present.

"It's a fission signature, sir - there's something coming."

Smith frowned. "What sort of something? Where?"

"I-I really don't know, sir. All I can tell you is that it's something big and it's not one of ours."

"Where?" Smith asked again, this time with greater urgency.

"Forty thousand klicks away, coming in at a similar altitude to us."

Smith stood, frozen. His jaw worked while his brain tried to figure out which words his mouth should say. A fission signature indicated there was something due to emerge from lightspeed travel in the next few seconds. The larger the signature, the larger the incoming vessel. Whatever was about to arrive, it was huge – far larger than anything Smith had seen before.

"Not one of ours," he said, repeating Larsson's words. The significance of it finally sunk in and he sprang for his seat. "Full alert!" he shouted. "Lieutenant Anand, load the Lambda and Shatterer batteries. Prepare the shock drones and Splinter interceptors. I don't know what the hell is coming, but I want to be ready for it."

"I'm sending a message to the *Juniper*, sir," said Rydale. "I'll coordinate with the *Stinger* and *Craster*."

"Recommend immediate launch of whatever warships there are already warmed up on the ground," Smith said.

"There's an emergency broadcast from the Tillos base, sir - telling us what we already know. We're ordered to intercept whatever it is that's incoming and take any action we deem necessary. That's a full authorisation for weapons launch," said Rydale.

Smith accessed the warship's AI and instructed it to commence evasive manoeuvres. The *Termination*'s gravity engines – their sound constantly present as little more than a background hum – grumbled loudly as they were made to generate maximum output. The warship's acceleration was brutal, though the occupants were shielded from the effects by the vessel's life support modules.

"The fission signature is fading, sir," said Larsson. "Whatever it is, it's almost here."

"Point the sensors towards it."

"You got it," said Rydale.

The main bridge viewscreen came to life – an image of the warship's front sensor arrays projected onto the bulkhead wall. At first, there was nothing – the blackness of space and a scattering of faraway stars. Then, something appeared, filling the display.

"Oh shit," said Larsson.

At that moment, the *ES Termination* lost power. The bridge lights remained on, but the four main consoles did not and the sensor feed faded away to nothing. Smith pushed at a few of the activation points, knowing at once it would be fruitless.

"We've got no weapons," said Anand.

"Our comms are down," said Rydale. "Sensors offline."

"Try the backup comms."

"Switching across now." She clenched a fist in triumph. "Yes! We have life from the backups!"

"Transmit that last sensor recording to the *Juniper*," said Smith, surprising himself with the calmness of his voice.

It was too late. A weapon struck the ES *Termination*. The warship's armour plating crumbled into dust and fell away, along with several thousand cubic metres of the central section which included the bridge and the people on it. The central Obsidiar AI core continued to function, but with the vessel's main power source unavailable it could do nothing to stave off the inevitable.

The unknown weapon was fired a second time and was followed by a high-intensity particle beam, which lit up the *Termination*'s hull in white heat.

The light cruiser wasn't able to withstand such punishment. A second particle beam strike split the *Termination* into three parts. The pieces tumbled and spun as they continued their voyage out into the depths of space.

CHAPTER TWO

LIEUTENANT MARIA CRUZ STIFLED A YAWN. It was coming to the end of her shift, after which she planned to get falling-down drunk to celebrate her twenty-seventh birthday. The evening would be no fun if she let her brain succumb to tiredness before the first drink was poured.

"Want me to cover for you?" asked 2nd Lieutenant Terence Reynolds, watching carefully.

Cruz tried not to meet his eyes. Reynolds was the last person she wanted to be indebted to. "Don't worry about it Lieutenant. Captain Chan will cut my throat if he hears I sneaked off early."

"It's only thirty minutes. He'll never find out."

"Yeah, you'd think."

Cruz slumped in her chair and stared at the bank of screens in front of her. Lists of text flew upwards in a variety of colours and quicker than the eye could follow, each one holding its own piece of information to be transmitted millions of light years to its intended recipient somewhere in the Confederation.

This was the operation area for the main comms hub on Atlantis – it was a big, dimly-lit, low-ceilinged, open-plan room located deep underground in the middle of the Tillos military base. Pretty much all of the planet's comms routed through here, via a large, central processor box. They were sent in by cable or bounced off one of the hundreds of orbiting satellites into the main array. The comms hub encrypted the millions of messages addressed to the other Confederation worlds and fired them off into space to be received by similar hubs on the destination planets.

Cruz looked around the room – there was a total of six personnel working here – four civilian operators and two from the military to oversee matters. Most of the civvies had their heads down and were likely counting time until the end of the shift in the same way Cruz was.

In years gone by, before the latest kit was installed, there'd been as many as two hundred in this room. When it came to new tech, humanity was getting better every year and each new generation of equipment was more reliable and faster than the stuff preceding it. In fact, there was hardly any need for six people in the hub these days. Cruz thought it her great misfortune that Terence Reynolds was one of them.

"Go on, get yourself away," said Reynolds, giving her a wink. "Have a drink for me and don't do anything I wouldn't do, if you know what I mean."

Cruz shuddered inwardly at the lecherous smile on his face and the way his gaze lingered on her chest. Reynolds was distinctly not invited to the evening's festivities.

"It's only another twenty minutes. Not worth the chance," she said firmly, hoping he'd get the hint and shut up.

The message got through and Reynolds fell quiet, though he didn't immediately take his eyes away from her breasts. Not for the first time, Cruz played through a mental scenario in which she punched her subordinate firmly in his scruffy, bearded face.

With ten minutes until the scheduled end of her shift, it

happened. Without warning, the lights went out and the screens on every console in the room went utterly dead. A moment later, the lights came back but the consoles remained off. The two exit doors were designed to open in emergency situations. One remained completely shut, whilst the other juddered a few inches along its metal runners before coming to a halt. A distant siren wailed.

"What the hell?" Cruz asked, too surprised to be alarmed.

She leaned forward and pressed the emergency reset button. Nothing happened, so she pressed it several more times for good measure. The others in the room were alert now – heads above the level of their consoles like mice looking for danger.

"Ramps, check the main power terminal!" shouted Cruz.

Manoj Ramprakash did as he was asked, taking three quick strides to a metal wall-mounted box with a single screen on one side. "It's dead, Lieutenant."

"Restart it."

"There's no response. I can't get anything from it."

Cruz was momentarily lost and panic rose within her. *Probably a test exercise* a voice inside whispered. The idea calmed her at once.

"What should we do, Lieutenant?" asked Reynolds. "The internal network is down. There are no comms in or out."

At that moment Cruz remembered something she'd been taught once, many years ago by one of the Space Corps' longest serving officers. She couldn't remember his name – at the time he was just another dodderer with a long list of improbable stories. He'd mentioned something to her which she remembered now.

"Residual power," she said.

"What?" asked Reynolds, his jaw hanging open stupidly.

"Let's find out if it works," she muttered to herself. She raised her voice. "Ramps, go and find someone. If this is an exercise, tell them I'm going to be really pissed off."

"Even if it's Captain Chan?"

"*Especially* if it's Captain Chan."

Ramprakash saluted limply and jogged towards the nearest exit door, still uncertain if there was any need for panic.

It took a few attempts and some experimentation before Cruz figured out how to tap into the tiny reserves remaining within the Tillos base's three massive Gallenium power generators. Her console fired up, each of the five screens awaiting input.

"There's no message queue," she said. "Shit."

"What do you mean, there's no message queue?" said Reynolds.

"There's nothing waiting to go out."

The remaining personnel gathered around her console. They exchanged worried glances, each experienced enough to realise what this meant.

"The whole satellite network must be offline," Operator Larry Keller said.

"Worse than that," Cruz corrected him. "We're not getting anything via the cable. There's nothing communicating."

"That's not possible," said Reynolds. "The whole planet can't possibly have shut down."

The words were logical, but the evidence in front of them couldn't be argued. The comms network across the entirety of Atlantis had failed. It was inconceivable, yet here it was happening.

She soon found the situation was even worse than a complete failure of the planet's comms.

"I can't get the doors open, Lieutenant," said Ramprakash, swallowing hard.

"There's no backup power?"

"I tried – everything's dead. I can't even get a light on the override panel. The south door's open a crack, but there're no lights in the corridor."

"We'll have to wait for someone to come and get us out," said Cruz.

"How long is that going to take?" asked Reynolds. "If this is as bad as it looks, we could be stuck here for hours. Days, even."

A sound reached them, distant and muted. It was like a thousand claps of thunder coming from a storm of unspeakable size. The rumbling continued for a few minutes, whilst the hub personnel remained frozen in place, unable to do anything but listen. The noise died off, to be replaced by a sporadic rumbling.

"Explosions," said Cruz.

"It can't be. Maybe it's a spaceship coming in to land."

"That's no spaceship."

With no answers to be found and the situation suddenly a whole lot worse, Lieutenant Maria Cruz crinkled her nose, grimaced and then swore.

———

SERGEANT ERIC MCKINNEY shivered in the chill of the air conditioning which blasted in through the vents of his armoured patrol car. He tried for the dozenth time to shut the system off, before accepting the undeniable truth – it was jammed open and the vehicle would require a visit to the Tillos maintenance yard. He cursed the missing soldiers who'd forced him out here and tried to convince himself he was warm instead of freezing cold.

An imperfection in the seat padding prompted him to shift position. The cockpit of the car was spartan and badly-worn, consisting of six seats clad in ripped beige cloth, a basic dashboard and a broken ventilation system. It smelled of sweat and stale grease, with an underlying edge of something metallic. McKinney peered out through the reinforced plastic windscreen which had begun to cloud as it reacted with whatever crap the environmental guys denied was floating in the air.

"Man, that feels good," said Corporal Johnny Li, holding out his hands to the vents. "Don't you think, Sergeant?"

"You must have balls of ice," said Rank 1 Trooper Martin Garcia from the back seat.

"Let's find these AWOL bastards and get back to base," muttered McKinney, his knuckles white on the control joystick.

"Yeah, I've got a red-hot date with that new replicator they installed over by the Obsidiar labs," said Webb, the final occupant of the car. "Some of the guys reckon they haven't locked down the alcohol dispensers."

"That's why we're out here, you shit-for-brains," said Garcia. "Someone probably got drunk and went missing."

"Not someone, *several* someones," said McKinney. He hadn't told the others the suspected reason nine of the troops stationed on the base were missing, but Webb had stumbled upon it. "On the off-chance they haven't repaired the replicator and I catch any of you going near it, I'll kick the crap out of you and have you docked a month's pay."

"I hear you, Sergeant," said Webb. He grimaced and rubbed his chin ruefully. "I'm out of leave for the next four months. I don't think I can stand to stay dry so long."

"Not my worry," said McKinney. "Now let's focus - if the colonel finds out what's happened, he'll have no choice but to sack everyone involved."

"It'll be their own fault," grumbled Li. "Not that I want them to be discharged, of course," he added hastily.

"There are times I wonder about the common man and woman," said McKinney, shaking his head.

He steered them along the deserted roads, past the main administrative building and then into the eastern barracks area. The Tillos base was not a place for romantics, nor those with an eye for beauty. Each building was a mundane cuboid, with the occasional window to break up the monotony. McKinney had long thought it was like living amongst a hundred square kilometres of prisons, except the base food replicators were marginally better and there was a bit more privacy when you needed to take a crap.

It was the middle of the night but the base was lit up in an average approximation of day, using a hundred thousand different sources of illumination. In times gone by, Tillos had operated around the clock, though extended shifts were no longer required and the base had fewer than one quarter its peak number of personnel. Forty years of peace resulted in steady cutbacks to the Space Corps' annual budget, gradually eroding the capabilities of some of the more far-flung bases.

Li pressed his face to the side window. "There's no way we're going to find anyone out here, Sergeant."

The patrol car left the last of the eastern barracks behind, emerging onto the edge of the main landing field. McKinney stared across the kilometres of starkly-lit, flat, reinforced concrete, the backdrop of rugged mountains lost in darkness. From the low height of the patrol car cockpit, it wasn't easy to spot any of the three vast docking trenches in which some of the Space Corps' largest vessels could berth during repairs and maintenance. The closest trench was only visible because of what was sitting in it.

"When is the *Impetuous* due to leave?" asked Garcia. "It's been sitting here for weeks."

"I'm not sure it's going anywhere soon," said McKinney. "Last I heard they'd taken some kind of super power source out of the hull and they're going to break the rest down for parts."

"Shame."

The *ES Impetuous* was only partially visible – two-point-five kilometres of the Space Corps' finest destructive technology. It was little more than an elongated wedge, with turrets and domes protruding through its plating. McKinney shivered again at the sight – the *Impetuous* was just one ship amongst many in the Corps. In the wrong hands it could wipe out entire planets with its incendiaries.

"It never saw battle," he said.

"And now they're pulling it to pieces," shrugged Li. "What else were they going to spend the money on?"

"My pension," said Webb.

"No sign of runaways, Sergeant," said Garcia, leaning forward to get a better look. "You'd have to be pretty stupid to set off this way."

"Your point being?"

"The replicator must be a couple of thousand metres behind us, Sergeant."

McKinney nodded. "You're right – we've come far enough." He gave one last, wistful look at the *ES Impetuous* and reached out for the patrol car's control stick. "Let's get back."

"What's that over there?" asked Garcia, pointing. "Is that the way into the underground bunker?"

"It is," said McKinney, squinting at the low, square building a few hundred metres away to their right. "That's the maintenance entrance."

"Somebody left the door open."

"Yeah," said Li.

"Maybe we should take a look."

McKinney took a deep breath – the underground bunker was off-limits, except for the specially-designated staff who worked inside. The Corps did its secret stuff in there, not that it was easy to keep anything hidden when there were so many mouths eager to reveal gossip.

"If we get caught." He left the sentence unfinished.

"What if *they* get caught, Sergeant? It'll be a one-way trip out of the Corps."

"I'm going to personally kick each and every one of them in the balls when I find them," said McKinney through gritted teeth.

Before he could turn the vehicle in the direction of the maintenance entrance, the lights went out on the Tillos base. One moment there was artificial daylight, the next there was an absolute darkness, as though nothing in the world existed. The engine on the patrol car died – there was no shuddering last gasp, it simply cut out, dropping the vehicle six inches onto the ground with a heavy thump.

"What the...?" said Garcia.

"A power cut?" said Li incredulously. "I didn't think that sort of crap happened anymore."

"Why is the car affected as well?" said McKinney, not really expecting an answer.

The four men sat for a few seconds and their eyes gradually adjusted to the night. Where there had previously been nothing, edges and hints of shapes became visible. McKinney reached for his gauss rifle without knowing quite why he did so.

"What now, Sergeant?"

"We should get back and find out what's going on."

McKinney pulled at the door release handle. Before he could open the door, something filled the night with a light so pure and so intense he was convinced his eyes would be left with permanent damage. A series of plasma explosions detonated along the length of the ES *Impetuous*, ripping enormous holes in its armour. Something else – a particle beam – struck the vessel, igniting the metal and melting it into a shapeless mass of alloys and pure, liquid Gallenium.

Inside the patrol car, the soldiers ducked instinctively. The *Impetuous* was a long way away, but the roiling clouds of plasma expanded with a roar, bringing an intense heat with them. McKinney closed his eyes and felt the patrol car shake as it was engulfed.

"Oh shit," said Li.

McKinney opened his eyes and blinked to try and clear the speckling of motes which danced elusively across his retinas. Far away, the *Impetuous* continued to burn and the glowing remains of its hull cast a sullen illumination by which McKinney could just about see. Where it had been freezing cold, now the air was warm and carried the scent of superheated metal, drawn in through the vents. He pushed the driver's door. It wouldn't open, so he pushed harder.

"Stuck," he grunted.

"Mine too," said Webb, banging a shoulder against his own door.

Swearing loudly, McKinney leaned back and kicked at the inside of his door with the sole of a foot. With a shudder, it opened, letting in a draught of hot air. He rolled out onto the concrete, pulling his rifle with him. The others followed by climbing over the seats and coming out after him. The exterior of the car was burning hot and they were forced to move away quickly.

"What now?" asked Garcia in a fierce whisper.

McKinney saw the man's face as a lighter shape in the darkness, his expression unreadable. Before he could respond, McKinney sensed something in the air above them – something vast and dangerous.

"Get to the bunker!" he said.

They ran from the smouldering ruin of the armoured patrol car, rifles clutched firmly in their hands. The entrance to the building wasn't far and McKinney hoped they'd make it without being targeted by whatever it was flying overhead. Luck was on their side and the four of them reached the building, where they sprinted through the open double doors.

Behind them, the semi-darkness was dispelled by a thousand plasma blasts, this time centred on the barracks and administrative areas of the base – the place where most of the personnel would be sleeping. McKinney could only watch numbly as further waves detonated amongst the buildings, blanketing the installation in flaming death.

CHAPTER THREE

FLEET ADMIRAL JOHN NATHAN DUGGAN felt as if he was under personal attack. Lights on his desktop communicator flashed to tell him no fewer than eight Priority 1 personnel were trying to reach him. Meanwhile, seventy-three new messages had arrived in his mailbox in the last sixty seconds. As if that wasn't bad enough, one of his security screens showed him there was a queue building outside the (presently sealed) door to his office.

He looked out of his window, half-expecting to find a carrier pigeon with a note attached to its leg waiting for him on the sill. Instead, there was only the sight of rain falling like a mist through the artificial light, drenching the thousands of buildings which comprised the Tucson Space Corps base on New Earth.

"I'm getting too old for this crap," he muttered angrily. Duggan was well into his eighties, though medical advances ensured he was physically in decent shape with aches and pains kept to a minimum. Certainly, his mind had lost none of its sharpness.

"Override request on main door from Councillor Dawson,"

announced his personal assistant Cerys. Cerys wasn't a real person - the infuriatingly friendly voice was generated by a node from the base AI, which was assigned purely for Duggan's use.

"Denied," said Duggan. "Keep that damned door shut!"

"Request understood," said Cerys.

"It's an order, not a damned request," he replied testily.

The AI was well-enough programmed to realise there was no requirement for it to respond.

"It's past bed-time. Why are these people still here?" Duggan continued, aware he was becoming what his wife called *cantankerous* in his old age. To add insult to injury, she took great delight in referring to his old age as *dotage*. The thought almost - almost - made him smile.

He stalked up and down the considerable length of his office. There was a vase of fresh flowers on a side table, filling the room with their scent. Normally, he'd have appreciated them, but today the smell was cloying. When the going got tough, Duggan preferred the sharp tang of cold metal. For some reason, being close to spaceship-grade alloy concentrated his mind. Not that he got to fly many of the fleet's warships these days, much to his chagrin.

Duggan was annoyed. He'd underestimated the strength of feeling from Roban and Liventor and the failure didn't sit well. With a bit more foresight, he could have likely nipped it in the bud by taking steps to prevent the hijacking of the warships stationed there. Admiral Talley – a good man – was already on his way in the Hadron battleship *ES Devastator* and was currently seventy days into the eighty-day trip.

Aside from that, the Confederation Council were doing the thing they did best in a crisis – squabbling and procrastinating.

Duggan could tell which way things were going; he could smell it like a pile of corpses rotting upwind. The bastards were going to piss around until Duggan took charge. If the outcome was favourable they'd be the ones on the front pages, basking in the glory. If the outcome was bad, they'd do everything possible to blame the Space Corps.

The trouble for the rebels was, there'd been no fewer than three solid Gallenium discoveries from the fleet's prospectors in the last six months. Soon, the Confederation would be awash with the stuff and the reserves on Roban in particular would no longer be so important.

If it wasn't for the loss of face involved in front of the Ghasts, there'd be no pressing reason to prevent the secession. The Ghasts probably didn't care either, Duggan thought sourly. All-in-all, it was a problem the Confederation neither wanted, nor needed and one to which the only acceptable outcome - whereby Roban and Liventor re-joined the political union - would lead to years of unrest on those two planets.

"On the plus side, it can hardly get any worse," he said. Duggan wasn't a superstitious man, but he was wise enough to know when he was tempting fate. "It can hardly get *much* worse," he corrected himself.

"Priority 1 communication – Admiral Carl Murray," announced Cerys.

Duggan hadn't blocked everyone's ability to contact him. His admirals were amongst the few exceptions to the temporary lockdown he'd imposed on his communicator.

"I will speak to Admiral Murray."

A voice crackled through the speaker. "John? It's Carl. Something bad is happening."

It was immediately apparent that Murray was worried. More than worried – petrified. Murray was one of the most competent officers in the Corps and Duggan had never once seen him flustered. A coldness seeped into his bones.

"What's the matter?"

"We've completely lost contact with Atlantis. All of the local fleet warships have gone offline and dropped off the network."

"How reliable is this information?"

"I'm seeking corroboration on the specific numbers."

"Clarify that for me. You're looking for verification of the details, but not whether we've actually lost contact with an entire planet?"

"No. That is a known fact, sir."

Duggan had a sinking feeling and memories from forty years ago came flooding back. "They've finally come for us."

Murray didn't need to ask questions. "What are we going to do?"

Duggan had no immediate answer to give. Only moments ago, the frontier rebellion had been a major issue, completely occupying his thoughts. Now the problems in the Tallin sector had become little more than a distinctly unwanted distraction.

———

ON THE BRIDGE of the Crimson Class destroyer *ES Determinant*, Captain Charlie Blake took a deep breath. "Powering up the engines. Lieutenant Pointer, please confirm we have clearance to depart."

"Yes sir!" she replied, her voice eager. Pointer made a few gestures across her console. "We have clearance codes from the *Juniper*'s flight AI. The hangar bay doors should open at any moment."

Blake closed his eyes for a brief second, wondering what he'd done to deserve having Caz Pointer as his comms operator for a flight as long as the coming one. He glanced across, taking in the expression of triumph on her face as well as the skin-hugging tightness of her uniform. He looked away quickly.

At the console to his right was 2nd Lieutenant Gabriel Rivera, an officer whom Blake had never met until just a few minutes ago. Rivera was of average height and build, with dark hair and a brow which stayed permanently lowered. Blake was sure the man was skilful enough with engines – the Space Corps usually weeded out the incompetents pretty quickly.

Commander Cain Brady made up the last of the destroyer's standard crew of four. Brady was tall and slim, with the features of a fiftieth generation New Earther.

Blake hadn't met Brady before today either. Some captains in the fleet were senior enough to insist on having their own crew. Others, such as Captain Charlie Blake, had to make do with a random selection from the personnel pool.

"Calculating journey time to Roban at maximum lightspeed," said Rivera. "Eighty-nine days."

Blake couldn't even pretend he was happy. "Nearly three months at lightspeed. Maybe the rebels will come onside before we get there. It's a long way to go for a simple show of strength."

"How many others are they sending?" asked Pointer.

"I don't think Admiral Murray knows himself. This is a last-minute job to make it seem like the Space Corps is actually doing something. I've been told to take orders from Admiral Talley on the *ES Devastator* when we arrive. Maybe it'll all be sorted out by then."

"You were *specially* chosen though, sir."

"Yeah." Blake didn't tell her he fully believed he was chosen simply on the basis he was on the *Juniper* when news of the rebellion came in and because he was the most familiar with the Crimson Class – not because he'd caught the eye of high command.

"In the meantime, there's the flight to look forward to," said Pointer. "A long, boring flight."

"A long, boring and vitally important flight," he corrected her.

"We won't need to shoot anyone, will we? I mean, they're going to back down as soon as the *Devastator* drops into orbit?"

"Anything can happen in situations like this," Blake replied with a grim smile. "Fighting is what you signed up for, isn't it?"

Pointer's look of confidence faltered. She talked the talk but wasn't long out of training and she hadn't encountered anything more dangerous than a malfunctioning food replicator. *Neither have most of us,* Blake thought to himself. *Peace has its downsides.*

Minutes passed and the last remaining personnel cleared from the floor of the hangar bay. The red warning lights continued to strobe and the bay doors remained closed.

"Why haven't they opened?" asked Rivera. "It's taking too long."

Blake agreed. "Lieutenant Pointer, kindly ask someone why we're sitting here waiting."

The answer wasn't long in coming. "Erm...our permission to depart has been rescinded, sir."

"That's not what I expected. Please confirm."

"I can confirm our permission to depart has definitely been rescinded," said Pointer.

"This is the part where you tell me why, Lieutenant."

Pointer's face fell at the rebuke. "I'll check, sir."

Not so tough after all, thought Blake, taking little satisfaction from the discovery. He gave her a few seconds. "Well?"

"There's a Priority 1 hold on our departure, sir."

"What the hell? Only Admiral Murray has the authority for that. He's the one sending us on this mission in the first place. You've overlooked something, Lieutenant – find out what it is and do it quickly."

Pointer looked miserable. "I'm sure that's what this code means." Something lit up on her console. "It's Admiral Murray, sir. He wants to speak to you – in private."

This wasn't expected. Blake put in his earpiece. "Sir?"

The tension in Murray's voice was unmistakeable. From his tone it sounded as if someone had his balls wired to a high-voltage generator and were threatening to flip the switch. "I'm changing your mission, Captain. You're no longer going to Roban – your new destination is somewhere far more dangerous."

"Where are we going, sir?" he asked, not caring if the others of his crew overheard.

Murray didn't answer directly. "We're under attack, Captain and have lost contact with Atlantis. We've been taken by surprise."

Blake opened his mouth while his brain raced through the possibilities. He could only think of one and he spoke it before realising it was surely wrong. "Is it the Ghasts?"

"No, not the Ghasts! Our alien cousins are keeping up their side of the peace treaty admirably. If it was the Ghasts, I might not be so angry." It sounded as if Murray wanted to hit something or someone.

Blake hated to appear stupid, but he'd been backed into a corner and given no alternative. "Then who?"

"That's where you come in. We think it's the Vraxar but have no way to confirm. It seems likely they've finally come for us."

"Have they..." It was hard to say the unthinkable. "Have they destroyed Atlantis, sir?"

"No. We don't think so. We've lost contact with the planet, nothing more."

"No contact at all, sir? How?"

"It's happened to us before, Captain."

Blake racked his brains, trying to recall what he'd learned about the brief Estral wars forty years ago. Admiral Murray wasn't in the mood to allow him thinking time.

"There's been a change of plan," he said. "The rebels will

have to wait for the moment. As I mentioned - you have a new destination, details of which I'm sending to the *Determinant's* navigational system."

Blake felt something clench in his stomach. It was an unfamiliar feeling and he couldn't decide if it was fear, excitement or both. "Are we going to Atlantis?"

"You will be joining a fleet of other Space Corps vessels – Response Fleet Alpha. We don't have many warships out here in the Garon Sector – we only have a few plus the *Juniper*. This orbital won't be taking part in the action."

"I understand, sir. Rendezvous with Response Fleet Alpha and then take appropriate action once we reach Atlantis."

"That's exactly what you're going to do, though in this case *appropriate action* means *blow the crap out of the alien bastards.* Captain George Kang has seniority and he'll be in command."

"Sir."

"Now get to it. At high lightspeed you should reach the rendezvous point in less than four hours. I've had the *Juniper's* AI upload some additional details to the *Determinant's* memory arrays. Make sure you become familiar with them."

"Sir." Another thought came to Blake. "What of the Ghasts? Will they help us?"

"Leave the Ghasts to us, Captain. Goodbye and good luck."

The connection ended and Blake removed his earpiece. The others looked at him, their faces as pale as his. There was little privacy on the bridge of a warship and there was no way they could have failed to get a good idea of what was going on.

"We've got clearance again," said Pointer.

The *Determinant's* front sensor feed showed the external doors in the *Juniper's* hull retracting into the space station's thick alloy walls. The process took less than a minute, with huge Gallenium-drive motors hauling the countless tonnes of metal into their recesses.

"I've got the details of our new destination," said Rivera. "Planet Atlantis, with a stop-off a short distance out."

Blake nodded in response. He activated the *Determinant's* autopilot and the spaceship rose silently from the bare-metal floor. The vessel's gravity drives thrummed and the smell of hot metal drifted in through the bridge air vents. The *ES Determinant* flew smoothly out of the hangar, emerging high above the surface of Nesta-T3.

"Loading up the fission drive for a jump to Atlantis," intoned Rivera.

Ten seconds later, the destroyer – an eleven-hundred-metre sleek wedge of near-solid metal – launched into lightspeed. The crew onboard were aware of the transition as a passing sensation somewhere between giddiness and nausea which was rapidly suppressed by the life-support modules.

"Two hundred and thirty minutes to our destination, sir," said Lieutenant Rivera.

"This is it, folks. We've been thrown in at the deep end. Lieutenant Pointer, we're carrying a standard contingent of forty-two soldiers who are in their quarters below, wondering what the hell is going on. Please advise them where we're going." He grimaced. "If this is the Vraxar, they've picked a bad time to come and say hello."

Pointer nodded dumbly in response. The enormity of the situation and the dangers ahead had evidently sunk in.

While Pointer passed on the message to the troops below, Blake lay back in his seat, finding it hard to get comfortable. The *Determinant's* data arrays had been populated with information relating to the upcoming mission, as well as the few details known about the alien race Vraxar. What stood out most for Blake was the lack of numbers in Response Fleet Alpha. *Seven warships,* he thought. *Four of them destroyers. It looks like Captain Kang has a Galactic – I suppose that's some good news.*

Whichever way he tried to spin it in his mind, the inescapable conclusion was that a tiny fraction of the Space Corps fleet was expected to take on what was surely an advanced, hostile alien foe. In the circumstances death seemed likely, if not certain.

CHAPTER FOUR

"HOW LONG WILL the batteries powering these lights work?" asked Manoj Ramprakash, looking about the room as if the answer was to be found etched into the ceiling or the walls.

"We should get a few weeks out of them, Ramps," said Larry Keller.

"Can't we divert some power to the doors or something?" asked Debbie Nelson, with her eye pressed to the gap between the south exit door and its thick frame. She thumped the door with the palm of her hand, hardly producing a sound from the thick, unyielding alloy.

"What do you think we're doing over here?" said Francis Akachi. He crouched over an access panel in the floor, next to Keller. They were studying something and Keller had a battery-powered diagnostic tablet in his hand.

"I don't like it," said Nelson. "There's something seriously wrong – I know it."

"It's just a power failure, Debbie. A bad one, but still just a power failure."

A few metres away, Lieutenant Reynolds was standing at

Lieutenant Maria Cruz's shoulder, leaning in a little too close. "How are you getting along, Maria?" he asked softly.

Cruz suppressed a shudder at both his proximity and use of her first name. "You will refer to me by rank, Lieutenant. As for how I'm getting along, you can see I'm still trying to get the main comms array back online."

She pushed fingers through her dark hair in frustration and dragged her chair a little further away from Reynolds. Whatever residual power remained in the base generators, it was sufficient to keep her console running at a very low level. The problem was, the really important stuff – like sending a distress signal to one of the Confederation's other hubs - required the main transmitter array to be online and there was nowhere near enough power for that.

"Did you hear that?" asked Nelson. "I think I heard another explosion!"

"I hope not."

There was a distant rumbling, deep and heavy. The reverberations from it caused some of the wall panels to buzz with the vibration.

"Crap, what is going on, Lieutenant?" asked Keller. "That sounded closer than the last ones."

"We're under attack," said Cruz, repeating the same line she'd already told them. "Someone's attacked the base."

"Who would do that?" asked Nelson. "This is the Space Corps you're talking about. There's no one capable of attacking a Space Corps base."

The sound of further explosions reached them – this time a series of blasts that went on for almost a full minute.

"Coming closer," said Nelson, her eyes wide with fear.

"It'll be the Ghasts again," said Reynolds. "I never did trust those barbarians after what they did to Angax and Charistos."

"That was more than forty years ago," said Cruz. "We're at peace."

"They're backstabbing bastards," Reynolds insisted. "If it'd been my choice, we'd have finished them when we had the chance. Now look what's happening."

"Lieutenant, be quiet," said Cruz, trying to keep a lid on her growing anger. "You're not helping."

She noticed something unusual and peered at her main screen. "When did they swap out that encryption processing module on the main array?" she asked. "You remember? When the old one burned out."

"Five months ago," said Keller at once. "They fitted a new single-core unit to replace the whole cluster. One core to replace a cluster! I had a look at the specs – we're getting thirty percent of our cycles from that single unit."

"We still have six of the old clusters, each with eight encryption cores," said Nelson. "When they told me the new core was close to twenty times faster than the individuals in the cluster, I was like *wow!*"

"What does this mean, then?" asked Cruz. The operators could be a gold mine if you asked them the right questions.

Keller came over and studied her screen. "The new core hasn't slowed down," he said.

"Is that expected?" she replied. "The other forty-eight have all throttled to five percent because they aren't getting enough power. The new one is still operating at maximum."

"It's an Obsidiar processor," said Ramprakash, as if that explained everything.

Cruz turned to look at him. She knew how everything worked and could operate the comms array blindfolded, but the operators knew the underlying tech far better than she did. "What's one of those? They didn't think to fill me in."

"New self-powering stuff they've started turning out of the fabs. Super expensive and super fast. I've got a friend over on the *Juniper* who reckons we're the last in line for a full upgrade. They've done the other hubs already. Typical eh? We're always the last."

"Oh yeah, I knew that," said Reynolds.

"Right," said Keller.

Cruz pursed her lips, wondering if having a self-powering encryption processor brought them any new options. The main transmitter array was still offline so there was nothing new to encrypt, yet the core was still churning away at something.

Keller saw her look of concentration. "The algorithms keeping the existing databanks encrypted change every few nanoseconds," he said. "That's what's using up all our processing cycles. It doesn't show up on your console, but the algorithm switch has slowed down since the other clusters went into throttle mode."

She looked at him and he smiled.

"Thanks, Larry. I'm glad you tech guys know your stuff."

"No worries, Lieutenant."

Keller moved off towards his own console, leaving Cruz with her thoughts.

"Shame about your birthday drinks," said Reynolds, getting into her personal space again. "Maybe you'd like to celebrate with me when we get out of here."

Her mouth automatically chambered the response *Piss off*. Her brain intercepted the words a moment before delivery and replaced them with, "Not going to happen, Lieutenant."

There was another explosion, this one seeming to be almost on top of the hub room. Cruz got the inescapable feeling something was coming and she wouldn't like whatever it was.

SERGEANT ERIC MCKINNEY felt like he'd entered a strange, parallel universe – a place in which the impossible happened frequently and where he was required to figure his way out of a combat situation in which he had no intel, no commanding officer and, worst of all, no idea what the hell he was meant to be doing or why. None of his squad carried a communicator and the one in the patrol car had stopped working when the power died. McKinney could handle himself, but he would have appreciated some advice right at this moment.

The four of them were still on the surface, hiding within the maintenance entrance to the underground bunker. Whoever it was attacking the installation, they'd not left much standing and every so often another plasma missile would strike what little remained.

"The lifts aren't working," said Garcia, kicking the featureless metal of the left-hand bank of doors.

"No shit?" said Webb, looking outside. Fading light from distant fires played across his high cheekbones and reflected from the sheen of sweat on his face.

"We've already established there's no power to the lifts," said McKinney. He cast his eyes around the darkness of the room, not sure what he was searching for.

"There's something out there," said Webb. "I can feel it."

"Of course there's something out there!" said McKinney angrily. "What do you think destroyed the base?"

Garcia crossed to the entrance doors, being careful to keep his back pressed to the interior walls. He lifted his gauss rifle. "I wish they fitted night sights to these things."

"Everything's built into the spacesuit visors," said Corporal Li. He flexed his arms. "I'd feel a whole lot better if I was wearing one."

"What do they do if there's a fire in the bunker?" asked McKinney, the question more for himself than the others.

"They come up in the lift," said Garcia. "The power never fails, so they come up in the lift."

"No, they have to come out of an emergency exit," said McKinney. "There are regulations for this kind of thing."

"There's no emergency exit in here," said Li. "We've checked."

McKinney had an idea about where the emergency exit might be. "Stay here," he said.

With that, he darted outside and crouched by the exterior wall, leaving Webb spluttering out questions. Doing his best to stay low, McKinney crept around the building. There'd been no chained explosions for the last few minutes and it seemed like much of the base was either ablaze or had been completely levelled by the initial onslaught. The air was warm and carried a peculiarly unpleasant scent which McKinney didn't recognize.

At the rear of the building, a few metres from the wall, he found what he was looking for. He counted himself lucky to have seen the gleam of metal, given how little light reached this side of the maintenance entrance.

The emergency exit was a square hatch, raised a few centimetres from the ground and with a mechanical release wheel on its surface. McKinney blew out in relief to find something that didn't require a power source for him to operate. He took hold of the grey metal. It was cold to touch and he turned it rapidly until it wouldn't turn any more. With a grunt, he hauled the hatch open, finding it easier to lift than anticipated. There was a shaft underneath, illuminated by low-draw lighting strips which he assumed must have their own power source. A ladder ran down the wall, descending into the depths.

Less than two minutes later, the four of them were climbing, grateful to be doing something even if they didn't know what their goal was. Corporal Li was the last man into the shaft and he closed the hatch behind him.

"Lock it," said McKinney, his voice muted by the solidity of the walls.

Li did as he was asked and followed the others.

The shaft wasn't as long as McKinney thought it might be. From chatting to the people working in the underground bunker, he knew the place was at least a thousand metres deep, as well as being four thousand long and fifteen hundred wide. It therefore came as a relief when they emerged into a room after little more than a hundred metres of climbing.

This room was lit with the same strips as were in the exit shaft. It was a large, square room with metal walls and four wide exit corridors. There were two operator consoles in opposite corners, their screens blank.

Garcia poked at one. "Dead."

"What now, Sergeant?" asked Webb.

McKinney knew the men looked up to him and he didn't want to let them down. He marshalled his thoughts.

"We face an unknown enemy. We're cut off from base and we lack a means of communication," he said. "There's got to be others down here. We need to find them and then see if we can get a message out to whoever is left alive."

"There'll be comms packs somewhere in the bunker, sir," said Li. "Plus weapons and protective suits."

"We've got to find them," McKinney agreed. "As well as food and water. They've got some sort of backup power running down here. We've got to hope the replicators are wired into it."

"What about the bastards who attacked the base?" asked Garcia. "There's got to be some payback for it."

"One thing at a time, soldier. If we're going to have a chance to strike, we need to be prepared first." McKinney raised his gauss rifle, thankful its internal power source was unaffected by whatever had shut down the base. "Something flew overhead when we were outside. I don't think one of these will do much good against it."

"There's nothing down here will do much good against a spaceship," said Garcia.

"I'm more concerned with what is going to get off that spaceship," said McKinney. "The bombardment has just about stopped. That makes me think our enemy believes it's time to come down for a look. When they do, I want to show those bastards the business end of a gauss round."

He didn't wait any longer. Sergeant Eric McKinney chose an exit passage at random and headed off along it. The others didn't stick around and hurried after.

CHAPTER FIVE

FLEET ADMIRAL DUGGAN was furious and it took every ounce of his strength to keep it from spilling over. He was standing in his office, facing a viewscreen on one of the walls. He'd been awake for over twenty hours and it was starting to take its toll. There was a robotic med-box at his feet. It was inevitable he'd require it to inject him with one of its many stimulants in the near future. For the moment, the med-box was unused and it bleeped softly to remind him of its presence.

"How could you let this happen, Fleet Admiral?" asked Councillor Watanabe, looking down his long nose.

"And what are you going to do about it?" said Councillor Kemp.

"Don't you dare ask me how this happened, Councillors!" said Duggan, struggling to keep his voice even. "I advised you time and again that we should keep the fleet warships equipped for every eventuality and that means they needed an Obsidiar core. Furthermore, we have fewer than half our peak numbers of active vessels currently in service."

"You've had decades and more than enough funding to find

an alternative source or material to the Obsidiar, Admiral," said Councillor Monkton. "And you can't seriously expect the Confederation's citizens to keep paying for the Space Corps to remain on a war footing. Forty years we've been at peace."

"Do you know how many digits there are in the yearly total of the Space Corps' budget?" asked Kemp.

"Eighteen," snapped Duggan.

"Nearly nineteen."

Duggan wasn't about to take the blame for the numerous failings which were beginning to surface. "Finding Obsidiar is and always has been, an issue for the Confederation - not specifically a Space Corps responsibility. The military's needs have been overridden and this is the result! If I'd been allowed my way, we'd have almost fifty combat-ready warships that could face a Neutraliser. As it stands, we have effectively none."

"Do we even know the enemy has deployed a Neutraliser?"

"Only by assumption. The known facts of the Atlantis situation point to the arrival of a vessel able to shut down any Gallenium power source."

"If you are so certain an Obsidiar-cored vessel is the answer, why did you order our single Obsidiar-powered battleship – the *ES Devastator* – out to the frontier, from where we have no access to its tremendous firepower and stealth capabilities?"

"The order was given in full cooperation with the Confederation Council, as you well know, Councillor Ancroft. I seem to recall the words a *show of strength to the frontier worlds* being bandied about amongst your colleagues. Unfortunately, the so-called Frontier League declared independence before the *Devastator* could get there."

"I do not accept your attempts to deflect blame, Fleet Admiral," said Councillor Kemp. "Where is the evidence of successful projects to produce Obsidiar? Now we face two terrible problems

– a rebellion and a likely alien attack. Perhaps the Space Corps would perform better under the guidance of another?"

"Councillors, you are queuing up to point the finger of blame at the military. The fact of the matter is, we need to put these disagreements to one side, else we may find our enemy destroys us utterly while we bicker over what we cannot change," said Duggan. "I require you to release the supplies of Obsidiar we hold here on New Earth so I can have cores installed onto as many of our compatible warships as there are available. This must be done as soon as possible."

The gathered councillors muttered amongst themselves. Duggan didn't hate them – he knew them for what they were. They were politicians, forever buffeted by whatever winds blew their way. Their priorities were different to his, but in this they needed to be pulling in the same direction.

"What happens if we permit the use of our Obsidiar only to find this unknown enemy destroy the ships carrying it?" asked Councillor Ellerson. "An irreplaceable resource would be forever lost."

"The people on Atlantis are an irreplaceable resource, Councillor."

"How long will they last without power?" asked Councillor Ancroft.

"There is no straightforward answer to your question," Duggan replied, wondering if he was being baited into something. "Primary facilities usually have a backup source of power. Those backups won't run forever, but the population will have food, water and heat for a time."

"It's a shame our fleet doesn't have backup power," said Ancroft. "Backup that doesn't rely on Obsidiar," she added hurriedly to avoid giving Duggan an opening.

Duggan wasn't prepared to explain the basics of spaceship design. It took billions of tonnes of Gallenium to achieve a high lightspeed. There was no widely-available alternative that you could simply bolt onto the back of a warship to take over the reins in the event of a complete failure in the main Gallenium drives.

"Do I have permission to access the Obsidiar reserves?" he asked.

Councillor Stahl stepped forward. "We cannot replace those reserves if they are lost. Obsidiar opens up new avenues for research in unexplored fields. Possibilities we could never have dreamed possible without it. If we gamble with our reserves, we are gambling with the Confederation's future."

"Nothing you say reduces the necessity to act with the greatest urgency, Councillor."

"Perhaps. I would prefer an opportunity to confer with my colleagues before we make any hasty decisions."

Duggan ground his teeth together. "Any delay increases the advantage our enemy holds over us."

"It seems to me they already have the advantage, Fleet Admiral," said Councillor Monkton. "I agree with my colleague – we should seek a consensus and only then will we be capable of acting with rational courage."

"I assume your *rational courage* will be appreciated by the several billion men and women you've placed upon your Obsidiar scales, Councillor."

"Don't seek to judge me, Fleet Admiral," snapped Monkton. "I suggest you explore other avenues to bring this situation to an acceptable conclusion. This is what we employ you for."

"We are not yet convinced there is a need to throw all our resources at the problem. You have your fleet, Admiral. I suggest you deploy it wisely."

Duggan couldn't believe the way the conversation was going. It was as though these intelligent men and women had stuck fingers into their ears in order to block out any words they didn't agree with. Duggan was a pragmatist and knew when it was time for a temporary withdrawal.

"How long until you come to a decision on the Obsidiar? I will need to divert warships to New Earth in preparation. I will not be pleased if I summon them, only to find I am not permitted access to the Obsidiar."

"The resources of the Space Corps are yours to juggle," said Watanabe. "However, I'm sure my colleagues will happily commit to providing you with an answer in forty-eight hours or less."

"That is longer than I hoped."

The Councillors muttered some more. Several of those gathered looked doubtful, whilst others nodded tentatively. In the end, the usual happened and the minority fell into line with the majority.

"Nevertheless, in forty-eight hours we will have reached a decision," said Kemp. "We expect to see evidence of firm action from the Space Corps during that time. There will be no sitting on your hands as you wait to hear."

Listening to those words made Duggan think he could cheerfully throttle Kemp. His strength was gradually fading as he got older, but he reckoned he could still overpower the Councillor if he wanted. *Why stop at one?* whispered the voice in Duggan's mind.

"You have been fully briefed on the formation of Response Fleet Alpha, Councillor Kemp. There are brave men and women on those warships who, in all likelihood, will die in the coming hours. You will show them some respect."

"They are doing their duty, Admiral."

The meeting ended and the screen went blank, leaving Duggan alone in the room. At his feet, the med-box bleeped soothingly. He was not a man who could stomach inaction and it didn't take long for him to make a decision.

"Recall the *Maximilian* – fastest speed to New Earth Central Command station."

"Acknowledged," said Cerys.

Having gone this far, there was no going back. "How long until the *Admiral Teron* can fly?"

"At what state of readiness, Admiral?"

"Countermeasures and missiles."

"Forty hours according to the shipyard records, with an additional twenty hours for the installation and activation of the new particle beam turrets."

"I want it off the ground as soon as the missiles and countermeasures are ready."

"I will relay the order, Admiral."

"How many other warships are there within a four-day radius of New Earth?"

"There is one Imposition-class cruiser, two Resolve-class light cruisers and six Crimson-class Destroyers, Admiral."

"Recall them all."

"I will see to it immediately."

Duggan felt the weight of uncertainty lift from his shoulders. The relief was short-lived and his next order was going to be a painful one – the type of order he hated giving and which he knew would make him feel like a coward no matter how much his wife told him only the bravest of men had the strength to issue them.

"Order Response Fleet Alpha to attack the enemy as soon as they are able."

"The fleet is at lightspeed. I will add the order to Captain Kang's queue."

"Thank you."

With a sigh, as though he were succumbing to a weakness he detested, Duggan reached for the med-box. It was going to be a long time until he could sleep.

CHAPTER SIX

"WHY HASN'T anyone come looking for us?" asked Debbie Nelson. "How long has it been now?"

"Four hours," Akachi replied. He'd given up trying to feed power into the doors and looked morosely at the floor.

"Closer to five," said Keller. "At least the toilets don't need Gallenium to flush." He grinned.

"Ewww," said Nelson.

"It's been quiet for a while," said Reynolds. "Maybe whatever was happening has happened."

"I don't think so," said Cruz. "We'd have been rescued in that case." She shook her head. "There's a lot more to go until this is over."

"Why would the Ghasts do this?" asked Ramprakash.

"Because they're war-mongering bastards who have never forgiven us for defeating them in the last war," snorted Reynolds.

"They weren't particularly subtle back then," said Ramprakash. "You mentioned Angax and Charistos yourself, Lieutenant. They just killed everyone. That's how the Ghasts wage war."

"Yeah, why would they act any different now?" asked Keller.

"Who the hell else is it going to be?" asked Reynolds. "It's the Ghasts, I tell you."

Cruz was only half-listening to the conversation. "It doesn't matter who it is. We need to ask ourselves what benefit there is in attacking a military base."

"I'd have thought that self-evident," scoffed Reynolds. "To destroy our warships and kill our personnel."

"We can build new warships, Lieutenant," she replied, ignoring his mocking tones. "New warships are something we can do *really* well. What about intel? What they wanted to find out as much about us as possible?"

"Like what?" asked Akachi. "If it *is* the Ghasts, they know where to find eight of our planets already."

"Only eight, Francis. Most of our strength is on the other eighteen – the Origin Sector and the remainder of Hyptron. If we lost those eight planets, we'd be hurt but we wouldn't be out for the count."

"Whoever or whatever it is, they might know everything about us anyway," said Reynolds, arguing for the sake of it.

"Yeah, but what if they don't?" said Nelson. "They'd need to find that information. Steal it from us, in other words."

"If I was an invading force, the information I'd find most useful would be the location of the people I was invading. If I knew where they lived, then I'd feel pretty sure I was on top," said Nelson.

"I'd be happy to have you on top," said Reynolds, hunting for laughs.

"Just shut the hell up, Tez," Akachi replied. "Everyone already thinks you're a creep."

"One more comment like that and I'll have no hesitation in requesting your demotion, Lieutenant," said Cruz. "That'll look great on your record, won't it?"

"Fine, fine, it was just a joke, that's all. Chill everyone. I'm sorry, okay? I'm a bad guy, what else can I say?"

Cruz wasn't fooled by the glib display of contrition. It wasn't the time to force a confrontation, so she continued where she'd left off. "Where would an invading force obtain the coordinates of other planets within the Confederation?"

"A comms hub like this one," said Nelson.

"Yeah, a comms hub," said Ramprakash. "If they got into our data arrays they'd be able to find all manner of top-secret stuff the military sends out as well."

"Wait a second, how would they know we're here?" asked Reynolds. "Last I checked, we were a hundred metres underground."

"There's a big antennae array above us, Lieutenant. You'd have to be blind or stupid to miss it."

"You can't just plug into our kit and suck out what you need," said Reynolds. "This stuff is highly encrypted. It would take weeks to hack into it."

Cruz had a sudden, unwelcome thought. "Oh crap," she said. "What was it you said about the encryption algorithm, Larry?"

"It's running well below its intended maximum. That shouldn't be a problem though – we're still talking about high-end, multi-layer twist encryption with nothing stupid like a back door that can be opened by entering the name of the base commander's pet dog."

"Our data is locked up tight," Nelson agreed.

"It would take weeks to break the codes, if not months."

"What happens when the residual power dries up?" Cruz asked.

"That Obsidiar processor just keeps on ticking, Lieutenant. It generates its own power."

"What if someone pulled it from the array so there was

nothing left creating that encryption algorithm? Wouldn't the data from our arrays be ready to download and make off with?"

"Not a chance. Any hostile attempts to gain entry into the data arrays would need to synchronise a breach attempt by matching the code from at least one of our processors at the precise time it generates the code. If you don't have that key, you don't get into the data."

"Once there's no processor creating those codes, the data falls into what we call a static state. For all intents and purposes, that means its irrecoverable," added Ramprakash.

"Unless you extract the physical data modules and analyse them at a molecular level," said Nelson. "That might take years."

"What if you tried to hack this Obsidiar processor using another Obsidiar processor?" asked Cruz. "What if you had a whole bank of such cores trying to hack in?"

The tech guys exchanged glances. A couple of them shifted, refusing to meet her eyes. None offered an answer.

"I thought as much," said Cruz.

Just then, there was a heavy thumping sound from somewhere outside the room. It sounded like a very heavy object impacting with another heavy object. The sound was repeated and then again.

"What's that?" asked Ramprakash.

"I don't think I want to know," said Cruz, wishing more than anything that she was out with her friends, enjoying those birthday drinks she'd been so looking forward to.

———

SERGEANT ERIC MCKINNEY had never been into the underground facility before. Now he was here, he was wholly unsurprised by what he found. There were wide corridors, stairs and rooms, with everything laid out in a logical way. Signs hung from the ceiling and most of the doors were numbered or labelled to indicate the function of what lay beyond. In the Space Corps fashion, there was hardly any decoration – no paint, no motivational posters and definitely no place to take a mid-day nap. The walls were clad in smooth alloy plates, either for reinforcement or simply because the Corps liked grey.

McKinney asked himself if he would have guessed this was underground if he'd woken up in here, having been somehow transported unknowingly into the bunker. By the appearance, it could have been within any Space Corps facility on any of the Confederation worlds.

"To think I was secretly jealous of the people who worked in here," said Garcia. He reached out for the panel adjacent to the door he was walking past. Like the others, it was powered off and the door refused to open.

"You'd think there'd be a few personnel down here," said Webb.

"The bunker has been kept on daytime shift for as long as I've been stationed at Tillos," said McKinney. "I'll bet it would be busy if we were at war."

"We *are* at war," said Webb. "We just don't know who with."

"I'm sure the base commander's doing his best to get a night shift organized as we speak," said Garcia sarcastically. "Before you know it, this place will be full of people."

"Piss off, Garcia."

"They've got a spaceship in here, haven't they?" asked Li.

"Yeah, a big one," said McKinney. "One of those Galactics. We'll be able to see it if we can get into one of the viewing rooms."

"A Galactic? Aren't they huge?" asked Webb. "How did they manage to fit it inside?"

"The stuff you can do with computers," said Li. "They must have landed it on autopilot."

McKinney could fly most transport shuttles, so had a general idea of how these things worked. "The Corporal's right. They probably don't need more than a few inches of clearance to park up."

"A few *inches*?" asked Webb incredulously.

"That's what I said."

"What's it in for?" asked Garcia.

"The ES *Lucid*," said McKinney, remembering the name.

"Yeah, the ES *Lucid*. What are they doing with it? And why haven't the enemy blown open the bunker doors to get down here? The *Impetuous* didn't last long."

"I've no idea what it's in for," said McKinney, pondering why the bunker hadn't been cracked open by an orbital strike.

"This whole place is meant to stay hidden," said Li. "Did you see the main overhead doors the last time you went over the base in a shuttle?"

"No," said Webb.

"Exactly. The Corps does stuff down here it doesn't want everyone to see. I wouldn't be surprised if there was some type of shielding around this whole bunker to stop anyone who's outside from looking inside."

"That's got to be it," said McKinney.

"Maybe we should hole up in here for a while," said Garcia hopefully. "I reckon everyone's dead."

"We ain't hiding from nobody," said Webb.

"That's right, soldier," said McKinney, giving him a clap on the back. "As soon as we get properly tooled up and find out if there's anyone still down here, we're going back up top. This is our chance to do what we signed up for."

"Where will we find the weapons?" asked Garcia. "What if they're locked up tight in a cabinet we can't access because there's no power?"

McKinney shrugged. "We'll deal with that problem when it arises."

"Did you hear that?" asked Garcia, cocking his head to one side.

The others shook their heads.

"I'm sure I heard…"

The sound came again.

"There," said Garcia, dropping his voice to a whisper.

"What the hell was that?" asked Webb.

"There it is again."

Something boomed in the distance, like a sledgehammer hitting a hollow metal surface with enormous force.

"What's that Sergeant?"

"Explosives," McKinney replied grimly. "Maybe the enemy has done a sweep and found the main entrance to the bunker."

"Shit," said Li. "We'd better find those weapons."

McKinney picked up the pace. He guessed they were maybe three or four hundred metres beneath the surface. He was working on the assumption there would be a security station somewhere on the hangar floor – if he was in charge that would be where he'd put one. After all, the Corps didn't want just anyone running onto fleet warships whenever they fancied. In truth, he was also hoping they'd pass a weapons station long before they reached the bottom. He felt distinctly under-equipped with just his gauss rifle.

The squad went down a long flight of steps, which led into an open area. There were more consoles here, as dead as the others they'd passed. The sounds of distant explosives came again.

"I can't believe this whole place is deserted," said Garcia. "If anyone got in here, they could burgle whatever they wanted."

"What if there *are* people in here?" asked Webb. "What if they got stuck behind some of these doors? I've not seen a single door with a window in it. There could be some poor bastards inside, waiting to be let out."

"This a complete screw-up," muttered McKinney angrily.

There were two exits from the room – a passage and another set of steps. McKinney led the way down the steps, taking them two at a time. The sound of the explosions left him worried that some unknown foe was pursuing them into the bunker. He'd never fought a Ghost before and he pictured one in his mind – a seven-foot tall grey-skinned muscular brute carrying a crude repeater that could shred flesh and metal alike. He put a hand on the railing and vaulted the last half-dozen steps, finding himself in a long, narrow room, with one entire wall made up from a floor-to-ceiling window. There was a row of metal benches in front of the window.

"A viewing room," he said, jogging across to look out.

The main hangar of the underground facility was an incomprehensibly vast space, thousands of metres long and fifteen hundred wide. The emergency lighting wasn't sufficient to illuminate everything, but it was enough to give the men an idea of what lay within.

"They're big bastards when you see them close up," said Garcia in wonder.

They stared at the spaceship. They weren't to know it, but the *ES Lucid* was one of the Space Corps' newest Galactic class heavy cruisers. At three-thousand nine hundred metres long and fourteen hundred across the beam, there was hardly any clearance in the bay and McKinney felt like he might be able to reach out through the glass window and touch the cool surface of the vessel. As he stood, transfixed by the world-destroying menace of its silhouette, a feeling he hadn't known for years came to him – the pure, wide-eyed wonder of a boy who first sets eyes upon the majesty of space and knew for definite that his destiny lay somewhere out there.

"It makes you feel...tiny," said Garcia.

"Shhh!" said McKinney, listening carefully. There were no more explosions, which was in itself worrying enough. However, there was something else – a low, humming vibration. McKinney pressed his hand against the glass window and felt it through the skin of his palm. "It's running," he said. "Everything else is out of power, but the *ES Lucid* is still running."

The men exchanged looks.

"Maybe it's why the base was attacked," said Webb, who wasn't nearly as stupid as he pretended. "Maybe there's something special about the *Lucid* that makes it so valuable that someone will attack us in order to get hold of it."

"We need to tell the base commander," said Li.

McKinney nodded. "This way."

The squad set off at a run, heading for the far exit from the viewing room. McKinney was convinced there was something of enormous significance happening here. In his head, the Ghasts were responsible and he was determined to throw a heavy spanner into the workings of their plans.

CHAPTER SEVEN

"HOW LONG UNTIL we reach Response Fleet Alpha?" asked Captain Charlie Blake.

"One hour," said Lieutenant Rivera without hesitation.

"Has everyone read through the details from Admiral Murray?" The files were classified, but in the circumstances, Blake preferred his crew to have as much information as was available. It could make the difference between death and failure or success and victory.

"I've just finished them," said Rivera. "Let me get this straight – we're facing some sort of *Neutraliser* which can shut down anything running off Gallenium?"

"That's what the report says. There's confirmed history of it happening before. The Estral sent two Class 1 Neutralisers into Confederation Space. One of them shut down Atlantis. This is the second time the planet has found itself without power and comms. Our intel suggests the Vraxar run a fleet of these things and now they've sent them our way."

"That's impossible," said Rivera. "No one's shutting down my engines."

"Those are the facts, Lieutenant. The existence of these Neutralisers is proven *fact*, whatever you choose to believe."

"We'll see what happens. I know a few tricks."

In the face of such stubborn denial, Blake didn't see any point in arguing. He switched his attention back to the warship's main console. There were no faults across any of the main or subsystems and everything was green, the same as it was a few moments ago when he'd last checked.

"They reckon Obsidiar is the answer?" said Commander Brady, keen to keep going with the conversation. "I thought the Confederation Council ordered all the fleet warships to have their cores pulled."

"They did," Blake replied - he'd done his research on the fleet's capabilities. "Until recently, there were only five left with Obsidiar backup power. The main being the *ES Devastator*, which is so far out into the Tallin Sector we have no hope of getting it back in time. The second – the *ES Rampage* – was stationed at Liventor and has been hijacked by the rebels. The third is the *ES Blackbird* – I'd like to call it a spy bucket but it's a lot more than that. The *Blackbird* is only lightly armed and not suitable to face hostiles except by surgical strike against known opponents."

"You said there were five *until recently*," said Pointer.

"The *Impetuous* and the *Lucid*," Blake confirmed. "They are both on the Atlantis Tillos base having their cores removed. Admiral Murray included the latest copies of the shipyard records, which confirm the work on the *Impetuous* is completed, whilst work on the *ES Lucid* is underway. The technicians were due to sever the links between the Obsidiar core and the rest of the ship yesterday afternoon."

"In other words, there are really only three of these ships in the fleet," said Pointer. "None of which are in a position to assist."

"Them's the breaks, Lieutenant. We're about to be thrown up

against an enemy who are likely to be more advanced than we are and who have a good chance of being able to shut down not just our engines, but everything that runs from those engines. Weapons, sensors and life support."

"Why have they done it?" she demanded in exasperation. "Why not leave the Obsidiar on our warships?"

"There are a million uses for a power source that is vastly more efficient than any other known material. The three AI cores on the *Determinant* are powered by Obsidiar. There are research stations with a hundred such cores running in parallel. With Obsidiar, we can miniaturise almost everything that requires a power supply. Think of it, Lieutenant – medical gear that is smaller than ever. Power stations that can power a megacity yet are small enough that you can carry them to new worlds. Processors that can solve problems a thousand times faster. There are countless uses."

"Augmentations," said Brady. "That's the big one. Stuff they can fit to the human body to make us bigger, faster, stronger, with the ability to think like a supercomputer."

"They'll never allow them," said Rivera. "The interest isn't there."

"It's changing," Brady replied with an enthusiasm which marked him out as a supporter of augmentation tech. "Mark my words – this stuff is already in the lab. That's what they need Obsidiar for."

"I don't care about augmentations or new medical packs," said Pointer. "We're about to be blown to pieces by a more powerful enemy. How are we supposed to win without Obsidiar if they can shut us down so easily?" she asked. "This sounds like it could be a suicide mission."

"What choice do we have?" laughed Brady bitterly. "We have to do something."

"Yeah, but this? There's got to be another way."

"If you think of something, tell me and I'll forward it to Admiral Murray as soon as we drop out of lightspeed."

With that, Pointer fell silent, though she didn't look happy. Blake hoped she wouldn't fall apart as soon as the missiles started flying. He didn't dare ask himself if he would cope. This wasn't the time for self-doubt, though he wasn't exactly known for a lack of self-confidence.

The *ES Determinant* flew on.

———

IT WAS silent within the comms operation centre. Whatever made the noises earlier had stopped, leaving the room's occupants even more worried about what was going on.

Lieutenant Maria Cruz banged her fist against the sealed door of the weapons cabinet. There was absolutely no give in the metal and she knew there was no way to force it open.

"I can't believe we're so vulnerable once the power is cut!" she said.

"Do we really want to fight?" asked Nelson nervously, her eyes on the locker. "Most of us aren't trained to fight."

"There are only three gauss pistols in there anyway," said Keller. "I saw inside last time they came to check everything was in working order. We're not going to fend off an army with three gauss pistols."

"Whatever it was made that noise, it's still outside," whispered Ramprakash, his ear pressed to the sealed door.

"Come away," hissed Cruz, waving him back. Realising she needed to do more to take charge of the situation, she pointed to the corner furthest from the door. "Everyone, over there! Quickly!"

The others did as they were asked and hurried around the banks of consoles to the place Cruz instructed.

"Get down!" she said. "They might try to blow the door."

"That will definitely incinerate us," said Ramprakash, matter-of-factly.

"We'll be piles of ash," confirmed Nelson solemnly.

"Quiet!" said Cruz.

The eight of them crouched in a circle, hidden behind one of the unused consoles. Maria Cruz found seven pairs of eyes looking at her for guidance.

"I need suggestions," she said. "Whatever is out there, it wants to be in this room. And maybe it wants to be in this room because there's something it needs that it can only obtain from here."

"The location of our other planets," said Akachi.

"Probably," said Ramprakash.

"Once inside, it could potentially interface with one of these panels and take what it wants," added Keller.

"Eventually."

"You're the tech guys. How do we stop it happening?" asked Cruz.

"I'm not sure we can from in here," said Akachi. "This is only the control room. There's no button to press that can shut the whole system down."

Cruz remembered an earlier conversation and returned to it, convinced she was missing something. "Debbie, what did you mean about needing to analyse the databanks at a molecular level if there was no functioning encryption processor?"

"Exactly what I said, Lieutenant. While there's a processor online, the databanks can – theoretically – be hacked. If the encryption algorithm stops working the data falls into a static state, making it effectively inaccessible."

"Like we said before - it would be like losing the key permanently," said Keller. "So if you could somehow stop the processors doing their thing, the data would be rendered useless."

"Almost useless," said Nelson.

"Why *isn't* there an off switch for emergencies like this one?" asked Reynolds.

"I'm not sure if you're being serious, Lieutenant," said Ramprakash. "In case you are, I'll remind you that disgruntled employees with sufficient clearance, who were having a bad day, might be tempted to press such an off switch as you describe."

"You wouldn't make it *that* easy," protested Reynolds. "I'm not talking about a big, red button attached to the wall next to the replicator."

Ramprakash ignored the response and forged on. "In addition, I very much doubt anyone considered the possibility of a scenario such as this one. They likely assumed that no attacker would get this far and if they did, would find it time-consuming to hack even a single, conventional processing cluster."

"Fine, fine. Maybe I shouldn't have asked."

"Do you think whatever is outside has gone away?" asked Nelson anxiously. "Maybe it saw the door and gave up."

"I don't think a door is going to be enough," said Akachi. "Even a metre-thick door made of warship-grade alloy."

"Come on, focus!" said Cruz, trying not to lose her temper. She reminded herself these were civilians and they'd only gone through the most basic of combat training required for them to work on a Space Corps base.

"Sorry, Lieutenant. We were trying to think of a way to sabotage whatever it is our enemy have planned, weren't we?" said Keller.

"The processing clusters for the comms hub are elsewhere," said Keller. "Debbie and I went with them when they swapped in the new core – there's a whole world under the Tillos base."

"The underground warren they don't want you to know about," said Nelson.

"Can we get to the processor clusters from here?" asked Cruz.

"Sorry. If you're hoping one of us knows about a secret maintenance tunnel you can sneak through, you're going to be disappointed."

"We took the stairs," said Keller.

"Stairs which are somewhere over *that* way," added Nelson, waving her arm vaguely to the left. "Through lots of doors."

"And even if the power came back, none of us operators have clearance to get into the hardware room," said Ramprakash. "You'd probably need authorisation from the base commander or one of his minions."

"We're stuck here and there's nothing we can do about it," said Nelson.

"I thought you were meant to be working on that *can't do* attitude?" said Keller, smiling.

"I have been. We're still stuck."

"Yeah."

"Let's hope our guys managed to repel whatever it was attacked us," said Nelson. "I could do with some sleep."

Cruz raised herself half-upright and looked towards the closest of the doors keeping the six of them trapped. She blinked. There was a green light on the access panel, glowing steadily.

"I think the power's back," she said in relief.

Without warning, the second blast door twenty metres away opened, gliding to one side with its familiar whoosh. Cruz opened her mouth to greet their rescuers. What she saw was definitely not human and it definitely hadn't come to rescue them.

She ducked down again quickly, hoping she hadn't been spotted.

"What...?" Ramprakash began. He saw the look on her face and went quiet.

Cruz was left with the memory of what she'd seen. Whatever

was beyond the door – a creature of some kind – was a mixture of flesh and dull metal. It was humanoid in shape, with thick, grey-skinned legs and pelvis. Above that, there was a grey-skinned torso and heavily-muscled arms. The creature's face was that of a Ghast, with its black hair patchy but mostly in place. However, it wasn't a Ghast. Half of its face was covered in metal, forming one cheek bone, part of the skull and much of its jaw. It had armour plates over its shoulders and covering parts of its upper arms and chest. Its eyes were those of something living and they glistened in the light of the room.

Lieutenant Maria Cruz closed her eyes tightly, but the vision remained.

CHAPTER EIGHT

DEEP IN THE UNDERGROUND BUNKER, Sergeant McKinney and his men continued their descent.

"We should be close to the bottom," said McKinney.

"I'm glad someone has a sense of direction," said Garcia.

The four men reached the bottom of what felt like the fiftieth set of steps and emerged into a rectangular room with four exit passages. They hadn't seen another soul, though Li had caught the sound of someone thumping at the inside of one of the sealed doors. With no way to prise it open, there had been no option other than to leave it and continue.

Otherwise, the only noise came from the four of them. McKinney was sure the enemy had invaded the Tillos installation with the purpose of stealing the *ES Lucid*. He didn't know how, but he was determined to stop them.

"Through here, Sergeant," said Webb. "This is the place."

McKinney ran across and looked through the doorway. The hangar lay beyond and the *Lucid* loomed overhead, its underside not much more than a hundred metres above. The thick pillars of the warship's landing legs rammed against the concrete like a forest of metal trunks. Even in the dim light, McKinney could make out the snaking fractures from the immense weight of the vessel. The bunker had probably been intended to contain much smaller craft than the one here now.

A whisper of movement in the room behind caused McKinney to whirl around, his gauss rifle pointing ahead.

"Hold!" commanded an unfamiliar voice.

There was a group of six soldiers, coming along the far corridor. They wore the new style spacesuits and had their visors down, making them look alien and threatening.

"Who are you?" barked the voice. "And what the hell is going on?"

"Sergeant McKinney. Who are you?"

The lead soldier lifted his visor revealing some of his face, though not enough to get a real idea what he looked like. "I'm Corporal Evans, sir, and these are my men. I hope you've got some answers."

"I hoped you'd have some yourself," said McKinney. "The base has been attacked and I believe whoever it is, they want the *Lucid*. How many are you?"

"Six of us, and another twelve on patrol, sir."

"Why are you still here instead of up there?"

Evans furrowed his brow, unsure if he was being criticised. The other five milled around a few metres away.

"We were assigned to the bunker, sir. We've had no orders to the contrary."

"You've had no communication from the surface?"

"No, sir."

"You must have noticed the power went out?"

"Yes, sir."

"You didn't think to check what was wrong?"

"No, sir. Our orders were to guard this bunker," Evans repeated. "We assumed someone would come to relieve us."

"There are people trapped in some of these rooms, Corporal."

Evans looked confused. "The bunker should be empty apart from us. No one is authorised for out-of-hours work."

McKinney was almost lost for words. "If this is what forty years of peace has reduced the Space Corps to, perhaps we should hope war is coming, Corporal. This is a screw-up from top to bottom!"

"Sir."

"Call everyone back from patrol. I assume you can do that?"

"Yes, sir. The suit comms are working fine."

"Have you tried to reach your commanding officer with the suit comms?"

"The bunker is shielded at surface level, sir. The built-in comms can't penetrate and the bunker comms array is offline along with everything else."

Confronted by so many examples of failure, McKinney did his best to be practical. "Corporal Evans, I'm in charge now. You will report to me, alongside Corporal Li."

Evans nodded and McKinney continued.

"My men need suits and I'd feel better if we had something bigger than gauss rifles with which to defend ourselves."

Evans saluted. "That is something I can help you with, sir. Follow me."

"Go! Run!" McKinney urged him. "Gather your men."

Evans did as he was ordered and set off the way he'd come at a sprint, lowering his visor as he ran. McKinney followed, entering a straight corridor which continued for a hundred metres. Just as he was becoming concerned their destination would be at the far end of the underground facility, the ten of them spilled into a new room.

"Suits, weapons," said Evans, his voice perfectly reproduced by the spacesuit's in-built micro speakers.

There was a weapons room leading away from this new room. The door had been jammed open by a metal bench.

"What is that?" asked McKinney, pointing at the bench.

"Only the lieutenants have authorisation to open the door. They tend to get a bit pissed off when we keep calling them down here in order to change out of our suits at the end of a shift, so we keep the door wedged open."

"Where are these lieutenants now?" asked McKinney.

"They only do 8am till midnight, sir. We're left to fend for ourselves during the other eight hours. The weapons are never left unguarded."

"They were unguarded when we arrived just now."

"Yes, sir. They were."

For once, McKinney didn't care about these monumental failings in procedure. If it wasn't for those failings, he'd be stuck outside the weapons room, probably kicking the door in anger.

"Inside," he said to Li, Garcia and Webb.

McKinney went first, stepping over the bench and into the weapons room. It was lit by the emergency backup strips and the light revealed racks of weapons fixed against the walls.

"Whoa," said Li. "What's all this stuff doing here?"

"They're guarding a thousand trillion dollars' worth of spaceship, remember?" said Webb.

"Only between the hours of 8am and midnight," said Garcia, his voice dripping with sarcasm.

"Suit up and do it fast," said McKinney.

He pulled the closest of the grey suits down from a rack. It felt like soft rubber in his hand, though he knew it was the hardest flexible polymer the Space Corps' labs could produce in sufficient quantities to meet demand. He stepped into the wide hole at the top, pushing his legs in first. He pulled the rest of the material up, feeling it contract about his legs to make a perfect fit. His arms went in next and he pulled the head covering up and over, taking care that the two earpieces were close enough to his ears. Inside, the material of the suit was perfectly smooth and it only took seconds to get comfortable.

McKinney dropped the thin visor into place, feeling the suction as it formed a seal. He breathed in the scent of the previous occupant's sweat. He was used to it – every suit he'd ever worn smelled the same.

A HUD illuminated inside the visor. The built-in processing units took over, providing a subtle boost to the light and over-laying information about his well-being. He noted his elevated heart rate. Otherwise, everything was exactly where it needed to be.

The suit's comms unit detected the presence of a local network. McKinney joined it and read through the names of the men and women stationed down here. Corporal Johnny Li's name appeared on the list, quickly followed by the names R1T Martin Garcia and R1T Dexter Webb.

"Hey Webb, you never did tell me why your mama gave you two surnames," said Garcia.

"Shut up, Garcia," McKinney ordered.

"Sorry, Sergeant. Just checking to see if the comms are working."

McKinney didn't answer and walked over to the weapons rack. He picked up a repeater. The main part of the weapon was a curved slab, slightly over two inches thick, which held the power cell and a few thousand rounds of ammunition. A two-foot-long barrel protruded – this barrel could be lowered to the horizontal when the repeater was firing. Afterwards, the barrel could be moved into a vertical position where it was slightly less intrusive for the soldier carrying the weapon.

There were self-fastening straps and McKinney pushed his arms through until the power/ammunition cell was positioned over his chest and stomach. It didn't take much adjusting and he slung his rifle over his shoulder.

The repeater interfaced with his suit. [Repeater ammunition: 100%] appeared on his HUD.

Corporal Li and Garcia took repeaters as well. It was no surprise to find Webb holding the six-foot tube of a plasma launcher.

"You sure you can handle that in here?" asked McKinney.

"It's what I was born to do, sir."

If it had been any other soldier, McKinney would have ordered him to put the rocket tube down. He'd seen Webb using one many times in wargames and there wasn't a man or woman on the base who had anything like the same skill.

"Just try not to kill us."

McKinney picked up a bandolier of miniature plasma grenades and went out of the room, to find Corporal Evans waiting with the other seventeen men and women. They were all suited and, in spite of the earlier signs of lax discipline, they stood alert and at attention. Every foot soldier in the Corps went through ongoing training in the form of off-world exercises, sometimes in exceptionally hostile conditions. The weapons might only fire simulated rounds, but the officers running the exercises made sure everyone took it seriously. Dismissals from the Corps for exceptionally poor performance were not unheard of.

"Why are none of you carrying repeaters?" was the first question McKinney asked. The repeaters were shatteringly effective in close-quarters combat. In fact, they were designed specifically for such conditions.

"They're too heavy to carry on routine patrol, sir," said Evans.

"You're not on routine patrol anymore, Corporal. Get in there and get properly kitted."

While the others filed into the weapons room, McKinney

continued to provide instruction. He was angry – not so much with these soldiers as he was with the whole situation. He'd grown up listening to the tales of the Space Corps' past conflicts, the bravery of troops thrown into combat against the Ghasts. McKinney had only ever wanted to be a soldier and though he hated himself for it, he always wished he'd been born in wartime instead of the longest time of peace ever recorded. Now that fighting had come, the Space Corps – or at least the Tillos base – had been comprehensively defeated.

"We're going to form two squads of seven and one of eight," he barked. "Your HUDs will show who you're with. It is my opinion the Ghasts have launched a surprise attack on us and equally, it seems certain they want to capture the *ES Lucid*. It's our job to ensure they fail in their mission."

"Sir, there are multiple entrances to the main hangar bay. We don't have enough men to keep them all secure," said Evans.

"What about choke points? Is there a place they'll have to come through to get here, or is there a route we can expect them to follow?"

"Third floor, breakout area six, sir. It's usually the busiest place in the bunker at 8am and again at 5pm."

The spacesuits' data chips held layouts for the bunker and McKinney tried to get an overall impression of the area. There was too much for him to absorb at the same time as giving instructions to the other men. "Where else?" he asked.

Evans thought for a moment. "Second floor, main viewing walkway. It's a long corridor and it acts as a funnel for people coming to work on the bay floor."

"Anywhere else?"

Evans shrugged. "This place is a warren, sir. Anyone coming here could flood through dozens of different corridors."

McKinney made his decision. "Squad B - Corporal Evans, secure breakout area six. Report any movement and shoot on sight. Squad C – Corporal Li, get up to the main walkway. Both squads fall back and defend the bay floor if you need to. Squad A, you're the lucky ones. You're coming with me."

"Where to, Sergeant?" asked Webb, the plasma tube held casually over his shoulder.

McKinney pointed at the heavy cloth pack one of the soldiers was carrying. "We're going to take this comms pack which Bannerman has on his back and we're going to attempt to get a message out to whoever is left alive on this base."

None of the gathered soldiers dared to make a wisecrack at the plan. Before they set off, there were a few other items McKinney wanted from the storeroom since he didn't know if they'd be able to return this way soon. One of the men was trained in explosives, another could use a medical pack and there was a third who professed himself able to carry and safely use a plasma tube. It didn't take long. Soon, the three squads separated and moved out at the double.

———

JERRY GREINER LEANED against the rusty, starboard railing of his boat and squinted into the distance. He could see plenty of low, rolling waves and plenty of pure, blue, dawn sky. The one thing he couldn't see was land.

"Shit," he swore. With no wife around to chastise him for using bad language, he repeated the word for good measure.

He ducked through the low doorway which led into the wood-walled cabin. There was a fixed wooden chair, a table upon which was an open can of beans, a stand holding fishing rods and, incongruous to everything else, a sophisticated all-weather navigation and control computer against the front wall.

Jerry sat in front of the computer and pressed a few buttons on the surface. The display remained steadfastly blank and the tiny vessel's Gallenium micro-engine stayed offline. The boat was equipped with a battery-powered emergency beacon. It bleeped every so often as it sent its automatic distress signal up into the sky. So far, there had been no response. He pulled the headset from its stand and put it over his head.

"Mayday, mayday, this is the *Maiden's Bounty*. Do you read?"

The earpiece hummed – if there was anyone receiving, they didn't reply. He switched the device off, not wishing to deplete its battery when there was no one listening.

He left the cabin, hawked and spat over the side into the water. Jerry had been stuck out here for hours – a fishing trip which now threatened to cost him his life. When his engine cut out, he'd initially thought the currents of the Plangaean sea would be kind and deliver him safely back to shore. Unfortunately, they'd done the opposite, carrying him away until eventually there was no sight of land.

"Piece of crap boat," he said.

A shadow fell across the sea, appearing so suddenly it made him jump. He looked up instinctively. Overhead, a spaceship flew quietly at an altitude of only a few hundred metres. Jerry wasn't really interested in technology anymore – he just liked to fish when he got the time. In his younger days, he'd served in the Space Corps as a comms man on one of the fleet's prospectors and he knew enough to be certain that whatever was above, it was definitely not built by human hands.

"Or Ghast hands," he said to himself.

Jerry was too old to be alarmed by much these days. Death would take him eventually and he'd die peacefully, without regret. Therefore, he studied this alien craft without fear. It was peculiar in design – something like a grey cube, a thousand metres to each side and with thick posts protruding from the centre of each face. Underneath, hung another cube, this one featureless and only five hundred metres to a side, attached to the parent vessel by invisible gravity clamps.

The alien ship flew on, with Jerry watching. A few kilometres away, it stopped unexpectedly, hovering motionless with its cargo dangling above the calm surface.

Then, the clamps holding the smaller cube were released and the object dropped into the water.

"Oh crap," said Jerry.

The splash was enormous, though it wasn't that which had Jerry the most worried. He watched with horror as the water rushed towards him, speeding away from the centre. Moments later, a huge swell took the *Maiden's Bounty* lifting it high up into the air. The small boat dropped down the far side of the swell, gathering pace as it raced towards the place where the cube struck the surface.

Then, it was over, leaving Jerry somehow, miraculously alive on the now-choppy surface. He had no idea what had just happened but it didn't take much imagination to realise it wasn't good. Jerry hurried into the cabin to see if he could work a few of his old tricks with the emergency beacon.

CHAPTER NINE

"WE'RE ABOUT TO EXIT LIGHTSPEED," said Lieutenant Rivera. "The *Determinant*'s AI calculates Atlantis to be a further ten minutes' lightspeed from the rendezvous point."

"Right on the doorstep," said Blake. "We'll meet up and be on our way."

The *Determinant*'s engines growled quietly and the walls of the bridge vibrated faintly. If you'd never experienced lightspeed travel before, the transition was subtle. Once you'd done a few trips, it was easy to detect the switchover.

"Lieutenant Pointer, get me the scans."

"Sir, the nears tell me there's nothing in our immediate vicinity. I'm switching to the fars." She didn't get a chance to complete the scan. "We're being hailed, sir. It's Captain Kang of the Galactic class *New Beginning*."

"Bring him through," said Blake, expecting a few brief formalities and a rundown of the plan before they took off back into lightspeed.

"You're late," said Kang without preamble.

"Sir, we're exactly on time."

"We've been waiting for you. Join our comms network – all orders will come from the *New Beginning* and I expect you to follow them without question or hesitation. I assume you know what we're up against. If not, please don't waste any of my time asking."

"Captain Kang, I have been briefed on this mission."

"In that case I won't expect any difficulties keeping the *ES Determinant* in line."

"Sir, I have been ordered here to assist in the destruction of hostile aliens, not to listen to you cast aspersions on my competence."

"I don't need a hotshot in Response Fleet Alpha, Captain Blake. I need a man who will follow the orders of a senior officer who has twenty-five years' experience commanding fleet warships. Do you understand?"

Blake had no idea why Kang was so hostile, since he'd never come across the man before at any point in his Space Corps service to date. One thing was for sure – even Kang's twenty-five years' experience didn't give him any more knowledge of real combat than Blake's eight years' experience. In fact, Blake didn't know if there were any officers left in the fleet who'd fought in anger, since there'd been no war in decades. If there were any such officers, they'd definitely be close to retirement age.

"I have been told to follow your orders."

"Good. We have fewer vessels than I would like, but still enough to take down a Ghast Oblivion if we were called upon to do so. Upon arrival, we will arrange ourselves in a standard formation – the *New Beginning* will be in the centre, with Imposition class vessels *Undertow* and *Hurricane* flanking at a distance of five thousand kilometres. You are in one of our four destroyers, Captain Blake – the *Sabre*, *Ransack* and *Lingard* are the others. Your vessel will range ahead with the other destroyers and act as a soak for the *New Beginning*. Is that clear?"

"Yes, sir."

"Very well. My comms man has provided coordinates to ensure we arrive at the same time and in the right place."

Blake looked over at Pointer. She raised her thumb to confirm receipt.

"We have the coordinates," said Blake.

"We're leaving in sixty seconds. Prepare for lightspeed."

"He's gone," said Pointer. "Not even a goodbye."

Blake suppressed a smile at Pointer's words. It appeared as though Kang was a grade-A idiot with a stick shoved in a place sure to cause eye-watering levels of discomfort. The tactics he planned to employ had been lifted straight out of a textbook, with one major exception which Blake hadn't failed to note.

"Lieutenant Rivera, you heard the man. We're going to Atlantis."

"Yes, sir. We'll leave the moment they do."

Precisely on schedule, the seven warships of Response Fleet Alpha entered lightspeed, travelling at the exact maximum speed of the slowest ship, which happened to be the ES *Sabre*.

Blake prowled around the bridge of the *Determinant*, his mind churning.

"It seems likely we'll be the first Space Corps vessels to take part in hostile action in forty years," he said. "I know we've all spent countless hours in the simulator, but as soon as we catch sight of a Vraxar ship, it's going to count for nothing. We need to be ready. We need to act with purpose and ruthlessness. The people of Atlantis are counting on us."

He looked at them in turn, only Lieutenant Rivera failing to meet his eye.

"Are you ready?" Blake asked.

The response wasn't quite as enthusiastic as he'd hoped. Nevertheless, the three members of his crew appeared ready for action. The testing would come soon enough.

"Sir?" asked Pointer. "I thought the newer Galactics were specifically designed and built to act as soaks, so our smaller vessels can engage in combat without being knocked out in the first exchange of fire."

"Well spotted, Lieutenant. You are quite correct."

"Why are we acting as a soak, then?"

"Do you need me to spell it out?"

"No, sir. I don't think I do."

After ten minutes at lightspeed, the fleet entered local space a little over seven million kilometres from Atlantis. The Obsidiar cores installed on every warship were so fast, they could calculate short journeys such as this one down to the nanosecond and could be relied upon to deposit a spaceship within a few hundred kilometres of a precise set of coordinates.

"Everyone on full alert!" shouted Blake. "Give me our status!"

"We're seventy minutes out on gravity engines," said Rivera.

"We have no enemy ships within a quarter of a million klicks," said Pointer. "I'm checking further out."

"The *New Beginning* has provided us with a trajectory."

The AI cores on the *New Beginning* sent instructions to each member of the fleet, keeping them in formation. Blake checked the tactical screen – the *ES Determinant*'s gravity engines were at seventy percent and the destroyer was on a course towards the distant planet. Blake didn't like giving up control of his ship, particularly when the area scans were incomplete. This was Kang's call.

Blake scanned the RFA comms network. Not all comms operators worked at the same speed and he wanted to find out if there were any hostiles within sensor range as soon as the details came in.

"Fars clear," said Pointer.

"Well done on being the first."

"The super fars are still going. I wish we had a Hynus sensor array."

"They've got three on the *New Beginning*. I don't know what's keeping them," said Brady.

"Put Atlantis up on the screen," Blake said.

The image appeared, projected onto the flat wall of the forward bulkhead. The distance was such that the forward sensor cluster couldn't quite produce a pin-sharp image, and the features on the planet's surface were grainy and wavering. The *Determinant* faced the night side of Atlantis, directly above the main land mass.

"No lights," said Brady.

"The power output of the planet is effectively zero when compared to its expected levels," said Rivera. "Even the major population centres are barely causing a flicker on the needles."

"Can you interface with any of their satellites?"

"No, sir. As far as communications go, Atlantis may as well be back in the dark ages."

"Whatever's caused the blackout, I can't find any trace," said Pointer. "It must be around the other side of the planet."

"I don't like it," said Blake. "We came in so close only a fool could have failed to detect seven fission signatures. It would have taken a star to shield us from sight."

One-by-one, the super-far scans from the ships in RFA came back clear. The *New Beginning* altered their course slightly. Blake looked at the projection on his navigational screen.

"We're going to come in a wide circle around the planet," he said. "Captain Kang is being cautious."

"That's for the best, sir," said Brady.

"I agree. No point in rushing in just yet."

Minutes passed and the *New Beginning* instructed an increase in speed to the maximum of the slowest vessel, this one again being the *ES Sabre*.

"Not even seventeen hundred klicks per seconds," muttered Rivera. "Fast in its day, not so much now."

Blake checked through a few of the sensor feeds – the *Determinant* had a total of eight arrays. There was nothing out there but space and stars. Pointer continued working hard at the sensors, whilst also juggling the inbound comms from the other vessels in the fleet. Comms work on a warship was the easiest to perform at a basic level and the hardest to excel at. Blake wasn't afraid to admit Pointer seemed to be doing a good job so far – she had a look of absolute focus and her hands flew across the indentations on her console as she made adjustments to the focus of the lenses.

"This is wrong," said Blake after another few minutes. He didn't know why he was so certain, but he couldn't shake the feeling that something bad was coming. "Lieutenant Rivera, please load a short-range lightspeed jump sequence onto two of our cores."

"Sir, procedure dictates no loading for an SRL until an enemy is detected. The cores might burn out."

"The Obsidiar cores don't burn out as easily as the old."

"Sir, but..."

"Do it, Lieutenant Rivera - we have three cores." Blake fixed Rivera with a hard look. "Don't question me again when we're facing potential hostiles. I won't tell you again."

"Sir," Rivera acknowledged, not trying to hide his own anger.

Blake didn't care what Rivera thought about it. He was furious he'd been asked to repeat an order. If his lieutenant had asked for confirmation at almost any other time, it would have been fine. In their current situation it was absolutely unacceptable.

An SRL meant instructing a warship's core do the preparations for a lightspeed jump in advance. Once the preparations were complete, the core would hold ready for the final command to go. The problem was, holding the processor in a state of readiness increased its utilisation, sometimes beyond its permitted maximum. The longer an SRL was held, the greater the chance of a core burnout. A ship without a core was effectively helpless – no weapons, no sensors and no lightspeed.

"Cores two and three are loaded, sir. Utilisation at eighty percent and ninety-five percent respectively."

"Keep me informed."

"Anything from the other vessels, Lieutenant Pointer?"

The sound of Pointer swearing made Blake turn.

"The comms have gone off, sir. I can't speak to any of the other ships."

Blake hesitated for a split second. Then, he remembered something about this in the mission briefing – the possibility the enemy could do something to interfere with the main comms.

"Switch to backups!" he ordered. "Let the others know something's coming!"

Pointer looked lost, her face scanning the front of her console. Then, her confidence returned and she stabbed with her fingertips at one of the panels. "Secondary comms active."

"Get us back onto the RFA network. Do it fast."

"I can't, sir. They're still offline."

Blake swore and clenched his fists. "We're under attack! How the hell can we respond without comms?"

"The *Undertow* and *Lingard* are now on backups, sir. The *New Beginning* is still offline – that's the ship we're meant to be routing through."

"Set us up as a hub. Invite the *Undertow* and *Lingard* to join."

"There's a decaying fission signature about two hundred thousand klicks to starboard, sir," said Rivera. "Something just arrived."

"What do you mean *just arrived?* You should have received warning."

Rivera stared back. "I missed it, sir."

Thoughts raced through Blake's mind, the most prominent of which was how badly prepared both he and his crew were to face the enemy. During the Ghast war, the Space Corps had been filled with officers who'd experienced dozens of engagements. Now, they were all dead or retired.

"Get me a fix! Find me a target!"

"Fixed!" shouted Pointer. "The enemy ship is jumping about like crazy! It's hard to keep the sensors locked onto it!"

The main bulkhead viewscreen showed a feed from the front sensor array. At first, there was nothing visible. Then, a space-craft appeared, moving fast. It was like nothing the crew on the *Determinant* had seen before – it was a black, tapering cylinder covered in hundreds of long, round metal posts, which aimed forward and ended in points. There was no obvious sign of weapons clusters, though Blake had no doubt they'd be housed somewhere within the Vraxar warship's hull. The alien ship was strange and somehow repellent to the eye.

As the *Determinant*'s crew watched, the enemy spaceship flickered, disappeared and reappeared a thousand kilometres away. Two seconds later, it did the same thing again.

"There are more of them," said Rivera. "Three...wait...four. I think."

"I've set a single ship as target. Fire Lambdas."

"Lambda X's refusing to lock," said Brady. "The *ES Sabre* has been struck by an unknown weapon."

"Damnit, we're stuck in formation with the *New Beginning*," said Blake. "Taking manual." He grabbed the control bars in front of him and pulled, bringing the *Determinant* around in a steep curve towards the closest of the enemy craft. He felt hints of nausea and the muscles in his neck strained against the pull. The life support modules stabilised the interior and the feeling quickly passed.

To his left, the *Determinant*'s tactical display showed a number of red dots, which moved erratically. Occasionally one vanished and reappeared a few thousand kilometres away.

"Holy crap, the *Sabre*'s breaking up!" said Pointer.

"Particle beam strike on the *Undertow*," said Brady. "Two more on the *Hurricane*."

"Where're those damned missiles?"

"Got a Shatterer lock. Forward tubes away."

"Nothing from the *New Beginning*," said Blake.

The *Determinant* was a fine warship, but it was still just a destroyer. It lacked particle beams, disruptors and most of the countermeasures found on larger Corps vessels. A destroyer was meant as a mobile missile battery, not as a backbreaker. The *New Beginning*, on the other hand, had overcharged particle beams, Splinter countermeasures, multiple Shatterer launchers and could fire a volley of eight hundred Lambda X missiles every fifteen seconds. It was also packing the latest stealth modules.

"The *New Beginning* has gone into stealth mode," said Rivera. "Thanks a lot, guys," he said bitterly.

Blake had no idea what Captain Kang was playing at. The Galactic should have remained on the tactical display of other fleet warships. With its comms offline, it simply vanished.

With the most powerful ship in the response fleet potentially out of the engagement, Blake got on with the job in hand. The fight was hardly underway and it already looked like a lost cause.

CHAPTER TEN

"WHAT THE HELL are we going to do?" whispered Manoj Ramprakash hoarsely.

Lieutenant Maria Cruz leaned carefully around the side of the console cluster. There was a narrow gap, through which she could see the alien creature standing in the doorway. A full minute had passed and the intruder showed no sign of movement – it remained in the same place, its eyes staring ahead. Every few seconds, it blinked.

Just as Cruz started to withdraw her head to confer with the others, the creature moved. It took a series of steps, which carried it out of sight behind the eight-feet-tall central comms control panel. The footsteps continued, heavy and thumping across the floor tiles. Cruz leaned this way and that but was unable to bring the alien into view. She crawled back to the group.

"It looks like a Ghast fused with a mech suit," she whispered.

"One of their shock troops?" asked Nelson.

"I have no idea what it is, but I don't think it's a Ghast. One thing I do know is that we've got to tell someone about it."

Akachi had his diagnostics tablet in one hand. "Oh crap," he muttered. "Look at this."

He turned the display around so everyone could see. The tablet showed a series of gauges and utilisation bars for the central comms processing unit. There was a series of progressively larger spikes across the entire cluster.

"Something's trying to hack in," said Cruz.

"Maybe that thing has plugged into one of the interface ports over there and now it's trying to brute-force its way through our encryption."

"Is there any indication how long that'll take from what you can see on the tablet?"

"How long is a piece of string?" Akachi responded. "There's no way to tell what sort of kit it's got – all I can tell you is that it's going to bring the whole cluster group up to full utilisation in the next few minutes. Whatever it's using, we can assume it's designed for exactly this sort of task."

"Where's it getting its power from?" asked Reynolds.

"I don't know," said Cruz. "If they can shut us down, it makes sense they have some control over the effect."

"Once it's unlocked those encryption routines, it'll be free to access whatever it wants," said Nelson. "From what we can guess, these *things* have knocked out a major Space Corps base without finding much to trouble them. Just think what will happen once they have the location of the remaining twenty-five planets."

"Yeah – we don't even know if anyone's aware of what's happened here," said Keller.

Reynolds snorted quietly. "If you think the Space Corps failed to notice the loss of an entire base, you're even stupider than you look."

"Pack it in!" Cruz warned, struggling to keep her voice low enough that it wouldn't be overhead by the alien.

Reynolds shot her a look but didn't say anything. Even he wasn't stupid enough to start an argument with a superior officer when there was an alien intruder in the main comms room.

"Larry – is there any way we can pull out the processing units if we get to that room you told me about?" asked Cruz.

"To render the hub data inaccessible?" he asked.

"Yeah."

"The processing room needs a high level of authorisation to enter. If we can get inside, then sure – we can pull out the units."

"You don't have that sort of authorisation, Lieutenant," said Nelson. "We're talking Colonel Tenney type of authorisation and maybe a few others."

"That door over there is open," said Cruz. "Maybe there are others open as well. They could have already hacked into the base mainframe to let themselves get everywhere without having to blow every door." She met their eyes one by one. "I need to act and I need to do it soon."

"Think we can get out of here without being seen?" asked Keller.

"Can't we overpower whatever it is hacking our kit?" asked Ramprakash. "There are six of us."

"I don't know if it's armed," said Cruz. "It's seven feet tall and it looked pretty strong. We don't know if any more are coming."

"Don't get me wrong – I'm not desperate to start a fist fight with it," Ramprakash replied.

"We're going to get out of here. I'll go look for the processor room, you others should try and get off base. Find somewhere safe and keep your heads down. The bad news is, I need someone to show me where the processor clusters are."

"I might be able to show you, Lieutenant," said Keller.

"I'll come along as well," said Reynolds. "That's what they're paying me for, right?"

Cruz did her best to keep her surprise hidden. Reynolds was one of the least committed officers she'd ever encountered and she expected him to split and run at the first opportunity.

With the whispered conference over, it was time to move.

"Come on," Cruz said. "Keep low."

Whatever the intruder was doing, it made no sound. Cruz kept her head below the top of the consoles and made her way along, sticking close to the wall. She caught a glimpse of the enemy as she darted across a wide gap between the maintenance console and the monitoring section. The alien creature had its arm extended and was touching the main supervisor console for the hub. It didn't look across, nor give any sign it had seen her. From this angle, she could see extra plating across its upper and lower back.

When she was only a few metres from the exit, Cruz stopped to let the others catch up. A green light nearby caught her eye and she realised the weapons cabinet door was unlocked. *Must have happened when the main door got power again.*

She pulled the locker open quietly and saw the three gauss pistols within. They had a handle, a short barrel and a small bore. Unlike a standard-issue gauss rifle, the pistols couldn't fire their projectiles over a distance of several kilometres, neither could they punch clean through several bodies at once if these bodies happened to be lined up conveniently. That didn't make the pistols useless – they were simply lightweight, backup weapons.

Cruz pulled one free and tucked it into her belt. Reynolds didn't wait for permission and helped himself to the second. The other four stared at the remaining pistol, as though it were a poisonous snake getting ready to strike.

"Ramps, you take it."

Cruz didn't spend any time waiting to see his reaction. She made her way towards the door, this time on all fours. She reached a point where the open door was to her left, whilst at the same time she had a clear sight of the alien.

Confronted by such an apparently straightforward choice, she drew the gauss pistol out. It was warm in her hand and smooth to touch. She aimed carefully. Her forefinger rested upon the firing button. She pressed the button and kept it held down.

The pistol whined as it launched three of its dense metal projectiles rapidly from the barrel. All three struck the alien where Cruz had intended – straight in the gaps between its back armour. It wheeled around with terrifying speed and something cracked in its hand.

Cruz fired again – the pistol limited to bursts of three. The enemy went down, slumping to the floor with a thud that spoke of its great weight. Cruz fired another two bursts into its body for good measure.

"I didn't give you permission to touch my console," she said.

She turned and found the others staring at a dead body. It was Ramprakash with half of his head blown off. There was a bloody smear across the floor and wall. Cruz shut her eyes. When she opened them again, nothing had changed.

Training took over. "We need to move," she said. "Someone take his gun. There'll be others coming."

"Lieutenant, there's still something chewing on the cores," said Akachi. His hand shook violently as he showed her his diagnostic tablet.

"Is there another place they could interface with the hub?"

"The Central Command Building - that's where Colonel Tenney and his staff work."

Cruz breathed in deeply and blew out. "Shit."

Tentatively, she walked towards the slumped form of the alien creature. Blood oozed from wounds on its body, merging with a clear fluid leaking from ruptures in its jointed armour. It had a gun of some sort, still clutched in one hand. The worst part of it was the smell – a sickly sweet odour came from the body, like badly-preserved meat. She fought down the urge to retch. She didn't back off immediately and had a look at the console. There was no sign of a physical connection between the creature and the hardware.

"Doesn't look like it was trying to interface with our kit after all," she said to the others. "Maybe this one got lost and wandered in here at random."

"And they've plugged in remotely at the CCB instead?" asked Keller. "If they haven't sent many ground troops into the comms hub, we should have a better chance of getting to the processing cores."

It sounded logical and Cruz nodded, trying not to look too hopeful. There was no point in staying around any longer. "Come on, we're going," she said.

Cruz led the way, taking the others into the corridor outside. It was cold in here – the cold of unheated night time air drifting through the underground complex.

"Maybe we should stick together," said Nelson, shivering.

The death of Manoj Ramprakash hadn't been part of the plan. Cruz realised she wasn't ready for the responsibility of looking after herself, let alone three civilians. Nevertheless, her sense of duty was strong and she could do little to resist it. She nodded at the others.

"We stay together for now."

They set off, deeper into the hub.

———

SERGEANT ERIC MCKINNEY brought the men of Squad A to an abrupt halt as soon as it became apparent he didn't know where the hell he was going. The HUD on his visor showed a perfectly accurate 3D reproduction of the bunker's interior, but it was hard to interpret on the run, especially when McKinney lacked any prior knowledge of the layout.

"What's the quickest way to the surface? I need someone on point."

"If you want to get to the surface, there's the secondary entrance away to our east," said Stein. The soldier talked with reassuring confidence.

"The secondary entrance is close to the main research facility, isn't it?" asked McKinney.

"Yes, sir. Not too far."

"When we came through the maintenance entrance, that part of the base was in flames. There could well be a strong enemy presence in that area."

"We could head back for the maintenance shaft if you want, sir."

"What other options are there?"

"There's the primary entrance. That's close to the central admin section and hard to miss – if I was an invading alien bastard I'd be all over that door like a rash. Assuming I wanted to come down here, that is."

"What other ways do we have to get in and out?"

"There's an entrance at the top end of Section D. That'll take us out right near the main comms hub. It's in the middle of the base, though, so we probably don't want to try that one."

"The comms hub?" McKinney asked with interest.

"Yes, sir. As I said, it's right in the middle of everything."

"We don't know who is left alive on the base, soldier. The Space Corps' high command may be grateful to have a squad in position to send and receive off-world communications."

"The power is down, sir," said Elder.

"We don't know exactly what is affected by the outage. We're going to the hub. If it's already secure, then we can use it to communicate much further afield than with this portable beacon."

"What if the hub is in enemy hands?" asked Garcia.

"I'll think about that when we get there. Stein, take us to the Section D entrance."

There was little relish in Stein's voice when he acknowledged the order and his reflective visor hid his expression. The man raised one arm and used the barrel of his repeater to point.

"That way, sir. It's a long run. The quickest way will be to cut diagonally across the hangar bay floor."

"Will we be visible from any of the viewing windows?"

"Maybe. If so, it won't be for long. The *Lucid*'s squeezed in tightly - we'll not be an easy target even if we're spotted."

"That's the way we'll go," said McKinney. It was the right choice in terms of efficiency and additionally he was secretly keen to see the heavy cruiser from close up.

Stein set off at a run, not once looking back to see if the others were following. The repeater he was carrying affected his gait and the man's shoulders swayed peculiarly with each stride. It looked as if he was forging a path through waist-high mud.

The squad pounded along a wide passage which was at the lowest level of the bunker. There were no windows, though there were doors in the right-hand wall at regular intervals.

"We're coming into the storage and maintenance area," panted Stein, evidently not in the sort of good shape demanded by the Space Corps. "It's something, all right."

The passage emerged into a square room, the dimensions of which caused McKinney to falter in his stride. His suit HUD calculated the place to be more than eight hundred metres along each of its metal-clad sides and close to seven hundred metres tall. Backup lighting strips in the walls, floor and ceiling weren't enough to fill the room and shadows reached into every corner, twisting the original shapes into new and irregular copies.

"The hangar is four thousand metres long," said Stein. "What most people don't know is that they also have this storage area here, another one at the far end, plus a third one in the middle. If anyone bothered to ask me about it, I'd tell them it was obvious that they needed a place to keep these cranes and all the other shit that you use to fix a spaceship."

McKinney was too busy looking to pay much heed to what Stein was telling him. Although the light was poor, it was ample to illuminate a row of three cuboid gravity cranes parked up along one wall. There was a flatbed lifter that looked as if it could carry fifty million tonnes of Gallenium.

McKinney had once been told that the Space Corps ships were modular – they assembled them from hundreds of different pieces flown in from factories across the Confederation to the shipyards, where they were fitted together like a jigsaw that could kill a hundred billion people.

"Behind that door is the cargo lift. It goes all the way to the surface," said Stein, continuing with his description. "Can you see that safety notice on the wall next to it? *Do not exceed rated capacity of four hundred million tonnes.* Imagine that shit! *Four hundred* million tonnes. When they fire up the gravity generators for it, you can feel it through the walls when you're taking a crap at the other end of the hangar. There's another lift just like it in the central storage area." Stein laughed as if he'd told the funniest joke imaginable.

"Lots of positrons," said McKinney, keeping one eye on the flashing amber alert on his HUD.

"Best if you don't think about it too hard, sir."

Stein set off again, casting shadows of his own to mingle with those of the smaller ground vehicles. Each of these vehicles looked as if it was designed for a specific purpose, though McKinney couldn't divine the functions from the shapes. As the squad rounded the side of the flatbed lifter, they found objects which had unmistakeable purposes.

Lying on its side was a huge turret of polished alloy, with ten thick runners still attached to the top, bottom and sides. A thirty-metre barrel pointed out through a wide, circular opening. McKinney found the half-metre muzzle opening was aimed directly at him and he stared into the infinite blackness within.

"Bulwark cannon," he said in wonder.

"They don't fit them on every ship these days, so I hear," said Stein, taking on the role of unofficial tour guide. When you worked down here and had an ear for gossip, it was easy to pick stuff up from the technicians. "Countermeasures that can destroy any ground armour in a single shot. Maybe one of the new Colossus tanks could take a few hits, but this baby can fire a half a million rounds per minute."

"Five hundred and thirty-two thousand rounds per minute for thirty seconds before burnout chance exceeds fifty percent likelihood," McKinney corrected him.

"Whatever you say, sir."

They were in a hurry and marched onwards as they discussed the array of weapons left almost carelessly in this storage area. Near to the Bulwark cannon was something else. A metal tube lay on the back of a smaller flatbed. The tube was over a hundred metres long, with a diameter of three metres. It had a rounded nose and a status panel on one side displayed a series of numbers. McKinney knew exactly what it was and even the insulating properties of his suit couldn't prevent him from feeling a terrible chill.

"I thought they banned these ten years ago," he said.

Stein shrugged. "Doesn't matter what the Council wants. If Old Man Duggan thinks his spaceships need to carry two-point-five gigaton nuclear missiles, then he can pull the right strings and make it happen."

"Lambdas over there," said McKinney.

The missiles were about forty metres long and a metre in diameter. Each had an armour-piercing head and a secondary, main plasma charge behind. There was a row of ten in the bunker, standing in a purpose-built half-magazine from which they could be easily moved and loaded onto a warship. Lights on the missiles indicated they were active.

The squad continued through the storage area until they came to the three-hundred metre opening which led into the hangar bay. McKinney looked up as he went through and saw a ten-metre-thick blast door, suspended in its recess high above him. Stein evidently caught the look.

"The door was up when the power went off. It's powered by the Gallenium generators, so they must have built in a lock to stop it falling closed when something like this happens."

"Good news for us," said McKinney.

They entered the hangar bay and almost immediately found themselves beneath the hulking shape of the *ES Lucid*. Its support legs were colossal, keeping the unimaginable weight of the spaceship above the surface. The stress fractures in the floor he'd seen earlier were much wider up close and McKinney had to keep a check on his feet to avoid tripping.

He tipped his head back – the underside of the vessel was little more than a hundred metres overhead. From this close, it was possible to identify the outlines of movable outer plates which concealed the Lambda X clusters and the Bulwark cannons. There was a single underside particle beam visible near the nose, its housing dome adding curves to the straight edges. The humming of the gravity engines sent a constant vibration through the floor.

"Over there," said Stein, pointing again. "There's a side exit a few hundred metres away."

"Shame we can't get inside the *Lucid* instead," said Garcia.

"Get inside, take off and then blow the Ghasts into little pieces," said Webb. "All we need is captain, a crew and a way to get those upper blast doors to open for us."

"It needs a code to get in," said Bannerman. "A code that people like us are distinctly not permitted to see or use."

"In case someone finds a malfunctioning replicator, gets drunk and tries to steal a fleet heavy cruiser," said McKinney, wondering briefly where the AWOLs he'd set out to find had ended up. *Probably dead by now.*

"They were meant to complete some big milestone in whatever work the *Lucid*'s in here for," said Stein, proving to be a goldmine of gossip. "That was meant to be yesterday afternoon. I don't know what happened – I think they had to abort for the day. There were a few pissed-off faces checking out at 5pm yesterday evening. They used to work late when there were problems. Not anymore. Anyway, the spaceship's sealed now, like Bannerman says."

"You're telling me the techs, scientists and engineers can't get onboard without having a fleet captain hanging around to open and close the boarding ramps every time they want to get inside?" asked Garcia.

"They've got keys," said Stein. "They'll be locked up tight, though."

"Yeah."

The side exit from the hangar floor wasn't far. When they emerged from beneath the *ES Lucid*, McKinney checked anxiously to make sure there were no Ghasts waiting to shoot them from overhead balconies and then he dashed into the comparative safety of a wide passage which led back into the personnel area of the bunker. He paused for a second and checked his HUD. True to his word, Stein had brought them much closer to the Section D entrance. There were several flights of stairs, a few corridors and they'd be there.

McKinney turned up the amplification on his earpiece. There was nothing unexpected – no sound of explosions, gunfire or an approaching army of Ghasts. For some reason, he didn't feel reassured and he waved the squad onwards, before setting off with renewed caution.

CHAPTER ELEVEN

"SECTION D ENTRANCE IS JUST AHEAD," said McKinney. He double-checked the overlay map on his HUD to make sure.

The squad gathered in one of the many open meeting areas found in the bunker. There were chairs and various consoles around the floor and the men stuck warily to whatever cover suited them best.

It hadn't taken long to get here and they'd met no resistance, nor seen evidence of an incursion into the bunker. Squads B and C had already established positions at their target locations. Corporals Li and Evans checked in at regular intervals – there was no sign of hostiles.

"We'll take it slow from here," McKinney warned.

"Got movement," said Corporal Li calmly.

The sound of a perfectly-machined repeater unleashing a short burst of projectiles came through the speaker.

"Corporal Li, please report!"

The repeater cut out and Li swore repeatedly.

"Shit, we got civilians down here, sir! Clifton got a jumpy and fired his repeater."

"Casualties?"

"One civilian dead, sir. The stupid bastard shot someone!"

"Damnit! Keep it steady, Corporal!"

"The doors are active now, sir – I have no idea when that happened. She must have been trapped in one of these rooms."

McKinney gritted his teeth. "No more crap."

"Sorry, sir."

"Corporal Evans, the internal doors are powered up again. Please be alert to the presence of civilians."

"Sir."

With a shake of his head, McKinney beckoned his squad over. "It sounds like we've got power back. Maybe our guys have asserted some control over the base. We're going to do whatever we can to assist them. Watch out for friendlies."

They set off, through one of the three exits from the meeting area. The passage went left ahead and McKinney crept forward until he was at the corner. He leaned out carefully – Section D entrance was visible and he saw the expanse of the lobby. The emergency lighting was still in place - enough for him to make out several of the unmanned security desks without needing to rely on his visor's image intensifiers.

"Wait!" he commanded.

The corridor offered nothing in the way of cover, so he sprinted along it in a burst of movement before crouching at the next corner, ready to use his repeater if necessary.

"Section D lobby is clear."

His suit's sensor detected nothing out of the ordinary. The entrance was in the opposite wall, fifteen metres away – the square blast door was raised and the activation panel glowed green. The angle wasn't good enough for McKinney to see anything of the base, since the Section D entrance was reached by a long, concreted slope which went up to ground level. His HUD registered a gentle breeze coming in from outside and he thought there might be faint flickers of orange light reflected from the metal of the door frame.

"Something isn't right," he said across the comms channel. "We're moving up."

While the squad advanced along the corridor he dashed across the lobby, vaulting over one of the security desks with its smooth laminate top. At the entrance, he pressed his back to one side and looked carefully around the edge of the doorway. The concrete ramp was about forty metres long and emerged somewhere in the base he couldn't immediately identify. The sky above had an orange glow to it and he guessed a significant part of the Tillos base was burning.

"Bannerman? Think you can get a signal out from this doorway? The rest of you, secure the area."

A figure ran over and crouched down. The HUD in McKinney's visor informed him it was Bannerman, though the presence of the portable comms pack also gave the game away.

"I can get you a signal out, no problems, Sergeant."

"Find out if there's anyone else alive on the base."

Bannerman lowered his comms pack reverently to the ground – the sign of a man in love with his kit. There was a flap on one side of the pack which he pulled open.

"Takes a moment to fire up and interface with the visor," he said. "Right, we're set. Who should I speak to?"

"Might as well go straight for the top."

"Colonel Tenney it is."

There was something in Bannerman's poise which told McKinney exactly what the answer was.

"He's offline, sir."

"These packs don't need to route through the base comms hub, do they?" asked McKinney doubtfully.

"No, sir. This baby can force a way through to any device capable of sending or receiving a comms signal. The hub doesn't need to be operational for it to work."

"Is there anyone online anywhere?"

"Scanning for receptors. It takes a few seconds."

McKinney waited impatiently. He flicked his gaze constantly around the room, checking to see where the others of his squad had positioned themselves. They were edgy too – he could see it in the way they moved and how tightly they gripped their weapons.

"There's no one out there," said Bannerman.

"What about beyond the base?"

"That's what I mean, sir. There's *no one*. There isn't a single military comms receptor anywhere within range. Plenty of civilian ones, so it seems like people are still alive somewhere."

McKinney tried to recall the names of the other military bases on Atlantis. The Tillos base was the largest, but there were three more. "They must have attacked the other bases as well. Tansul and Teklo."

"And Tivon. I can't reach any of them."

Just then, something passed overhead – a dark shape travelling languidly as if it had all the time in the world. The magnitude of the problem struck McKinney with the force of a hammer blow. He'd brought the squad here in the hope they could be of some use to an imagined resistance upon the surface. As well as that, he'd wanted to find someone who could relieve him – someone to take charge and tell him what he needed to do. He smiled inwardly. *Looks like I'm going to get that chance to prove myself after all,* he thought. A different voice asked him if it was a chance he really wanted.

"Can you get a signal out to one of the other planets? Or that orbital. What do they call it? The *Juniper*?"

"I can send a birthday greeting to your great aunt on Roban if you want me to, sir. The trouble is, she won't receive it for a few years. The stuff they pack into warships like the *Lucid* – that can get a signal to most places in a few seconds. Some sort of trans-dimensional crap they use. These packs are meant for comms between squads on the same planet. Maybe a planet and its moon."

"What about that comms hub out there on the base?"

"It's a comms hub, sir," said Bannerman, trying unsuccessfully to prevent himself from sounding as though he thought his superior officer's knowledge was sorely lacking. "It has the same comms arrays as the *Lucid*."

"That trans-dimensional crap?"

"Yes, sir." Bannerman kept an admirably straight face.

Having caught the implication that he was asking stupid questions, McKinney ploughed on with what might have been another. "Can you patch this field pack into the comms hub and get a signal out through its antennae? Even if there's no power to the hub?"

"I don't know. It's not showing as a receptor. Maybe if I plugged straight in through a port in the control room. I've never been asked that question before."

The sound of a detonation – low and heavy – reached them. It was followed by another and another. The harsh, metallic clinking sound of high-velocity projectiles followed.

"Someone's still fighting," said McKinney.

"Whatever just flew overhead must have come to give air support," said Bannerman. "Could be that's why the Ghasts haven't come into the bunker yet – some of our guys are fighting back."

"It's sporadic," said McKinney. "This is just a mop-up exercise before they move on to the real reason they came here."

"The *Lucid*?"

"Yes."

"Strikes me they'd have found it by now if that's what they were looking for, sir. They might be here for something completely different."

"Like what?"

Bannerman shrugged. "You tell me, sir. I'm only a pack mule."

McKinney lifted his visor and smiled. "Yeah, and I'm a captain's lapdog."

"Are we going for the hub?"

"You bet we're going for the hub."

"This bunker is heavily shielded. Once we're out we won't be able to get a signal to the other two squads," said Bannerman. He pulled a rectangular piece of blue metal from the top part of his comms pack and with a twist extended a long aerial rod. "Want me to leave this booster here?"

McKinney nodded. It was the little things like this which were easy to overlook when you lacked real battlefield experience. "Good idea, thanks."

"No problem."

With that, Sergeant Eric McKinney ordered the others of his squad to join him at the entrance. He gave them details about what he planned. When he was satisfied they understood, he stepped out into the warm night.

———

FLEET ADMIRAL JOHN DUGGAN'S meeting with the Ghasts wasn't going to plan. Duggan's opposite number in the Ghast navy stared impassively through the viewscreen, his pale, grey eyes giving away nothing that could be used as leverage.

For his own part, Duggan stared back, knowing that to look away for even an instant would be seen as a display of weakness. Subjos Kion-Tur was big, even amongst his species and Duggan imagined the Ghast to be at least eight feet tall. He was broad and muscular with it, his dull blue uniform hardly able to contain his thick arms and legs. His face had similar features to those of a human – nose, mouth, eyes, but mixed with something unmistakeably alien.

"It would be seen as a great favour amongst the people of the Confederation if the Ghasts were to offer some assistance in this matter."

"The terms of our treaty do not encompass military aid," said Kion-Tur. "We are neighbours at peace, not brothers in arms."

Duggan had been a frontline captain when the peace treaty was finalised. Even as a younger man he hadn't been especially naïve, but he'd still been filled with hope that some kind of bond would develop between humans and Ghasts. A real friendship would forever be a step too far after the war. Even so, both species knew how insignificant they were in a universe which seemed to be filled with empires of advanced, warlike aliens. Human ingenuity, combined with the Ghasts' ability to advance their tech at a tremendous speed, would have left both species much more secure. For many reasons, it appeared as if those closer ties would never happen.

"The Vraxar have come for us. The Ghasts will be next."

"You say they have come looking for Obsidiar. We have little of it for them to find."

"We only guess it is Obsidiar they want. You say the Ghasts lack reserves. You have enough to fuel a number of your warships, Subjos," said Duggan. "They have found Atlantis, perhaps as a result of the Oblivion *Teskinir*'s broadcast forty years ago."

"You don't know this for certain, Admiral Duggan. You don't even know if this is the Vraxar."

"Who else might it be? Your ancestors – the Estral – are gone."

A hint of a smile appeared on Kion-Tur's face, showing a flash of the same bright, white teeth all Ghasts appeared to possess. "Some amongst us would argue the Vraxar's defeat of the Estral makes us friends."

"They are no friends of the Ghasts."

"I am sure you are correct. Nevertheless, they are not yet our enemy."

"You will send no ships?"

The Ghast didn't answer directly. "What of your own Obsidiar warships, Fleet Admiral? You have led us to believe there are more than thirty amongst your fleet. Could it be that you have sent them elsewhere? I am advised the Confederation has additional problems out on its frontiers."

Duggan had absolutely no idea where the Ghasts had found out about the rebellion at Roban and Liventor. He kept his face neutral, fully aware Kion-Tur could be doing no more than fishing for information about both the Space Corps fleet and the frontier issue.

"The people of the Confederation are as happy as they have ever been, Subjos, safe in the knowledge that the Council has their best interests at heart. You are aware Confederation Space is vast and even with a hundred Obsidiar warships, it would not be easy to bring sufficient numbers to bear against the Vraxar."

Kion-Tur laughed, the sound not entirely pleasant even with the hard edges smoothed off by the language modules. "You are poor at deflection, Fleet Admiral. Where you attempt diversion, I will provide truth. We do not have a significant warship within three days of Atlantis. Even if we did, I would not order it to assist."

Duggan cursed inwardly. The Ghasts were not accomplished liars. When asked a question to which they couldn't give an honest answer, they generally answered a slightly different question to the one asked. Sometimes they changed the subject and occasionally they would point-blank refuse to give any answer at all. Duggan realised Kion-Tur had easily seen through his partial answer.

"No *significant* warship?" he asked. It was tantamount to an admission that the Ghasts had other, less significant, resources closer.

"The movement of our fleet is our own business. I'm sure the Space Corps has vessels parked near to every single one of the planets populated by the Ghast Subjocracy." Kion-Tur looked intently at Duggan. "Vessels equipped with surface-cleansing incendiaries."

"The movement of our fleet is our own business," said Duggan, parroting Kion-Tur's response. In truth, he was shocked at how well-informed the Ghast was. The Space Corps maintained a constant, covert presence near to each of the Ghast worlds. Entire planets had been destroyed during the war and the Confederation had no intention of letting it happen again, even if it meant extensive subterfuge against the Ghasts.

"I wish you success in defeating your attackers," said Kion-Tur.

"You will not reconsider?"

"We do not see the requirement for us to become involved."

Duggan nodded. "Very well. I hope the Ghast Subjocracy does not come to regret its decision."

"A life without regrets is a life which has been wasted."

"I don't care for platitudes," said Duggan.

Kion-Tur wasn't bothered by the comment. "If you were to give us some of your Obsidiar, we would assist."

In a way, it was surprising it had taken the Ghast so long to bring the matter up, given their reputation for straight talk.

"I can't authorise that," said Duggan. "We have precious little of it our stores."

"We estimate you to have something in the region of two-point-five million tonnes in total."

The guess was exceptionally accurate, if indeed it was a guess. Duggan had no intention of giving the game away by confirming or denying. "How much of our Obsidiar do you expect to receive for your promised assistance?"

"Enough for ten of our warships – approximately half a million tonnes. That would be sufficient for us to put three of our Obsidiar-fuelled Oblivion battleships at your disposal, as soon as we can recall them."

"You ask too much, Subjos. Besides, Atlantis is under attack now. We can't wait for your ships to return from wherever in deep space you have them."

The Ghast smiled. "Perhaps we don't ask enough, Admiral. It is not we who are under attack. Perhaps if you were to ask later our price will be higher. You may regret spurning this opportunity while the cost is so low. An agreement reached now would ensure our resources are at your disposal immediately in the event the Vraxar come to Overtide or Pioneer."

Three Ghast battleships would make a fearsome attack group but it was galling to listen to the demands, especially given the likelihood the Vraxar would come for the Ghasts at some point. Duggan had long suspected the Ghasts were angry to have found themselves with so little Obsidiar at the end of the Estral wars. On the other hand, it was the Confederation which had done most of the fighting.

Duggan wasn't happy but knew he couldn't let pride or a sense of betrayal stop him from acting in the best interests of the Confederation.

"I will speak to the Council," he said.

"We await your answer with interest."

The Ghast didn't speak further and Duggan gave the command for Cerys to close the secure link. The viewscreen went dark and he returned to his desk to sit in the ancient, battered chair in which he did most of his best thinking. He opened the top drawer in his desk and pulled out a framed photo of his wife and three children, taken back in their younger days. With a sigh, he returned it, keeping it hidden to stop the never-ending barrage questions he received about his family when he left the picture on display – a lesson taught him by a man long-dead.

With the comms link to Atlantis unavailable, the response fleet facing what was sure to be a vastly superior foe, his other resources in transit and this double-edged offer from the Ghasts to help, Duggan experienced a terrible feeling of helplessness.

CHAPTER TWELVE

LIEUTENANT MARIA CRUZ brought the group to a halt while she did some rapid thinking. The three civilian operators milled around uncertainly, whilst Lieutenant Reynolds did his best to look like this was the kind of situation he encountered every day. They were in a compact room with bare, metal walls and cheap carpet tiles on the floor. There was no reason for the room to be here and it had absolutely no apparent purpose, other than to break up a long corridor.

"I think the CPU room is a couple of levels below this one," said Larry Keller. "Somewhere over there."

"*Think?*" sneered Lieutenant Reynolds "I thought you knew where you were going?"

"It's been a while, Lieutenant. I came a different way last time."

"I thought they paid you to know this stuff?"

"No, they pay *me* to troubleshoot and monitor the hub encryption algos. They pay *you* to kill the bad guys."

"Knock it off!" said Lieutenant Maria Cruz. "This is screwed up enough already without you two arguing."

They were lost, somewhere underground. In fact, none of them even knew if they were still in the comms hub area or if they'd inadvertently wandered off into another zone on the Tillos base. The problem arose from the fact that during normal operation most of the doors remained closed for the majority of the time. You either didn't have authorisation to open them, or you simply didn't have a need to see what was beyond. The Space Corps absolutely did not encourage exploration, so in the end, personnel walked to where they were required to be at the start of their shift. At the end of their shift, they walked the same route in reverse.

Since the enemy had released the locks on every single door, the group was able to roam freely, yet without an idea where they were going. Up until recently, it had been silent. A few minutes ago, a series of explosions had shaken the walls. Cruz was sure they were far underground, so whatever the source of the blasts, it likely carried a fairly high yield. There were only two positives she could take from their situation – firstly, they were alive, Secondly, no more of those skin-metal creatures had shown up. In the absence of birthday drinks, Cruz accepted what she was given.

"I think the residual power is gone," said Nelson, brandishing her own diagnostics tablet.

"What've you got, Debs?" asked Keller, crossing over to look.

"The processor clusters have just died. Except this single, remaining unit."

"The Obsidiar core."

"It's nailed on one hundred percent," said Akachi.

"They're still trying to get through the encryption."

"Yup. A standard brute force attack," said Keller. "Since the other clusters shut down, the hub just got a little easier to break into. On the other hand, we only need to pull out the Obsidiar core now to put the databanks into a static state."

"That's good news?" asked Reynolds.

"Probably as good as we're going to get, Lieutenant."

"Shh!" said Akachi. "I heard something."

Reynolds looked as if he wanted to say something dismissive.

"I can hear it," said Nelson.

Cruz picked up on it too. It was the heavy thud of footsteps, muted only by a thin covering of cheap carpet tiles. "Quick! Move!" she said, as loudly as she dared.

They ran for the far exit corridor. Dim light pooled on the floor, its overlapping patches insufficient to dispel the darkness, leaving them to dash through alternating places of shadowed gloom and cold, meagre white. Cruz tripped over something – an object low to the floor hidden in the dark. She swore under her breath, her mind waiting for the pain to come rushing into her bruised shin. She limped onwards, as the others stretched out a lead of a few paces. Keller looked over his shoulder and dropped back to help. He put an arm around her shoulder and hauled her upright.

"Thanks, Larry," she said.

"No worries, Lieutenant."

While Cruz tried to get back into her stride, the others reached the entrance to a stairwell. Reynolds was in the lead and he turned without hesitation. The rest followed, vanishing from sight. A few seconds later, Cruz and Keller reached the place. The steps went up and down, the sound of receding footsteps making it hard to tell which way the others had gone.

"This way," she said, setting off downwards.

She stopped, sensing Keller's hesitation.

"You said it was down, right?" she asked.

"Yeah." He flashed a look at the upwards stairs. "I think they went up. I don't think I'm cut out to be a hero, Lieutenant."

"I need you to show me what it is I'm meant to do, Larry. Where I'm meant to go."

Suddenly, he smiled. "For you, Lieutenant? Anything."

With a start, she realised he meant it. He followed her at once and they took the stairs two at a time, haste competing with the need for silence. After one flight, the stairs switched back and descended another twenty metres. They emerged into a room, this one packed with banks of consoles. There was a series of gauges on one wall, along with other instrumentation. The power was off and everything was dead. There was a damp, mustiness in the air as if the ventilation in the room was poor.

"They're not here," said Cruz, cocking her head to listen. She swore. "Damnit, I bet Reynolds went up those steps like a champion sprinter."

"The man is a coward," said Keller.

"I shouldn't comment on a fellow officer."

"He's always trying to undermine you, Lieutenant. Even when you're not there."

"I know, Larry. It's my own fault for letting him get away with it."

It wasn't the best time to talk about the difficulties she had with stamping her authority. Cruz knew she was well-liked, but when it came to expert well-poisoners like Reynolds, she was out of her depth.

"I think I know where we are now," said Keller. "See that sign?"

He ran across the room, heading for another of the seemingly identical passages. The sign in question hung from the ceiling. *Hub Core Processing Area. Authorised Personnel Only.*

Aside from the sign, there was evidently something in the layout which told Keller where he was and he picked up the pace, turning left and then right, with his diagnostics tablet clutched in one hand. The explosions came again and this time they were followed by the metallic sound of a repeater, somewhere ahead of them. Keller came to an abrupt halt.

"Let me go in front," said Cruz.

She raised the gauss pistol, realising how small it looked. She walked on, Keller following a few paces behind. He looked close to panic and Cruz berated herself for getting into a position where she required the assistance of a civilian.

"We need to go that way," Keller whispered, pointing to a passage in the right-hand wall. He didn't need to remind her that the sound of repeater fire had come from the same direction.

She looked around the corner and pulled her head back. "Bodies," she said.

There were five of them, all human and each of them clothed in a military-issue space suit. The soldiers were contorted in death, their blood spilled on the floor and the walls. Their bodies were shredded, with limbs and huge chunks of flesh torn away.

"Hand-held repeater," she said. "They must have been caught by it."

Keller peered around the corner and his face turned white. "Messy."

"How far away from the processor room are we, Larry?"

"Not far."

"Think you can give me directions?"

He nodded. "Left at the end of here, second right, across an open space and it should be straight in front of you."

"Once I'm in the room, what do I need to do?"

"Look for the handles. You just need to find the right handle and pull out the processing unit."

"As easy as that?"

"Yes, Lieutenant. They should be marked. You want unit number five. That's the one that burned out and got replaced by the Obsidiar processor."

"What if they bring the power back after I pull the core? Won't they be left with a bunch of easily-hacked old cores?"

"No. Once all the processors are offline, the data goes static.

It doesn't matter if you fire the encryption processing clusters up again – by that point it'll be too late."

"Think you can find your way back to that stairwell?"

"I should stay with you, Lieutenant."

"It's too dangerous, Larry. I'm the one with the training and the gun."

He was torn – she could read it in his face. Larry didn't want to leave her, but he didn't want to die either and he clearly knew he stood a better chance if he went in the opposite direction to the bodies.

"Maybe we can have a drink when this is all over, huh? Just me and you," she said.

The change of subject cut through his fear and focused his mind. He smiled. "That sounds like a plan I can go with."

"I want you to go back to the stairs and see if you can get out of here. You're no good without a weapon."

"Those guys out there were carrying rifles. I could use one."

"I want you to go back, Larry."

Something changed in his face – a hardening as if he'd discovered a new resolve he didn't know existed.

"I'm staying with you. Two of us doubles the chance of success, right? And I've already got the promise of a date out of it. In my eyes, that's a result already. Anyway, how could I look at myself in the mirror knowing I'd been given the chance to stop these bastards finding out where everyone else in the Confederation lives and I'd been too scared to do anything about it?"

They both knew their chances of survival were slim and it was unlikely they'd ever get out for that drink. It didn't seem right to say it.

"Come on, then. We'll stick together," she said.

Whatever had been the source of the earlier gunfire, it was now silent. Feeling exposed, Cruz made her way along the corridor, keeping her shoulder to the wall. She reached the closest body, doing her best to avoid looking into the dead eyes. They didn't cover this in training and the exercises the Space Corps put its troops through was no substitute. When the sharp scent of blood reached her nostrils, it took every ounce of her willpower to remain strong and for the first time since she'd joined the Corps, Maria Cruz wished she'd chosen a different path.

The soldier's gauss rifle lay across his torn chest. She stooped and pulled it free in one movement. Larry was behind and she handed it to him. A few seconds later, she was holding a second rifle. The pistol was now effectively useless, but she tucked it into her belt anyway.

"Grenades," said Larry.

Four of the soldiers carried grenades in bandoliers. Cruz managed to get one of the straps free and put it across her chest, doing her best to ignore the wetness of the blood. She was willing to trust Larry with a rifle, but there was no way he was allowed to handle grenades. The Corps made its soldiers go through an extended course before they were allowed to use them and they were a lot more sophisticated than the old pull-pin-and-throw type. The civilian course in firearms Larry attended didn't qualify him to handle explosives, no matter how many aliens there might be hiding around the next corner.

"Along here and turn left?" she said.

"Yes."

Before they could take more than a dozen paces, the sound of gunfire came again. This time it was much closer than before. Without knowing what she'd find, or if she stood a chance of overcoming whatever was ahead, Maria Cruz pressed on, her gauss rifle braced against her shoulder and the muzzle pointing unerringly in front.

CHAPTER THIRTEEN

SERGEANT ERIC MCKINNEY stared in horror. The Tillos base looked like something from a madman's nightmare. Piles of rubble reached dozens of metres above the ground, extending as far as the eye could see. Red-orange flames licked up into the sky with such ferocity that the sensors on the spacesuit visors struggled with the contrasts of heat, light and darkness.

Across from the Section D exit ramp, there was a series of deep craters covering the visible area of the landing pad, their edges scarred by plasma. The *ES Impetuous* continued to burn with an intensity that gave the impression it would continue for a hundred years or more. Positrons spilled from the area, setting off alerts on the watching soldiers' HUDs.

To the east the explosions continued, their blasts hidden by mounds of rubble, twisted metal rebar and charred bodies. There was a small craft in the air a good distance away and only visible with assistance from the spacesuit visor. The shuttle's design was alien and unfamiliar. Light flashed from a weapon mounted on its nose. Tracers streaked to the ground, projectiles spilling heat into the air as they travelled.

McKinney was most of the way up the Section D exit ramp, using the lip as cover. This was the first time he'd been confronted by the reality of war and it left him numb. He'd grown up reading heroic tales of the Ghost wars, but this was the first time he'd seen it for himself.

Before the attack, the base had been home to tens of thousands of personnel. They'd lived and worked in the countless buildings which covered many square kilometres. The base had been in place for decades and now it was reduced to flames and rubble.

"They hit the barracks hardest," said Webb grimly. "The bastards must have known that's where most people were sleeping."

"Where's the hub?" said McKinney. The base he remembered was no longer reflected by the reality. "Hang on, let me check the HUD."

The tiny computer in the spacesuit visor showed him a topographical view of the base as it had been a few hours before. It showed McKinney's squad as a series of orange dots and then added a vector which pointed towards the comms hub.

"Six hundred metres! Stein, I thought you said we'd come out right on top of it!"

"It's the closest entrance to the hub, sir."

McKinney got himself oriented. There was a hundred metres of clear ground before the nearest piles of rubble started – huge quantities of rubble, with no clues as to what lay beyond. He zoomed in the visor's sensor and tried to figure out the best way to proceed. At the top of the Section D ramp was a wide, pedestrian walkway. The walkway branched off into several directions. The northern path looked as if it came within a short distance of the hub building, though it was hard to be sure since it was piled up with yet more debris.

There was no movement on his visor sensor and the only

visible sign of an enemy presence was the shuttle. His HUD told him it was three thousand metres away and when he zoomed in, McKinney saw it was a boxy thirty-metre vessel of dark metal, vaguely slug-like in shape and with four landing feet. The shuttle's nose cannon continued to spew its projectiles at something on the ground.

"I don't like it," said McKinney. The shuttle would chew up his squad if it caught them in the open. He waved Webb forward. "Think you can hit it from here?"

Webb spun the plasma tube around in a smooth action, resting it on his right shoulder. Two blue lights glowed faintly at the middle of the launcher – the only visible adornment.

"I can hit it, sir. The question is, will it go down in one shot? There's a ten-second recharge on the tube."

"That gets you two shots easy."

"And alerts every enemy soldier on the base that we're here, sir."

It was a decision McKinney didn't enjoy making. He knew perfectly well what the capabilities of a Space Corps' shuttle were, but he could only guess what the alien equivalent might be able to do. If it was heavily-armoured and two shots failed to bring it down, they'd be forced to retreat into the bunker.

The decision was taken from him.

"Movement," said Elder. "Six hostiles. What the hell are they?"

From the north, six figures emerged into view. They came along the remains of a road and began walking over an area of comparatively open ground about two hundred metres from the top of the ramp.

"Shit, they're coming this way!" said Boon.

McKinney gave an angry wave of his arm to silence the men. He put his head over the edge of the ramp again to get his first sight of the enemy.

Mechs was his first thought. *They've sent machines to do their dirty work.* When he looked more closely, he saw that he was mistaken. The approaching enemy was made up from more than simply metal. They gave off a heat signature consistent with that of a living organism. They had the appearance of Ghasts in that they were broad and strong. They were also different, having metal plates embedded in their faces and chests, with more covering their shoulders. One of them had an arm made entirely of alloy.

McKinney stared with revulsion. Each one of the creatures was slightly different to the others. Some were well in excess of seven feet tall, others were closer to six. Some looked shrunken and atrophied as if they'd sent the oldest members of their species to fight alongside the youngest. Two were bald, others had hair. One had hardly any biological face, the rest being metal formed into a poor copy of a mouth and nose.

"What are those cannons they're carrying?" asked Garcia.

"I don't want to find out," McKinney replied.

The *cannons* Garcia referred to were thick tubes about two feet long, with short stocks and an uncomfortably wide bore. Each of the aliens carried one.

"That's what we're facing, folks. Those are what killed our men and women."

Rage surged up in McKinney. He crawled a little way further up the ramp and crouched down so that only his eyes were showing at ground level. The tube of his repeater was in his hand and he ached to use it – to spray his opponents with a deadly arc of projectiles. The repeaters weren't subtle and he unslung his rifle instead.

"Elder, Stein, Boon, McCall, Garcia. Rifles only."

The soldiers crowded in alongside McKinney, forming a line. They aimed their gauss rifles over the ramp's edge. McKinney glanced across, trying to gauge their state of readiness.

The tiny delay was enough to spoil their surprise. As a unit, the approaching enemy dropped into a crouch.

"They've seen us," said Boon.

"Fire!" said McKinney, surprising himself with the calmness of his voice.

Six gauss rifles whined as their coils hurled slugs of dense alloy across the intervening space. Something made a cracking sound on the far side of the ramp channel. McKinney felt shards of stone pinging away from his back. He fired again and again, pressing the activation trigger on his rifle, feeling the thud-thud-thud of its recoil as it kicked into his shoulder. There was a second and third sharp crack from behind as the enemy's response fire struck the concrete edge of the channel.

The enemy fell beneath the withering hail of gunfire. They toppled over without sound, thumping heavily onto the concrete. The men of Squad A didn't let up, firing volley after volley into the prone bodies of their opponents.

"Stop!" shouted McKinney at last.

The gauss rifles fell silent and there was a moment during which nobody moved and nobody spoke. McKinney broke the spell.

"Up! Move!" he said.

As a group, the soldiers of Squad A sprinted along the last few metres of the ramp, emerging onto open ground. With the die cast, McKinney didn't hesitate. He got his head down and ran to the north, aiming for the cover offered by the ruins of the nearest building. The bodies of the alien soldiers were in front of him. Such was their aura of strangeness, he half-expected them to stir, to raise their snub-nosed hand cannons and begin shooting again. They did not and McKinney looked into the open, staring eyes of one as he jumped over it. The part of the creature that was flesh looked like it was taken from the body of a Ghast and joined with metal components created in a factory.

Without knowing quite what made him so sure, Sergeant Eric McKinney was suddenly convinced these weren't Ghosts at all. They may have contributed the flesh, but they'd done so unwillingly. He wasn't used to having insights and it wasn't the time to think about where this one had risen from.

The squad reached the edges of the rubble, their pace slowing as they wended through the larger pieces. A fire simmered somewhere deep beneath the ruins, as though waiting for its chance to burst free. Dust floated in the air, motes of it highlighted in the wavering orange light.

"We have to go over," McKinney said across the open channel.

He looked up – the Tillos base had been a visual monstrosity – a shrine to mundanity. That didn't mean it was built from anything less than the strongest concretes, fixed and reinforced with a hundred thousand kilometres of steel bars. Here, slabs of concrete made a series of overlapping slopes, leading to a height of fifty metres or more. There was a twisted chair, precariously balanced halfway up, along with something which may have been a bed or a desk.

Trying hard to ignore the unspoken tales of this tragedy, McKinney began the climb. From below, it looked like an easy scramble up the slope. It wasn't long until he realised the surface was treacherous with loose grit and the slab he climbed bounced underfoot as if it were suspended by overstressed rebar.

The others came after him, their weight and footfall increasing the bounce until McKinney became concerned something would give. Whatever was holding the slab held and he jumped across to the next, working his way ever higher. McKinney prided himself on staying fit, but his breathing sounded loud in his ears. His HUD told him his heart rate was high and his adrenal glands were working flat-out.

Just below the top, he looked back and saw his squad had

fallen behind. While he waited for them to catch up, he crouched below the top of the pile and looked away over the landing field to the south and west. He zoomed in his suit sensor and searched for signs of the enemy or any indication there was continued resistance.

The darkness of night combined with running at maximum zoom ensured the cut-down sensor model fitted into his visor struggled to cope. He saw speckled green shapes that were so indistinct he had no idea what they were. He activated his movement tracker. Here and there he saw flickers of orange, far away in the distance.

The first of his men – Webb – joined him, hunkering down awkwardly on the slope.

"What a shit job this is, Sergeant," he said.

It wasn't clear exactly what Webb was referring to and McKinney was too preoccupied to ask. He crawled up the last few metres to the highest point of the rubble and looked cautiously over. The enemy shuttle was hovering to the north-east, closer than it had been before. Its nose cannon was still and McKinney's brain registered the fact that there were no more explosions and the previously constant sound of small-arms fire was now little more than the occasional shot.

"We're losing," said Bannerman.

"We lost this one long ago," said McKinney.

Bannerman stood a little higher and leaned forward to point. "There's the main comms hub, Sergeant. I see they left it well alone."

McKinney had seen the comms hub hundreds of times. It was a low, square construction, close to three hundred metres along each side. All across its roof there was a series of dull pillars made of metal and varying in length from a couple of metres to fifty or more. These pillars were the antennae – from atop the rubble they appeared slender and delicate.

The hub was set in an area of ground which was mostly unoccupied, aside from two buildings which McKinney remembered housed generators. These equally low buildings were also intact, presumably saved from destruction by their proximity to the hub.

There was movement around the building. McKinney counted four separate groups of six enemy soldiers. More appeared – dozens of them coming from amongst the ruins or whatever was left of the original roads and footways through the base.

McKinney spoke over a private channel. "Bannerman, get on the comms again and see if there's anyone out there."

The soldier put down his pack. "Let's give it a go, Sergeant. I think it's probably a waste of time."

"What else can we do?"

"I'm not giving you an argument, sir. Nitro Bannerman doesn't argue with his superiors. I'm just telling you how I think it is." Bannerman kept low as he operated the comms pack. It didn't take him long. "There's some of our fleet up there!" he said excitedly.

"Can you get a signal out to them?"

"Yes, sir. It'll take a few minutes for it to reach them. There are seven spaceships operating on a closed network. Which one should I send the message to?"

"How should I know?" asked McKinney, trying not to sound angry. "Send it to the biggest one. Tell them we're stranded down here and the Tillos base has been overrun by some kind of mech-suited aliens that look like Ghasts but might not be. Tell them they've come for the *ES Lucid*."

The ground comms pack was an exceptionally robust piece of kit, with an incredible amount of functionality. However, it couldn't access a spaceship fleet's closed comms network in order to find out which was the most important ship. Bannerman knew all this, but he didn't bother to tell Sergeant McKinney. The soldier simply picked one of the seven warships at random and sent his message.

"That's done, sir," he said. "A few minutes and they'll know we're here."

McKinney felt like a weight had been lifted from him. "We might get out of this yet." He crawled back to the top of the rubble pile and studied the comms building again.

Bannerman joined him. "There's no way we're getting through all those soldiers."

"Maybe we should back off, Sergeant," Garcia suggested.

"Why would they leave the hub alone when they destroyed the rest of the base?" McKinney pondered. "Look – they've established positions all around. It's like they're keeping it safe."

"It's just comms stuff, sir," said Bannerman. "Anything that goes off world comes through here."

"That would include our most important military secrets?"

"Yeah, Sergeant, good point. Also, the routing data for the other Confederation hubs is held in there as well." Bannerman paused, lost in thought. "If they lifted that stuff, they could go to anywhere else in the Confederation. If they haven't already done so."

"That must be what they've come for," said McKinney. "Maybe not the *ES Lucid* after all."

"We can't let them have access to our data," said Bannerman. "They could wipe us out if they knew where the rest of the Confederation planets were."

"If we get in there, can we blow the arrays up or something?" asked McKinney.

"I wish I could tell you, sir. I've only been inside the hub a couple of times and they keep people like me away from the sensitive stuff. It goes a long way underground and it could be filled with those metal bastards already."

McKinney ducked out of sight and sat on his haunches,

thinking. The place was crawling with the enemy and he was sure the most experienced of troop commanders would have second and third thoughts about charging in. He had another fourteen men in Squads B and C, but it would take them a good few minutes to get here. Since the last pockets of human resistance were evidently overcome, it was minutes they didn't have to spare. In addition, he wasn't quite ready to relinquish the idea that the *ES Lucid* was the main target – or an important secondary one.

Endless training is no replacement for experience, he thought, not for the first time. He was struggling with the situation and his limited options to make it better. Just when his mind was closing in on a decision, Doug McCall provided some unwelcome information.

"There's a second shuttle coming, sir," he said.

McKinney's eyes darted left and right across the sky. The far horizon was becoming the perfect blue of dawn, but it was still too dark for him to easily find an approaching object and it took a moment before he saw the orange blob of a distant craft.

"That's not a shuttle," said Boon. "Crap! Look at the size of it!"

The bad news didn't stop.

"The first shuttle is moving, sir," said Bannerman.

It was. The vessel accelerated slowly, before banking through the air in a wide arc which would carry it directly to the place Squad A sheltered.

Sergeant Eric McKinney found himself in the most unwelcome of situations – a vastly superior enemy approached from more than one direction and he lacked the weapons and numbers to do anything about it. The stream of expletives from his mouth was hidden behind his visor.

CHAPTER FOURTEEN

RESPONSE FLEET ALPHA'S encounter with the Vraxar was going badly, catastrophically wrong. The enemy ships were carrying jammers which confused the targeting on both the Lambda X and Shatterer missiles carried by the Space Corps vessels. The guidance systems on these missiles were incredibly advanced and in some cases were able to adapt. Unfortunately, only one warhead in ten would lock on and launch.

To make matters worse the Vraxar had energy shields, against which those few warheads detonated harmlessly. Blake knew how an energy shield worked – hit it with enough high-yield explosives and it would eventually crumble. The trouble was, the response fleet wasn't able to launch enough of those explosives to accomplish this feat. Nukes would take out a shield in most cases, except they weren't carried by fleet warships anymore.

"The *Hurricane* isn't going to last much longer," said Blake. "Damnit!"

He had no idea how the cruiser hadn't broken up already. Three-quarters of its hull was aglow, whilst the remaining quarter had simply disintegrated. The Vraxar ships carried an unfamiliar weapon, which fired a beam of dark energy. Where this beam struck, it caused metal to become brittle and fragment into dust. The *ES Hurricane*'s crew were certainly dead, but its AI continued on, firing missiles in sporadic bursts from the few clusters which remained active.

Two of the four enemy ships broke away from the combat, turning in a wide circle which suggested they were less agile than most things in the Space Corps. It didn't really matter – their particle beams burned repeatedly into the vessels of Response Fleet Alpha. At the same time, the dark energy weapons came amongst the fleet and where they struck, millions of tonnes of armour plating and Gallenium engines scattered into rough dust.

"One of our cores has burned out," said Rivera. "Kept it going too long, sir."

Even in battle, the man was trying to score points. Blake told himself there'd be a reckoning soon.

"Load up the last core," he said.

A short-range lightspeed jump wasn't always intended for escape – it was a good way of breaking a missile lock or getting out of range when enemies threatened to overwhelm.

"Acknowledged," growled Rivera.

"There's another twenty of our Lambdas got a lock," said Brady. "Firing."

"For all the good it'll do," Blake spat.

The *Hurricane*'s resistance ended. A series of particle beams ripped into its centre section in an area already weakened by the dark energy beams. The warship split, two large pieces tumbling away from each other.

"Positron output at twenty percent," said Rivera. "It's gone."

"We've got lucky so far," said Brady. "They're focusing on the bigger ships."

"None of what's happening here is good, Commander," said

Blake. "Is there anything you can do to get more of our missiles away?"

"I've not figured it out yet, sir. I think it needs more than a simple reprogramming from the weapons panel. The guys at the lab will need to fix this one."

"Lieutenant Pointer, who is the most senior Captain left in the fleet?"

"Captain Kang, sir."

Blake gritted his teeth. "Apart from Captain Kang. I mean someone who's been able to figure out how to turn on the damned backup comms!"

"Captain Edwards, sir. He's on the *Undertow*."

"Tell him we need to order a withdrawal. We need to get out of here *now*."

"Hold!" she said. "The *New Beginning* has come online. They must have worked out how to use the backups."

"Speak to Captain Kang. Get him to order the withdrawal."

It took only a short time for the message to be sent and the response to arrive.

"Sir, he's refused the request. We are to continue with the engagement."

"Damn the man!" Blake shouted. "What sort of fool is he?"

"Something just one-shot the *Lingard*," said Brady in disbelief. Notes of fear clung to the man's voice and Blake realised his crew were on the verge of outright panic.

"Focus, Commander!"

"Yessir! I'm trying," Brady stammered.

"Stay calm and we'll get through this."

Blake patched into the weapons systems to see if he could help out. The missile control system had a thousand errors, with new ones appearing each time a warhead launch was aborted because of a failure to lock-on.

The *Determinant* was equipped with three Bulwark cannons,

currently dormant. They weren't intended to be used against anything other than missiles, but since the enemy showed no sign of deploying any, it seemed pointless to ignore their potential. Blake set the Bulwarks to track targets of any size. This facility wasn't widely-used, yet it was disappointing to find Brady hadn't learned about it.

The Bulwarks started up immediately, each of the three turrets thundering along runners which carried them through thirty metres of armour plating and into their external positions. An unmistakeable grumbling started at once and they threw thousands upon thousands of hardened Gallenium rounds towards the closest Vraxar ship.

"Tell the others to set Bulwarks to full auto and remove the target size constraints," Blake ordered.

"Letting them know," said Pointer. She sounded far more secure than either Brady or Rivera.

The targeted enemy warship spun away and Blake turned the *Determinant* to follow. Bulwark fire continued to crash into the enemy's shields. With no way to tell how effective the attack was, Blake tried to keep close to the Vraxar. They were less manoeuvrable and slightly faster than the destroyer. In terms of outright speed, it was nothing that would put some of the larger Corps vessels to shame.

"They're ignoring us," Blake realised. He checked his tactical and saw that all four of the Vraxar were converging on the same place. "They've found the *New Beginning*," he said.

He was right. The stealth modules were amongst the most effective technologies anywhere in the Space Corps. However, they weren't completely proof against detection and were generally meant for scouting purposes or to allow a surprise attack. The Vraxar had somehow managed to locate the *New Beginning* and also realised it was the most powerful of the warships arrayed against them.

"Maybe Captain Kang will start doing what we've come here to do," said Pointer.

Forced into action, the *New Beginning* shut down its stealth modules and put its extensive arsenal of weapons to use. Captain Kang had clearly understood the benefits of using the Bulwark cannons. The Galactic was equipped with seventy-two turrets, though it was unable to bring all to bear at the same time. Projectiles ripped through space, joining those from the *Undertow*, the *Ransack* and the *Determinant*.

With the *New Beginning* engaged, the numbers of missiles in flight increased fivefold. The Lambdas and higher-yield Shatterers exploded in waves against the Vraxar energy shields.

The Vraxar fired in response. Two of the dark beams hit the *Undertow* and another struck the *Ransack*. Particle beams flickered between the Vraxar and the *New Beginning*. The hull of the Galactic glowed as it absorbed and dissipated the heat.

"We might do this!" said Blake, his hands clenched in a death-grip on the *Determinant*'s control bars.

"I think the *Ransack* is out of action, sir."

"Core two is fried," said Rivera. "Disengaging core three."

"Hold!" shouted Blake. "Lieutenant, please acknowledge that order!"

"Acknowledged, sir. Core three is still loaded for lightspeed."

For a short time, it looked as if the two sides were evenly matched. The Vraxar energy weapons struck the *New Beginning* time and again, heating the heavy cruiser's armour plating until it seemed as if the entire spaceship was alight. As the Galactic banked and turned in response to the movement of the enemy, it left an orange trail for a thousand kilometres behind, like a meteorite with its own source of ignition. There were lights sparkling within the trail as dust from disintegrated armour flared up in the intense heat, before rapidly dwindling away to nothing.

"One of the enemy warships is breaking off!" shouted Pointer in excitement. "Come on, guys!"

A red circle on Blake's tactical vanished and the *Determinant*'s AI overlaid a symbol to indicate the enemy vessel had escaped into lightspeed. He felt a surge of furious triumph. The *New Beginning* continued to soak up the punishment, exactly as it had been designed to do. Chunks of its hull were missing, exposing the dull grey of the engines beneath.

Then it happened. Without warning or notice from its comms team, the *New Beginning* launched into lightspeed, leaving the few remaining ships of Response Fleet Alpha to face the enemy.

"They've...gone," said Pointer in disbelief. "The bastards have run out on us!"

Blake heard the words but couldn't bring himself to make a response. Another vessel had appeared on the far edges of his tactical screen. It was far, far larger than anything else in the current engagement and its current course suggested it was aiming for the *Undertow*.

"What the...? That's got to be the Neutraliser! Why has it decided to join in?"

A thought came to him – perhaps if the approaching Neutraliser came far enough away from Atlantis, power would return for the people on the surface. He didn't have time to pursue the idea. An already very bad situation was in the process of going rapidly downhill.

"Sir, the *Undertow* has lost power!" said Pointer. "They've got comms and nothing else."

The Vraxar warships closed in on the cruiser, their beam weapons raking across its hull. With its Gallenium engines shut down, the spaceship could do nothing to respond and it drifted at a speed of several hundred kilometres per second on a course that would take it into deep space.

"The *ES Ransack* has just dropped off the comms network," said Pointer. "I have no idea why. Lieutenant Rivera?"

It looked like Rivera had more or less given up. "Hardly any output from them. Maybe they've been shut down."

"One of the Vraxar is coming our way," said Pointer. "I've fed the details onto your tactical, sir."

The warning came too late to take action, even had the *Determinant* possessed a means of defending itself. Blake's console lit up in a sea of red alerts. The bridge lights dimmed and an alarm emitted a shrill howl.

"We just got hit," said Rivera flatly.

"Lieutenant, you had better get your crap in order!" Blake said. In truth, Rivera had already gone way beyond the limit.

Blake scanned his console to see what damage they'd taken. The cause appeared on his left-hand status screen.

[Particle Beam Strike, Aft Sections 15-28. Critical Damage to All Major Systems. Heat Penetration Into Main Quarters]

It was bad – very bad.

"We've lost rear engines and sustained damage to five Lambda clusters. Life support system operational with a predicted time to failure of fifteen minutes," said Rivera, having evidently decided to offer some input.

"What of the soldiers we're carrying?" shouted Blake. "What about them?"

"Dead," said Rivera, as if he didn't mind at all.

Blake prided himself on his calmness. Now he was beginning to find how difficult it was to live up to the reputation he gave himself. He swore angrily, the words flying from his mouth without control.

"Sir?" Pointer's voice cut through the clouds of his fury. "I've received a message from a comms ranker on the Tillos base. He says they've been attacked by a force that's come to steal the *ES Lucid*."

Blake didn't really have time to listen to this. The *Determinant* was badly damaged and the control bars shook in his palms. The enemy ship which had fired upon them was in range to do so again and he didn't have any idea how long its beam weapons took to recharge. "The *Lucid*'s got no core," he grunted, trying his best to keep his breathing steady.

"The message says it's online, sir."

"How would a soldier know?"

Pointer didn't answer the question. "Captain Edwards on the *Undertow* has issued the order to withdraw," she said. "Except they have no power to go to lightspeed themselves."

"About time we got out of here," said Rivera, galvanised by the news. "I'm taking us back to the *Juniper*."

Blake's mind raced. The *Lucid* was meant to have no Obsidiar core. If it was still running, that meant the work hadn't been done yet. The shipyard records stated the core had already been removed, but it wasn't entirely unheard of for these records to be subjected to a few subtle *amendments* or even to tell a few *outright lies* in order to ensure project milestones were met.

On his tactical, the closest Vraxar warship came to within one hundred thousand kilometres. A few missiles sputtered towards it, but it was clear the engagement was over. The huge, unknown Vraxar spaceship was now a good distance from Atlantis, its crew having evidently decided they needed to come for a closer look at the human fleet.

With his mind made up, Blake reached out with a finger and pressed at an area on his console.

"I'm locked out of my panel!" shouted Rivera.

"We're going to Atlantis. We need the *Lucid*."

"We are *not* going to Atlantis, sir! Captain Edwards has ordered us to withdraw!" Droplets of spittle flew from Lieutenant Rivera's mouth, a tiny cloud of them falling over his now-dead console.

"Sit down, Lieutenant! That's an order!"

"No, sir! I will *not* sit down!"

Rivera lunged across the intervening space, his hands open and reaching for Blake. With a final sweep of his index finger, Blake activated an SRT. The entire ship juddered and something shrieked deep in the hull. Blake noted they'd taken a second particle beam strike. The *Determinant*'s life support modules were too badly damaged to keep the ship's interior stable and the transition to lightspeed was sickeningly violent.

Three of the crew were seated, whilst Lieutenant Rivera was on his feet. When the *Determinant* entered lightspeed, he was thrown across the floor of the bridge and into the rear bulkhead wall with a tremendous thump. The others were pressed hard into their seats and Blake felt something stretch within his ribcage.

The warship emerged from lightspeed, hardly any time after entry. The alarm siren continued to sound and the alerts on Blake's console had multiplied until there was no screen which wasn't covered in them, each warning vying for his attention.

Fighting against the overwhelming urge to be sick, Blake struggled to focus his mind. The control bars were unresponsive in his hands. He pushed and pulled at them, before realising their connection to the engines had failed. The altimeter showed they were at a height of five thousand kilometres and heading in rapidly. The SRT had brought them in closer to the surface than he'd intended.

"Where are we?" he asked, the words coming out thickly.

Lieutenant Pointer didn't answer at once. He looked across and saw her rousing. "One second," she mumbled.

"Quickly!" he urged, his voice stronger. "Find me the Tillos base!"

"Coming in fast," she said.

Blake glanced to his other side. Lieutenant Brady was still in his chair with his eyes closed. Blood trickled from his mouth and one of his ears. He didn't move and there was no indication whether he was alive or dead.

"Our altitude is four thousand klicks," said Pointer.

"We don't have enough power to slow down. There's less than five percent of our engine output available."

He worked hard at it. The autopilot wouldn't activate, either because the AI knew there wasn't enough power to stop them crash landing or because the system had failed. He attempted an override – the core wouldn't accept his authorisation codes. He tried to force it to restart the manual control system. Everything was running much slower than usual and it took him seconds to get a response.

"Three thousand klicks. Forward sensor feed now available."

The bulkhead screen showed nothing but a blur of colours, ever-changing and shifting. Abruptly, it cleared to show the planet Atlantis below, a paradise of oceans and forests. Then the image returned to the distracting blurred mess again.

"Turn it off," said Edwards.

The left control bar jerked in his hand. He pulled at it firmly, producing a thunderous vibration which shook the *ES Determinant* violently. The right-hand bar shuddered too, fighting in his hand as he attempted to exert some control over the plunging warship.

"There goes two thousand klicks. We're coming up on the Tillos base, sir, or what little remains of it."

At an altitude of fifteen hundred kilometres, Blake felt the ship respond to his commands. It was sluggish and reluctant, but it did its best to obey. The safest course of action would be to bring the *Determinant* in to land as slowly and steadily as possible. On the other hand, everything was failing and Blake was increasingly aware of the passing time – the Vraxar might not have guessed the *Determinant* had made for Atlantis, but they would surely have detected the faint double fission signature of the short-range transit.

"We're coming in," he said. "Hold on."

At five hundred kilometres, there was a new noise to add to that of the siren and the howling engines. It took Blake a moment to realise what it was.

"The underside Bulwark is firing at something."

He tried to look at his tactical screen from his periphery. There was nothing showing on it, so he dismissed the Bulwark's firing as a symptom of the warship's operational degradation.

In spite of his best efforts to bring the *Determinant* down on the cratered surface of the Tillos landing field, Blake overshot, flying over at a height of a few hundred metres. The engines failed entirely and the *Determinant* fell into a dive. With no way to control it, Captain Charlie Blake and Lieutenant Caz Pointer braced for impact.

CHAPTER FIFTEEN

SERGEANT ERIC MCKINNEY was pretty sure he and his squad were about to die, though he had no intention of going down without a fight. The smaller shuttle, which he'd observed laying down fire only a short while earlier approached leisurely, crossing over the undamaged comms hub as it came towards the squad's position on the far side of the pile of rubble. High above, a much larger craft – this one over two hundred metres in length – floated menacingly. McKinney was certain this second vessel was directing the first.

"Webb, shoot that smaller one down," he said.

"Yes, sir."

Webb was a few metres below the top, staying out of sight. He climbed to his feet, lifting the plasma tube onto his shoulder. With a sudden movement, he strode closer to the top of the pile. The launchers had a brief warm-up time and McKinney heard a whine as its coils powered up. The tube whooshed and a projectile burst from the wide muzzle. Webb dropped out of sight quickly.

"Direct hit," he said with confidence. "It's going to need a second."

His words were drowned out by the thumping sound of a plasma detonation.

"How long till recharge?" asked McKinney.

"Not long."

A shape flew overhead, plasma still burning across its front quarter. McKinney looked up and saw the glint of something hanging from beneath its nose – a weapon with many barrels. He fired his gauss rifle instinctively, sending a short burst of slugs to clatter against the armoured underside. The other men did likewise, though it was easy to see it was too little, too late.

Webb fired again. The plasma rocket crossed the intervening space in a split second and detonated against the shuttle's hull. Droplets of white-hot flame burst away, falling towards McKinney and his squad below.

"Got them," said Webb in satisfaction.

"No you haven't," said McKinney.

The shuttle was badly damaged and its engines thrummed unevenly, but the pilot didn't break off. Instead, he rotated the craft jerkily around, bringing the nose cannon to bear. The men below shouted in defiance and continued their fusillade of gauss fire.

"Not going to be enough," said McKinney grimly. A blob of metal and plasma landed at his feet, spitting and writhing. He ignored it and fired at the shuttle again.

"Still got the big one to deal with after this, Sergeant," said Webb.

McKinney didn't respond. Though he kept firing, his gaze was transfixed by the nose cannon, which was now aimed directly towards him. His mind idly noted the peculiar design – it was a collection of three distinct sets of three barrels, each set arranged in a triangular pattern and then arranged into a cluster.

He had no idea how it worked and had better things to worry about. McKinney didn't want to die, yet he refused to look away.

Fate had other plans for Sergeant Eric McKinney. Just as the moment appeared to be on the verge of becoming a barrage of high-calibre slugs, something hit the shuttle with such ferocity that the vessel was pummelled sideways across the sky. Its side wall crumpled as though a giant fist had struck it with appalling force. The noise was incredible, like a steel sledgehammer crashing into the side of a hollow metal barrel. The shuttle was hit again and again until it was hurled to the ground on the other side of the rubble.

"Look!" said Stein.

McKinney hardly needed to turn his head to see. The larger of the two craft suffered a similar onslaught. A hundred huge-calibre Gallenium slugs punched into it, crumpling it out of shape. Dozens of holes appeared through its armour, easily visible from the ground. The sound of it reached the squad, distant hailstones upon a metal roof.

With his mouth open in awe, McKinney watched the enemy spaceship as it was destroyed and thrown towards the ground, ruined as easily as the shuttle.

"What the *hell* was that?" asked Garcia, his voice distant with shock. He raised his hand and made the sign of the cross over his heart, something McKinney hadn't seen in years.

"I have no idea, soldier."

The answer was revealed soon enough. A shape descended through the air, this one far larger than the two alien spaceships. This vessel glowed with a brightness that confounded the sensors on McKinney's suit until they were able to adjust. Heat spilled away and a trail of orange reached as far as the horizon and beyond. The spaceship passed directly over the base, the wave of sound yet to reach the squad.

McKinney recognized it – even through the burning heat and

with its hull misshapen, he knew it was a Space Corps destroyer. He could also see it was so badly damaged that any landing was unlikely to be a smooth one. He saw the hillside, a few kilometres away, a dark silhouette against the steadily-lightening sky.

"Get off this rubble!" he shouted, certain it was already too late.

Their position on top of the rubble was precarious given what he felt sure was to come. Taking the lead, McKinney slung his rifle across his back and scrambled his way downwards, his feet struggling for purchase. The others caught on quickly and they came afterwards – men in fear of imminent death.

The noise of the spaceship's passing finally reached them as the air carried the sound in the vessel's wake. The rumble of tortured engines was terrifying and the rubble shuddered, some of the smaller pieces tumbling away ahead of the squad as they slithered down the myriad of different angled slopes.

Then, the ground started to shudder. There was no build-up – the whole Tillos base shook violently as if it were suffering the most powerful earthquake ever felt on Atlantis.

McKinney tried to go faster in his headlong flight. A piece of broken wall detached itself from the mound to his left and bounced past him, leaving a colossal shroud of dust blossoming into the air. He lost his footing and put out a hand to steady himself. It was no good and McKinney found himself sliding at an ever-increasing speed towards the ground. All the while, he felt the earthquake from the spaceship's nearby impact build in intensity.

Just when McKinney thought he might make it unscathed, one particularly large convulsion cast him up into the air. He came down again – hard – and rolled the final few metres until he struck a block of steel-reinforced concrete which brought him to a halt.

He coughed and tried to roll to his feet. His visor HUD

provided an evaluation of his physical condition, but he was too dazed to make sense of it. He felt a sharp pain in his chest as his spacesuit injected him with a drug – battlefield adrenaline he guessed. One of the squad took his arm and dragged him towards the ramp leading to the underground bunker's Section D entrance.

Eventually, the ground stopped shaking, except for a few much fainter aftershocks. Crouched halfway along the ramp, McKinney patted himself down, scarcely able to believe he was still alive. He was bruised and winded, though fortunately nothing was broken. In fact, he felt sharp and alert as a consequence of the synthetic adrenaline coursing through his bloodstream. Apart from a few superficial scrapes, the exterior of his suit looked undamaged. He gave mental thanks to the men and women in the lab who'd figured out how to make the combat suits so damned tough.

"I can't see Boon and Stein," he said across the open channel. The two rankers had vanished from the comms network, but there was a chance they might have suffered a visor malfunction and be alive somewhere.

"A slab fell on them, sir," said Bannerman, somehow still carrying his portable comms pack. "Poor bastards didn't stand a chance."

The first men I've lost, thought McKinney. In the aftermath of the quake, the pile of rubble was lower than before and spread over a wider area. It made him angry to think he'd recently taken his squad to the top of it and now here they were on the Section D ramp, back where they started except with two of their number dead. He knew he'd feel sorrow later. For the moment, he was energised by the battlefield adrenaline. There were rumours the drug was designed to numb emotions, to help a soldier carry on in the face of the worst imaginable horrors and he was starting to believe there was some truth to it.

"Bannerman, try and reach that spaceship," he said. "It was a Corps vessel."

"It didn't look in very good shape," Garcia replied. "It's probably in even worse shape after hitting that hillside. Everyone on board has got to be dead."

"What do you think shot those enemy shuttles down?" asked McKinney. "Bulwark cannons, that's what. If there's anyone alive on that warship, we owe it to them to help out."

"I'm unable to reach them, Sergeant," said Bannerman. "There are no open receptors on their comms system."

"Does that mean they're dead?"

"It means nothing more than I said, sir."

McKinney was torn. He felt as if he had a debt to the crew of the crashed warship. Equally, he believed the enemy were up to no good in the comms hub and it was incumbent upon him to do everything possible to stop them.

He saw an opening – a way to put off the difficult decision for a few more minutes.

"We're going up that pile again," he said to the others. "We can see what's happened to the hub. If there's no way in, we can skirt around and go looking for the spaceship."

It wasn't the most well-thought of plans. The others didn't need a promotion to see it, though they kept their mouths shut, glad they weren't the ones having to make the decisions. The enemy soldiers had surely been stirred up when their support vessels were shot down. Luckily, they hadn't yet come to check out the Section D entrance ramp.

"Doesn't look as if they have a crapload of troops on the ground," said McCall. "I thought it would be crawling with them."

"Maybe," said McKinney. "They know they've won – could be they only sent a few down to check the place out."

"If they're going for the comms hub, why not pack it with their troops?"

"These are *aliens*," said Webb, going out of his way to emphasise the word. "They probably don't think like we do."

"Yeah, well they took out the base pretty easily, so they must have something going for them militarily," said Garcia. "And for all we know, they could have dropped a hundred thousand of these metal soldier things off at Tansul, Teklo and Tivon. Maybe Tillos isn't the main target."

"Tillos is the primary Atlantis base," said McKinney. A sudden thought came to him and he welcomed it, since it made the looming choice a much easier one to make. "What about the Central Command Building?" he asked.

"Yeah, what about it?" asked Garcia, clearly not understanding.

"It's about eighteen hundred metres over that way," said McKinney, pointing across the broken slabs of concrete. "We wouldn't have been able to see it from our position up top. What if that was the main target, rather than the comms hub? The aliens around here might only be hunting survivors – they've probably got significant numbers holding the CCB."

"Are we going into the hub, then, Sergeant?"

"No. I wouldn't know what the hell to do when I got in there anyway. Let these bastards have it – we're going to see if there are any survivors from that crashed destroyer." Another thought flashed into his head, illuminating in its perfection. "Maybe one of them knows how to get onto the *ES Lucid* and maybe they'll know how to fly it. They could shoot down a few of the enemy. Maybe save Atlantis."

"Yeah, Sergeant," said Webb eagerly. "I've never been on a Galactic before."

With his mind made up, McKinney checked in with Corporals Li and Evans.

"We've seen a Corps destroyer come down nearby. We're going to check for survivors. We lost Boon and Stein."

"They were good men," said Evans. "I hope they gave as good as they got."

"They brought hell to the enemy, Corporal," McKinney lied. He didn't know what else to say. "Any sign of hostiles in the bunker?"

"It's quiet down here, Sergeant," said Li. "Most of the doors are open, but we've not found any more personnel."

"We believe the main attacking force may be concentrating on the CCB. We've seen them – they're aliens all right. Dressed in some kind of metal, like robots and flesh in one. If we're lucky, they might not have a clue the *ES Lucid* is down there."

"A new theory every minute, Sergeant," said Li.

Li had a knack of making his wry comments in a way that was entirely inoffensive.

"It's an ever-changing situation, Corporal."

"What do they want at the CCB?" asked Evans.

"Probably trying to tap into our databanks or something," McKinney guessed. "For us, it's secondary. We're going for the destroyer."

"Good luck, sir."

"Hold your positions. If things work out, we'll come back with someone able to fly the *Lucid*."

"Then we'll blow the crap out of them."

"Yeah. Then we'll blow the crap out of them."

McKinney closed the comms link and did a scan of the area with his visor's heat and movement sensors. Daytime was approaching rapidly and the squad would soon be able to rely on their eyes alone. There was no sign of the enemy. He stared in the direction the destroyer had come down and tried to plot a route in his head. It was pointless – the destruction of the base was so complete he had no way of knowing what lay beyond the broken buildings surrounding his squad.

After one final check of the area, McKinney clambered over the edge of the ramp and onto level ground. The others followed, spreading themselves out so as not to be an easy target for repeater fire. They set off at a jog, trying to keep the sound of their footfall to a minimum. Running at point and with his gauss rifle held across his chest, McKinney felt a relief that stemmed from more than just the battlefield adrenaline. He'd made his decision and now all he had to do was follow this path to the end.

CHAPTER SIXTEEN

"MORE BODIES," whispered Lieutenant Maria Cruz.

She didn't need or want to examine them in detail. A repeater weapon had ripped the two humans to pieces, leaving bloody chunks spread across the floor. It was hard to tell if they were male or female, though enough of their uniforms remained to tell Cruz these were civilians rather than soldiers.

She tipped her head to one side and listened carefully. There were noises which seemed to come from all around, some far away and some at an indeterminate distance.

Realising she and Keller were exposed in the middle of the corridor, Cruz advanced quickly. Her heart beat rapidly in her chest and so heavily it felt as though she was being punched on the inside of her ribcage. She tried to put her training into practise. *Long, deep breaths,* she thought. *Keep my mind focused. Death is death. It comes to us all.*

Something clicked inside her mind and body. The beating of her heart slowed, dropping close to a normal level. *Slightly elevated. That's to be expected.* She saw things in greater detail – the tiny imperfections in the bare, metal walls. Scuffs on the carpet tiles. The rapid flickering of the lighting further along the corridor. The faintest of humming from the gauss rifle's coils and the metallic odour which it expelled through tiny vents on top.

"It's the second right turning, remember," whispered Keller. He sounded sick to his stomach.

At the first right, Cruz heard something – footsteps either coming or going. She leaned out carefully and quickly withdrew her head. She made a signal with her fingers which she'd learned in training, letting Keller know there were two enemy soldiers twenty metres away and walking in the opposite direction to their position. He stared at her blankly.

She put one finger over her mouth. "Shhh."

He nodded in understanding.

Cruz leaned out again. The light was poor, disguising some details and altering others. The two enemy soldiers continued at a measured pace, heading away. From the back they were nearly the same as the one she'd killed earlier – grey skin in parts, alloy plates and patches of ragged, filthy hair. With disgust, she realised their bare skulls were exposed. Trying not to think too hard about it, she squinted past them – the corridor turned right a little further along and she hoped they'd follow it until they were out of sight.

She waited a long ten seconds. The sound of footsteps receded further and Cruz risked another look.

"Gone," she whispered, closing her eyes in relief and breathing out.

She didn't hesitate - three quick strides took her past the opening to the corridor. Keller followed, one of his feet making a loud scrape across the floor in his haste. He cringed, whilst Cruz was once again left regretting her decision to allow him to come along.

The second right turn was another twenty paces away. The corridor continued past, reaching a T-junction at the end.

Once again, Cruz checked carefully before heading along the turning. It appeared as though Keller's memory was accurate so far – the new passage continued for a short distance before it opened into a room filled with curved banks of operator consoles.

There was no sign of enemies ahead and she was reluctant to wait any longer than necessary in the corridor, so Cruz set off along the new passage. She walked in a half-crouch, with her shoulder close to the left-hand corridor wall and her rifle pointed ahead. Keller followed along a few steps behind, clumsily attempting to copy her stance.

The closer she came to the room, the more she could see - it looked like a large space, which had presumably seen use back in the days of the Ghost wars. The consoles looked ancient and a layer of dust clung to them – the forgotten technology of a war long ago fought.

From her crouch, the view was obscured. Carefully, she lifted her head slightly in order to see the passageway opposite which Keller believed would lead to their goal. A sign hung from the ceiling, a near-repeat of the one a few hundred metres behind. *Hub Core Processing Area. Unauthorised Personnel Will Be Incarcerated.*

There was no sound here – even the distant noises elsewhere in the hub were muted. She took another few paces and stopped in her tracks. There were two of the aliens in the centre-left of the room – visible through a wide gap in the consoles. With a whispered curse, she dropped out of sight and kept her rifle steady, hoping they hadn't seen her.

Keller saw her stop and did the same, lowering himself into a crouch of his own. The action caused his diagnostic tablet to spill from the wide pocket in his uniform. Cruz watched it happen in slow motion. The heavy tablet turned in the air as it descended towards the floor – she saw its display showing the utilisation bar of the Obsidiar processor, still pinned at maximum. There was no way the carpet tiles would muffle its landing.

Quick as a flash, Keller reached out and caught the tablet in a pinch-grip between fingers and thumb. It was like he was so used to dropping stuff he'd developed superhuman reactions to stop himself from breaking his equipment. Cruz looked at him and he winked back, though it wasn't enough to disguise the fact he was mortified.

Once the diagnostics tablet was tucked away, Cruz did her best to make Keller aware of the situation. She raised two fingers, at the same time as she mouthed the words *two soldiers – we wait*.

He nodded in response and hunkered down next to her. He was desperate to talk – to ask questions that would allay his fears. In a way, Cruz was relieved he wasn't able to speak. She had no truthful reassurances to offer him and she wasn't about to lie.

There was no way to sneak into the room without being seen, so they waited – desperately hoping the aliens would move on. As the seconds went by, Cruz found memories from her training swirling around her head. The thing which interested her was the limited number of enemy soldiers in the comms building. The Space Corps taught that you hit a primary objective hard and once you'd taken the objective, you held it with tenacity and high numbers of your best troops. She didn't know how many of the enemy were in the underground complex, but she was sure the numbers weren't sufficient to take or hold the area if they met any significant resistance. It was as if they were mopping up or simply investigating what they'd captured.

Her thoughts led inescapably to the conclusion she'd discussed with the operators earlier on – the invaders' main target was likely to be elsewhere on the base. That left one place, which was the Central Command Building. The CCB couldn't send comms, but it had access to everything. If this was nothing more than a surprise strike by the aliens, they were unlikely to have huge numbers of troops with them. It made sense for them to focus their efforts on one main objective.

A minute passed. Cruz wasn't sure which way the two enemy soldiers were facing – she'd only caught a glimpse. She'd already witnessed how quickly they could react when the one in the control room shot Ramprakash, so she wasn't keen to stick her head into the line of fire if it wasn't necessary.

After two minutes, Cruz was getting edgy and no amount of regulated breathing would calm her down. Each second felt stretched out, though her brain operated at normal space within this distortion of time. She chanced another look – the aliens were still in the same place, as though they'd been positioned exactly here with the express purpose of pissing her off.

Keller reached out and patted her urgently, several times on the shoulder. She turned her head and that's when she heard it – something was coming from behind them. Heavy footsteps came down upon the floor tiles. At first, Cruz wondered if it was the patrol they'd sneaked past earlier coming back along this route. There were too many footsteps – there were four or six of the aliens coming, not just two.

Cruz was torn by indecision. Part of her wanted to crouch in place and hope she and Keller went unnoticed. The realist within her knew that was the coward's way out. *It's what Lieutenant Reynolds would do* an insidious voice tormented her.

Without humour, Cruz realised her own mind knew exactly where to poke in order to produce action. She shuffled closer to Keller so he could hear what she was about to say.

"Two targets, fifteen metres to the left of the doorway. I'll take the right, you take the left. Aim for the chest. Press and hold the trigger button. Understand?"

Keller looked petrified, but he nodded all the same.

"You move up to the edge and prepare to take aim. I'll get in position when you're set. When I nudge you with my foot, go. They're fast – whatever you do, don't miss."

This time, she didn't wait for a response. She moved to let him pass and he brushed by. Close in, Keller smelled of aftershave and sweat. The scent clung to her nostrils and she breathed it in, while listening to the approaching footsteps. They were close now and it sounded like six or eight of them, instead of the four or six she'd first guessed. Her eyes rested on the grenade bandolier across her chest, with its coating of drying blood. *A plasma grenade would bring every one of the bastards in the hub running towards us and we'll still have these other two at our back,* she told herself. *Let's see how Larry performs with the rifle first.*

Keller was in position, kneeling on one knee and with his rifle held vertically so it wouldn't protrude around the corner. Cruz came up close behind, standing upright. The edginess was still present, but it didn't affect her as much as before. The trembling in her muscles was gone and her grip on the gun barrel was solid. She raised her foot and gave Keller a nudge with the instep of her military-issue boot.

As soon as she sensed Keller respond, Cruz took a sideways step, with her eye looking along the length of the barrel. The targets were in the same place, as though they lacked interest in moving even an inch from where they were standing. The aliens reacted with terrifying speed, thick grey arms bringing short hand cannons upwards, swinging them towards the corner of the exit passage.

Cruz pressed her finger on the activation button. The rifle's coils whined softly and it thumped with gentle force into her shoulder. Slugs spat from the muzzle with incredible, lazy speed, punching through the air with their distinctive hum. The first shot missed its target by a hair's breadth. The second punched through the metal plating over the left-hand side of the alien's chest. The third round followed a moment later and six inches to the side.

The two enemy soldiers fell at the same time. It was like a strange, synchronised dance in which their knees buckled, their backs arched and they fell onto their fronts.

Cruz strode quickly into the room, keeping out of Keller's arc of fire. As she walked, she fired in controlled bursts, sending round after round into the two prone bodies. She heard Keller come after her.

"Hold fire," she hissed, all the while continuing to fire her own rifle. The last thing she wanted was to watch one of his gauss slugs rip a foot-wide exit hole in her chest if he was jumpy enough to try and copy her.

The aliens were dead, but Cruz didn't stop moving. She swung around, checking for movement, in case there were others in the room sitting out of sight somewhere. They were alone. She looked at Keller to check if he was keeping it together. Something had changed in his face, though she didn't know quite what it was.

"Keep watch," she told him.

She darted across to the entrance passage and listened. A grenade had found its way into her hand – a cold, five-inch cylinder of high-explosive with a timer and a proximity sensor. She knew it would feel good to throw it into the middle of a squad of the enemy soldiers and had just about made her mind up to do so if they ventured this way. The two she and Keller had just killed were far too heavy to drag out of sight and they'd be discovered immediately.

The patrol didn't come towards them. Cruz found relief and disappointment vying to be her primary emotion. She put the grenade into her pocket and crossed over the room, beckoning Keller to follow.

"How far?" she asked, standing a metre inside the corridor leading from the room.

"Just down here, Lieutenant." He pointed ahead to where three corridors converged. There was a doorway in the wall at the end, twenty metres away.

"It's open," she said. "Looks like our security didn't stop them for long."

"Ever get the impression this is something these *things* have done many times before?" he asked.

A memory of something Cruz couldn't remember learning came to her. She had no idea where it sprouted from – maybe she'd seen it in a file somewhere, or heard it mentioned in a lesson long since forgotten. "Vraxar!" she said. "That's what these are!"

"I'll take your word for it," he said with a shrug. "I'm sure they won't mind if I refer to them as *alien bastards* or whatever else comes to mind."

"Call them what you like, Larry," she said. "Come on, let's get that processor pulled before any more of the *alien bastards* show up."

They hurried along towards the open doorway, wary for sounds that would indicate there were Vraxar close by. A sign dangled above the entrance. *Hub Core Processing Area.* There were no additional warnings of punishment for unauthorised transgressors into the area. If you'd come this far, you were probably looking over your shoulder already.

At the junction, Cruz looked both ways. The right-hand corridor was deserted. To the left at a distant junction, there were shapes, twisted in death. She stared hard – there'd been a big fight here and both human soldiers and Vraxar had died. The walls were scarred from repeater or gauss fire which had left countless furrows and gouges. There'd been at least one explosion and several of the wall plates had melted away, before solidifying into new, uneven shapes.

Cruz looked away from the mangled bodies. In contrast to the nearby carnage, the interior of the processing room was mundane and apparently empty. There was no sound from within except for a low humming, emanating from an unknown source.

"Wait," she said.

Cruz dashed over and through the doorway, her rifle sweeping into the corners of the processing room. To her relief there were no Vraxar soldiers, waiting patiently out of sight to shoot any humans who might happen by. After the effort it had taken to get here the room itself was surprisingly small, especially considering the importance of what was within. There was a single, modern console to one side, whilst the centre of the room was taken up by a smooth, floor-to-ceiling square-edged pillar of metal which was a little less than a metre wide.

Keller joined her in the room.

"Around this side," he said, heading straight around the pillar.

Cruz joined him, shivering in the cold of the room. From this side, the pillar had a row of square handles jutting from its surface. Each was clearly numbered in red, starting from number one near to floor level and going up to number fifteen which was high enough that a ladder was required to reach it.

"We don't have fifteen clusters," she said.

"Redundancy. Or maybe if they ever wanted to beef it up." He raised his hands in a *who knows?* gesture. "It's always better to have the option to add more processing grunt if you need it."

"Number Five?"

"Yep. Just grab the handle and pull."

"That'll put the data array into a static state?"

Keller pulled out his tablet and showed her the screen. "There's only one core running. Once that's removed we can all go home and put our feet up."

"Funny guy," she said.

"Go on, Lieutenant."

Cruz put out a hand and wrapped her fingers around the handle. It was ice-cold and damp. She pulled and a square block slid partway clear.

"There," she said.

"Keep going," Keller urged.

She pulled it further, until the entire unit came free. It was heavier than she was expecting and the end of the drawer fell, striking the floor hard.

"If you break it, just hope they don't start docking the cost of a replacement from your pay."

In spite of the situation, Cruz couldn't help laughing. "Is that it done?"

Keller brandished his tablet at her. "All clusters dead, gone and offline. Well done, Lieutenant, you just saved humanity from the rampaging Vraxar hordes."

It was a success, but Cruz couldn't help feel like they'd only accomplished a part of what was needed. She put the processor drawer carefully onto the floor. It didn't look like much – a flat slab of metal with a six-inch square etched into the middle which she presumed housed the core.

"It's small."

"Every generation is smaller than the one before. These Obsidiar cores are something entirely new."

"What will the Vraxar do now?" she asked. "This should slow them down until the Space Corps can get its act together and send a fleet here."

"Maybe they'll fly away home and leave us be." He saw the seriousness in her face. "They'll have to take the data arrays. Get them to a facility that can analyse the molecular arrangement of the units. Then, they'll need to piece it together again. It won't be easy, especially since the last encryption lock will remain in place."

"Hard, not impossible."

"With the right gear, they could do it."

"Where are the arrays?"

"You don't want to know."

"The CCB?"

"Not hard to guess, was it?"

"Seems not. How would we get there?"

"Out the door, turn right, according to the sign hanging over the passage. There must be an underground link."

"I didn't see the sign. Too many bodies."

"You're not seriously thinking of going to the CCB? The place must be crawling with Vraxar."

"Yeah. Do you know exactly where the data arrays are located in the CCB?"

"I haven't got a clue, Lieutenant. I was here to work on the hub – they don't give guided tours of the Colonel's office. Besides, the arrays won't be small like this CPU stack – they'll fill a big room. All those grenades you're carrying probably won't be enough to wipe it out."

Cruz sighed. Having come this far, she was reluctant to give up. On the other hand, she knew they'd been lucky to get as far as this. Once they started running into big groups of Vraxar, she and Keller would be killed in no time. Bravery was encouraged in the Corps, suicide generally not.

"We've done our bit, Larry. Let's cut and run."

Keller didn't ask if she wanted to change her mind – he'd clearly had enough.

"Back the way we came," he said.

She gave him a half-hearted thumbs-up in response and tried to smile. It didn't feel quite like a failure under the circumstances, but she couldn't shake the feeling of disappointment.

The corridors outside were clear and the pair of them set off with caution, retracing their footsteps.

CHAPTER SEVENTEEN

FLEET ADMIRAL JOHN DUGGAN was still in his office, though he wished he was elsewhere. He was frustrated beyond measure - every time he came up with a new idea or approach to this catastrophe, something outside his control interfered with his plans. The most galling aspect was that the largest obstacles were put in the way by his own side.

"What came from your informal meeting with Subjos Kion-Tur?" asked Councillor Stahl. "Our attempts at negotiation through the standard channels are ongoing. I assume you obtained a more straightforward response?"

"The Ghasts will help, Councillor. In exchange, they want Obsidiar."

Stahl's expression didn't change, nor did the tone of his voice. "They can't have any. The Confederation Council has plans for our reserves and those plans don't involve giving it to the Ghasts."

"They will put three Obsidiar-cored battleships at our disposal in return for half a million tonnes — twenty percent of our stocks."

"I hope you left the Subjos suitably rebuffed, Fleet Admiral?" asked Councillor Watanabe.

"I told him I would bring his offer to the Confederation Council. Three Ghast Oblivions would provide an incredible boost to our offensive capabilities."

"We have six operational Hadrons, do we not?" asked Stahl.

"Only one powered by Obsidiar, which is too far away to be immediately useful. You already know this." Duggan paused. "There is news from Response Fleet Alpha. Not ten minutes ago I received a communication from Captain George Kang on the *New Beginning*. Response Fleet Alpha was defeated – destroyed - and Captain Kang was lucky to escape."

The group of Councillors arrayed against him shuffled uncomfortably – something they were getting good at. Duggan knew them well enough to realise they'd pinned their hopes on Response Fleet Alpha outperforming expectations. Whilst that operation was ongoing, they could put off the more difficult decisions. Now, they no longer had the luxury of wasting time.

"Do you have details?" asked Councillor Kemp.

"I will provide a full report later this morning. In summary, our warships were attacked without provocation by a superior foe. Alien ships equipped with energy shields, Councillors." Duggan faced the group through the video screen – these were the most influential members of the Confederation Council and could usually sway the others if they desired it. "Please bring forward your decision on whether we can refit our fleet from the Obsidiar reserves. You should also reconsider the ban on nuclear missiles. They are an efficient way to disable an energy shield."

Councillor Monkton stepped forward. "The utilisation of nuclear weapons is a touchy subject. Our citizens do not like to think we rely on such outdated, dirty methods of warfare."

"I think they would prefer to know we are using every means possible to ensure their survival."

"We will add it to the agenda. In addition, you will have our answer on the Obsidiar in due course, Admiral. Rest assured we are aware of the importance." His eyes narrowed. "I hear the *ES Maximilian* has been diverted from its usual patrol route."

"One of our planets has been attacked," Duggan replied. "Of course I am making preparations for the unknown."

"Then why have you summoned it to New Earth, Admiral?" asked Monkton, a note of triumph creeping into his voice.

Duggan kept his expression fixed, though he was shocked at the extent of Monkton's knowledge. It was natural for the Council to have contacts within the Space Corps, but the *Maximilian* was running silent. He trusted the battleship's captain implicitly. The only alternative source of the leak was unthinkable – it would need someone of Admiral rank to access the flight plan of an off-grid warship.

"When the Council comes to the correct decision regarding our Obsidiar, what use would it be if none of our fleet was in the vicinity for the shipyard to begin installation?" Duggan responded smoothly.

"Just make sure you respect our wishes, Fleet Admiral," said Monkton. "Whichever side our decision may fall."

"These are our people. How can there be uncertainty in the outcome?"

"We have many things to balance," said Councillor Dawson. "Rest assured we will act in the best wishes of the wider Confederation."

"What happens when the Vraxar come for the other seven planets broadcast by the *Teskinir*?"

"There is no proof the aliens have those details," said Kemp. "If they do, the Council expects the Space Corps to be more successful in the defence of those planets than it has been for Atlantis. The military commands fifteen percent of our *entire* budget – failure will not be accepted."

The meeting ended, leaving Duggan numb. He'd always been aware the lead Councillors were ruthless and ambitious, but understanding their behaviour was on this occasion beyond his grasp. He wasn't certain what plans they had for the Obsidiar, but he was starting to believe they were a higher priority than the lives of the people on Atlantis. Whatever those plans, they would doubtless be designed to bring glory to the Confederation Council as well as its members individually.

They're hanging me out to dry, he thought. *They don't want me to fail, but they can't bring themselves to give me the resources to succeed.*

He needed to get away from it all for a few minutes. Duggan marched across the floor of his office, through the door and out into the carefully-landscaped grounds he had personally ordered be created. It was a warm morning and birds sang in the trees. Space Corps personnel walked here and there, enjoying the sunshine. In spite of the pleasant surroundings, Duggan couldn't calm down. It seemed increasingly likely he was going to have to sort out the mess with the Vraxar using the Space Corps' existing resources. In the likely event he failed, he'd be the one blamed. Not for the first time, he cursed the existence of Obsidiar and wished it had never been discovered.

The worst thing of all was that he didn't have concrete proof telling him what the Vraxar wanted. Then, it came to him – a memory of a conversation decades ago, with a man whose intellect could encompass an infinite array of plans and possibilities. The now-dead Fleet Admiral Teron, who once told Duggan he believed there was something special about the planet Atlantis – something which meant Obsidiar could be extracted from its core under the right circumstances. Those circumstances were invariably easy to predict – destroy the planet and the right type of spaceship could pick up the Obsidiar as it formed.

Duggan felt the energy flow out of his body, leaving him

completely drained. The more he experienced of the universe and the beings living within it, the more he despised the unending thirst for annihilation he witnessed amongst them.

———

SERGEANT ERIC MCKINNEY and the remaining five men of Squad A picked their way warily across the wasteland of the Tillos base. The exit ramp for Section D was ten minutes back and lost from sight behind a million tonnes of debris. This new area of the base had been particularly badly damaged by enemy missiles and somehow the concrete retained heat from the initial onslaught. In places it was enough to generate warnings on the suit HUDs.

A short distance away, fires still burned, their anger lessened and their contrast with the sky reduced by the arriving day. McKinney was worried – darkness brought with it a sense of security, albeit an illusory one. The rising sun made him feel exposed and he was beginning to doubt if he could lead his squad to their destination without putting them at an unacceptable level of risk.

McKinney wasn't lazy, but like most Tillos personnel he was accustomed to travelling around the base in one of the many pool vehicles. Consequently, when he was forced to use his feet, the size of the base became all the more apparent. He squinted at the range of high hills where he believed the fleet destroyer had come down and his visor HUD provided him with an estimation of the distance: seven thousand metres, with no guarantee the warship wouldn't be another few thousand metres beyond that.

"That's a lot of open ground to cross, Sergeant," said Bannerman. "I used to spend my free time up in those hills. They're nice enough to look at, but the Corps pulled down all the trees when they built this base. Now, there's just lots of grass."

Bannerman seemed to have a few ideas of his own – he'd probably have made corporal or higher if he wanted. McKinney paid attention to the man's words.

"We've got little choice, Soldier."

"I know that, Sergeant. Just saying we might have a rough time of it. We'll be easy pickings if another one of those shuttles comes down. I don't want to rely on there being any more guardian angels watching over us."

McKinney was digesting these words and trying to figure out a better way to complete his objective when he caught sight of movement in his periphery – a wedge-shaped, grey alloy object flew across the skies a few kilometres away. Wherever it was going, it appeared to be in a hurry.

"Get down!" he yelled through the open channel.

The squad was already tracking a path close to a ruined building and there was plenty of cover. McKinney got himself behind the burned-out remains of one of the base's small transport vehicles. It still smouldered and he was grateful his visor filtered out the odours of soot and char.

"It's heading towards the destroyer," said Bannerman.

"I hope not," said McKinney.

He looked into the sky and traced an imaginary path from the craft. There was no doubt about its destination.

"That little spaceship isn't big enough to do much against a fleet destroyer – even a crashed one." said McCall.

"They must be confident it's out of action, given what that Bulwark cannon did to their other shuttles," said Elder.

"Bannerman, try reaching the destroyer again."

"Right you are, Sergeant."

McKinney waited, not expecting there to be a change from the previous attempt to reach the crew.

"I've got something!" said Bannerman excitedly. "Military

vessel *ES Determinant* acknowledges our signal. I'm speaking to a Lieutenant Caz Pointer."

"What's their status?"

Bannerman didn't respond at once. Whoever he was speaking to they were evidently passing on a lot of information in one go. At last, the soldier got a chance to repeat what he was told and he spat out the words quickly.

"They're running on residual power – whatever that is. No weapons, engines or long-range comms. Lieutenant Pointer is patched into the ship's main comms systems using a spacesuit. The hull has absorbed a lot of heat and they're expecting to be hit by an orbital strike so they don't want to stick about for that."

"They're abandoning ship?"

"Looks like it."

"Damnit! Tell them there's an enemy shuttle heading their way."

The wedge-shaped craft vanished from sight at the far end of the base.

"They've seen it, sir."

"What are they going to do?"

"Lieutenant Pointer doesn't know, sir. She's waiting to see if the ship's captain has any ideas."

"The captain is alive?"

"I doubt she's lying sir and I can hear him talking in the background."

McKinney tried hard to think of an intelligent suggestion – something that might help the *Determinant*'s crew. His brain failed him and even if it had not, it would have been too late.

"The signal is gone. I've lost her," said Bannerman. He pressed the signal booster on the pack and held the button down. "Hang on a minute, there's something else."

"What is it?" asked McKinney.

Bannerman snorted. "It's a civilian device. I've got no idea how it managed to connect to this pack – we're meant to be invisible to anything non-military."

With his single objective snatched away from him, McKinney was fighting despair. "Who is it?" he asked.

"Sounds like an old feller, calling himself Jerry Greiner. He's rambling on about aliens."

"Nothing we don't know – cut him off. We haven't got time for this."

"That's him gone." Bannerman covered up the pack and shrugged it onto his shoulders. "Are we sticking with the plan and going for the *Determinant*, sir?"

The truth was, McKinney didn't have any idea what to do next. The enemy had managed to deliver a real sucker punch, he told himself, and always seemed to be several steps ahead. *They fooled far better officers than Sergeant Eric McKinney. It's time to retreat.*

"Let's get back to the bunker," he said. "Maybe we'll sit it out until help gets here."

"Or maybe one of the technicians left an access key for the *ES Lucid* lying around, eh?" said Bannerman jokingly. "Get onboard, press a few buttons and off we go. How hard can it be to fly one of those things, eh?"

McKinney laughed bitterly. "It took me ten months to get accredited for shuttle flight. It's another four years on top of that before they let you loose on anything bigger."

"I'm sure they spend half of that time in the bar, sir."

"We'll go back," said McKinney despondently. "In a minute."

He rose from cover and watched the sky. For some reason it was important to him that he see the shuttle on its return flight, as if witnessing it would close the loop and allow him to accept it was over for the crew of the *Determinant*.

Five minutes went by and the squad became restless. A few

of them started muttering that it was time to get moving. Then, it appeared – a black dot against deep blue.

"There's that shuttle again," said McCall. "Going back the way it came. I wonder if they killed the people on the destroyer."

"Best not to think about it," said Garcia. "Poor bastards."

"Move out," said McKinney. His anger spilled over and he kicked at a fist-sized chunk of stone, sending it bouncing away. "We're going to the bunker. We've run out of options."

None of the men complained or suggested an alternative. It was clear their morale was low and McKinney couldn't blame them – the Space Corps had suffered defeat after defeat, without offering anything in the way of significant resistance.

Before the squad had made it halfway towards the bunker entrance, the unexpected happened - a figure came scrambling out from beneath a canted section of collapsed wall. McKinney spun towards it, his finger resting on the activation trigger of his repeater.

"Help!" called the figure. It was a man dressed in civilian uniform, his face, hair and clothing covered in dust.

"Hold fire!" McKinney roared across the open channel. The men were jumpy and it wouldn't take much for them to accidentally start shooting.

Under the grime, man had sandy-coloured hair and looked to be in his late twenties. It was no one McKinney recognized, not that he expected to know everyone on the base.

"Who's in charge?" the man asked.

"That's me. Sergeant McKinney." As he said the words, McKinney waved his squad towards the rubble where the man had emerged. "Over here!" he ordered.

"Come quickly! This way!" said the civilian, beckoning frantically.

There was a gap between the canted wall and the pile of rubble it leaned against. The man went through. McKinney ducked beneath the edge, twisting to avoid the jagged edges of protruding rebar. The rest of his squad came after, unsure what to expect.

There was an enclosed space – an area beneath the rubble. It was dark and dust floated in the air, suspended in apparent defiance of gravity. There was a woman in here, sitting with her back to a block of stone, her uniform covered in grey dust. Her face was twisted in a grimace and she clutched her ankle.

"Who are you?" asked McKinney.

"I'm Larry Keller," said the man. "This is Lieutenant Cruz. We just got out of the comms hub."

McKinney raised his visor so his face was visible. "Lieutenant? You're hurt."

Cruz raised her head. "I got all this way and then I broke my damned ankle crawling through this rubble. It hurts like hell." She laughed bitterly.

McKinney reached for the emergency pack at his waist. He pulled it open and unclipped one of the silver-coloured injector tubes held within.

"Take this," he said, walking across with his hand outstretched. "Painkiller."

She reached out gratefully and accepted the tube. She pressed it to her thigh and activated the switch on top. The injector hissed faintly and Cruz closed her eyes as the anaesthetic flowed through her veins.

"Thank you..." she studied McKinney's insignia. "Sergeant."

"McKinney, ma'am."

"How many are you?"

"Six of us in this squad, with another fourteen holding position in the underground bunker."

She looked drawn and tired. "You're all that's left on the whole base?"

"I can't tell you. If there are others, they aren't in any position to repel the Ghasts."

"Vraxar, Sergeant. These aren't Ghasts."

"I don't know who the Vraxar are, ma'am."

She smiled. "Alien bastards, Sergeant. That's all you need to know. Where were you going?"

"A fleet warship crashed down nearby. We were intending to rescue the crew, but they got captured or killed."

"What did you plan to do after that?"

"The *ES Lucid* is still active, ma'am. Near enough everything else has stopped working, but the *Lucid* is online. You can feel its engines when you get close."

"It's a cruiser, isn't it?"

"A heavy cruiser, ma'am. Built to take a beating and give back twice as much. At first, I thought the enemy had come to steal it. Now I think they came for something entirely different."

Cruz studied him with interest. "Such as?"

"I don't know for certain, ma'am. If you insisted on knowing what I think, I'd tell you this is a limited attack force and they're after something in the Central Command Building. Maybe they're hoping to find out where all the other Confederation planets are located."

She smiled. "Well, Sergeant, I'm glad someone agrees with me. Aside from Larry, that is. There're data arrays in the CCB. Military stuff as well as coordinates for every asset within the Confederation. There's probably all sorts of other stuff we really don't want the Vraxar getting their hands on. We – Larry and I – managed to shut off the processing cores to stop them getting into the live data. That leaves one option open for them."

"I don't know what that option is, ma'am."

"They need to remove the data arrays, Sergeant. It's unlikely they'll want to stick around here long enough to unravel the contents, so they'll have to steal them – take them off-world."

McKinney put the pieces together. "Can we destroy the arrays?"

"I hope so. Because if we can't, it seems likely humanity is going to be much deeper in the shit than it already is."

There was something about Lieutenant Maria Cruz that left McKinney feeling calm. He could see at once that she respected people and would treat them accordingly. Even a fool could foresee what she was going to ask and McKinney helped her out.

"What can I do?" he asked.

"I have an idea, Sergeant McKinney," she replied.

CHAPTER EIGHTEEN

CRUZ AND MCKINNEY spent a short time talking, with the former giving an outline of what she hoped to achieve. The plan wasn't the most fully-fleshed one ever devised. McKinney didn't care – he'd been given a new objective and one which he could tell would have a significant positive impact on the Confederation's chances of dealing with the Vraxar. *Assuming we succeed,* he thought.

For once, the pessimistic voice inside his head didn't carry much weight. He was absolutely determined to beat the odds. He found himself gripped by a fervour – the same feeling he'd experienced as a young man reading and hearing about tales from the Ghost wars.

"Corporal Li, Evans, report," he said, once the talking was done.

"Wherever the enemy are, it isn't here, Sergeant," said Li.

"Nor here," said Evans. "We rounded up a couple more technicians. They're happy to wait it out."

"Are any of them able to get the *Lucid* open?"

"Wait on, I'll ask."

The asking didn't take long.

"No, sir. None of them have the clearance."

"Never mind. It might not be important now. Do you have explosive packs with you?"

"Clifton says he's carrying enough plasma charges to blow your wife's chastity belt off, Sergeant," said Li.

The unmarried McKinney chuckled. "We won't need quite that many. Tell him to leave half behind in case the weight slows him down."

"Alvey's got a plasma tube," said Evans.

"That's good enough. I want you to bring your squads across to the Section D entrance. Do it fast and do it now."

"Already moving," said Li.

"What about the civilians, sir?" asked Evans.

"Tell them to keep below ground and leave them behind. We've got a mission and it's a dangerous one."

"Like a real, proper mission where we get to shoot genuine aliens?" asked Li, his breathing heavy as he ran.

"Exactly that, Corporal. Real, flesh and metal aliens. Vraxar they're called."

"Just point me in the right direction, Sergeant."

McKinney closed out of the channel. "Did you get the details of that, ma'am?" he asked.

Lieutenant Cruz was in the same place on the ground as when they'd first met. "I heard enough, Sergeant. How long until your men get here? The Vraxar have proved themselves extremely decisive in their attack on Tillos. I can't imagine they'll sit on their hands for long."

"We'll be ready in less than twenty minutes. I'm going to send four of Squad A to the bunker entrance to guide the others here. I'll get one of them to help you back. You'll be safer underground."

Cruz looked torn for a moment until she saw what the risks

were to the men. "I'll stay here. I can't move very fast and I'll put my escort at risk if there's a firefight."

"I can't guarantee we'll be able to come back this way."

"I'll figure something out. I've got Larry to help me and I'm aware of the possible consequences."

"We'll do our best."

"Are you clear on what you're looking for?" Cruz asked.

"Clear enough. The visor HUD has layout plans for the whole base. We should be able to get from the hub to the CCB without getting lost."

"I wish I could come with you. Of all the lousy luck to snap an ankle."

Cruz's expression was sincere and McKinney believed what she said. "On the other hand, if you hadn't ended up stuck here, we'd never have found you and wouldn't have learned about the data arrays." He looked up at the countless tonnes of rubble overhead. "Or about the entrance to the hub hidden under all this crap."

"A man who looks on the bright side of things? Doesn't that make you an optimist? What are you doing in the Space Corps, Sergeant?" asked Cruz in mock surprise.

"I'm as pessimistic as the best of them, ma'am. I'm just trying to learn new tricks."

Cruz chewed her lip for a minute, lost in thought. "Larry and I got separated from some others down there. It's possible they found a way to the surface and are hiding out on the base. Or they could still be under the hub."

"Civilians?"

"Two civilians and Second Lieutenant Terence Reynolds. If by any chance you happen to come across them, there's a chance Lieutenant Reynolds might order you to do something contrary to what we've planned."

"He'll want you to save his miserable hide, whatever the

cost," said Keller. When he caught the others looking at him, he shrugged. "I'm a civilian – I can say what I like about him."

McKinney wasn't certain if that was strictly true. It didn't matter – he'd heard the warning and would keep an eye out. "I'll stick to the mission."

"It's not you I'm worried about, Sergeant."

He caught on. There were some in the squad who might choose to obey the orders of an officer superior in rank to a sergeant. "You could give them a direct order before we go, ma'am."

"I could, but I'm aware of what changes circumstances can bring."

"Shoot the bastard if he tries any funny business," said Keller.

"I'll treat anything which arises on its merits, sir," said McKinney drily.

With the details more or less ironed out, McKinney sent four of his squad to the Section D entrance to rendezvous with the other soldiers. They moved out and he tracked their position using his visor HUD. Squad A arrived at the entrance first and they waited on the ramp. Squad C arrived next and lastly Squad B.

"On our way," said Li.

"Take care," McKinney warned. "We shot a few of the Vraxar – they're fast and I wouldn't like to be surprised by them."

The soldiers made the trip without encountering the enemy. They entered the area beneath the rubble which McKinney had started to think of as a *room*. There was plenty of space for them to stand in four rows of five, their suits and reflective visors making them appear every bit as alien as the Vraxar, albeit considerably less ugly. They were armed to the teeth with repeaters, rifles and grenades.

McKinney outlined the plan in a few short sentences. After it was done, he said farewell to Lieutenant Cruz and led his squad towards a narrow vertical gap at the far end of the room. At first glance, it appeared to lead nowhere but when he squeezed through, it opened out again into a wide, low space with pieces of overhanging concrete waiting to catch the heads of the unwary. Hardly any daylight reached this area and McKinney turned on his visor torch. A beam of yellow light danced around, bobbing with the movement of his head. He'd already scouted through here and knew exactly what he was looking for.

"There," he said.

There was a hole in the ground. It was a square opening, three metres to a side and with a smashed console lying halfway across. McKinney stooped uncomfortably low to avoid injury from the ceiling and crabbed his way to the opening. There were steps going down and they were intact. At the bottom of the steps was the dull metal of a thick doorframe. The door was in its recess to one side and the way was clear for them to proceed.

"If we're lucky, there'll be no immediate resistance. It's more than a thousand metres until we get close to the CCB. After that, we're likely to be knee high in the crap."

"I'm going to get me a medal for this," said Garcia.

There were a few laughs and McKinney waved the men into silence. "Let's have no pissing about, unless you want to go on point."

"Sorry, Sergeant."

"Hold here. I'll scout."

McKinney turned off his suit light. The visor sensor switched on the image intensifiers, turning everything to shades of black and green. Sharp edges became rough and the finer details blurred together. He turned on the movement detector as well – in the training exercises he'd learned it was the motion of the enemy which was easiest to spot.

Leaving the soldiers standing motionless behind, he descended the steps, trying to keep his footfall as quiet as possible. The room at the bottom was large, with three wide security desks arrayed across the middle. There were chairs fixed to one wall and a refreshments replicator nearby, its selection menu screen blank.

There were two exit corridors from the room and McKinney crept over to the one which would lead them most efficiently to their destination. The HUD on his visor showed a tiny map of the immediate vicinity, with him as an orange dot in the middle. This first room was dark, but about halfway down each of the two corridors, the emergency lighting was in operation. It was a mixed blessing and, all things considered, McKinney would have preferred darkness.

The corridor stretched away into the distance, with doors to the left and right. It ended at a T-junction. McKinney stopped and listened carefully, giving the visor an opportunity to pick up any sounds. It was absolutely quiet, except for the occasional scrape of movement from the men on the steps.

"Move up," he said.

Something caught his eye in the moments it took the men to file cautiously into the room - it was a photo frame on the desk. He reached out a hand with unexpected trepidation. There was an image of a young boy in the frame, his expression of happiness expertly captured by the photographer. With a feeling of intense sorrow, McKinney put the photo back, exactly where he'd found it. Anger came quickly to replace the sorrow and he clung to it.

"We're going along this corridor and turning right at the end," he said. "Garcia, with me. We'll go first. Clifton, Mills, cover us with your rifles."

This was a lot of soldiers to bring through the confined spaces beneath the base. If they didn't play it right, they could find themselves vulnerable to explosives or repeater fire. McKinney ran as fast as he could along the passage whilst still keeping the noise to a minimum. The barrel of his repeater was comforting in his hands and he kept it aimed straight. His finger stroked the activation trigger in anticipation.

At each right-hand doorway, he stopped and looked inside, with Garcia doing the same for the left. There were offices beyond the doorways with identical desks, chairs and shelf units - the epitome of the Space Corps' disregard for visual flair.

"Clear!" shouted McKinney over the open channel.

"Clear!" said Garcia, in his own rhythm of run-check-run.

The pair of them arrived at the end of the corridor. McKinney looked both ways, sticking his head out into space and withdrawing it quickly. "Nothing."

"No sound," said Garcia.

"Agreed," said McKinney. He looked at the layout again – the right-hand passage would take them to room 1415A. The map didn't explain what the room's purpose was intended to be – it was just one of many such spaces.

"Listen up – Garcia and I are moving to check out 1415A. The rest of Squad A, move up to our present position. Squads B and C hold until I say so."

McKinney looked again, trying to see what lay ahead in the room. The emergency lighting was to provide guidance only and wasn't meant to be sufficient for day-to-day operations. Consequently, it was hard to be certain exactly what the room contained. There were dark, square shapes, which he assumed were operator consoles.

Staying low, he set off. He covered the distance in fifteen rapid strides and repeated his procedure of stopping at the entrance and looking inside. Once again, there was no movement or sound. He chanced a look over the top of the consoles. A sign hung from the ceiling over the middle of the room. *Breakout Area C*. A collection of utilitarian chairs were gathered underneath, clad in a bright blue cloth. The blue was the high point of this room and there were no Vraxar hiding.

Garcia waited on the opposite side of the corridor, his reflective visor pointing directly at McKinney. The two men shrugged in unison.

"1415A is clear," McKinney said. "All squads move up and we'll secure the area."

A minute later and it was done – twenty soldiers were arrayed about the room, covering the three exit corridors with repeaters.

McKinney oriented himself – the next target was room 1720M, which was to be found at the end of the corridor straight ahead.

"Garcia, with me," he said.

The two men did the same again - advance, scan and secure. Two minutes later, the same twenty soldiers were in room 1720M, arrayed in slightly different positions around a similar set of furniture.

"Where the hell are they?" asked McCall.

"Maybe they've left already," said Zack Chance.

"They're here, soldier. We simply haven't found them yet."

McKinney double-checked the map. They were still some distance from the CCB's underground complex but it was a little surprising they'd not encountered any of the enemy so far, especially given Lieutenant Cruz's report about how numerous they were. McKinney didn't like the unexpected and each step they covered without an engagement made him ask if there was a nasty surprise somewhere up ahead.

He was conflicted – the part of him which felt the pressure of time was gripped with the urge to run onwards, shooting at anything which moved. The cautious side of Sergeant Eric McKinney, the side which was fully aware this was still his first proper engagement with a real enemy, advised him to take his time and ensure nothing went wrong. Balancing the two approaches was important, but also difficult.

"We've got to reach the bottom of Stairwell North-C, which is way over there," he said. "After that, two more open areas and we'll be at the outskirts of the CCB complex."

"I'm going to take a shit in Colonel Tenney's toilet," said Huey Roldan, sparking a few laughs.

McKinney found himself boiling over. He marched across and shoved the man. McKinney was strong and the push sent Roldan stumbling into a wall.

"Everybody is *dead* you idiot!" McKinney yelled at him. "Can't you understand? It's not the time for laughs! If we don't fix this, these Vraxar will find out where our other planets are located and then they might kill everyone!"

Roldan got to his feet. McKinney didn't know what the man's reaction would be and he held himself ready.

"Hey, Sergeant, I'm real sorry. Sometimes you've just got to joke, you know? It wasn't meant as anything against the dead. If you can't laugh, then there's nothing left."

As quickly as it came, McKinney's anger subsided. "Yeah. Let's keep it together, Soldier. Me included. We might be the only ones who can do this."

Ten minutes later, McKinney was reassured Stairwell North-C was clear of hostiles and he ordered the men to descend into the room below. This was a large space, filled with consoles. Instrument panels were fitted to one wall and there were two replicators. At one time this area must have been a hive of activity.

The dividends of peace had let much of the base fall empty and it occurred to McKinney how much harder it would have been for the Vraxar to overcome the base if it had been working around the clock. The aliens could have destroyed everything on the surface easily enough but when it came to putting their troops on the ground, they'd have encountered a lot more resistance in these underground warrens. The time of peace had come to an end, that was clear enough to see.

"Got movement," said Grover urgently. "Coming our way."

Instantly, the men tensed up, holding their repeaters tightly, their eyes darting about.

"Where?"

Grover blew out, the sound of his relief apparent to everyone. "Don't shoot – it's one of the base personnel."

They heard the sound of man's voice, coming from one of the side passages. "Wait! I need help!"

"Shut up!" hissed Brogan. "You'll let everyone know we're here."

The man emerged into the room. "Soldiers – am I glad to see you," he said loudly. "About time you got here."

"Keep your voice down," McKinney told him.

The man got the message. "Who's in charge?" he asked, speaking quietly this time.

McKinney lifted his visor out of politeness. "I am. Sergeant McKinney."

"Lieutenant Reynolds. You're going to get me out of here, Sergeant."

McKinney studied the new arrival. Lieutenant Reynolds was pushing forty, wiry, with a thick, unkempt black beard and long hair. There was something dislikeable about the man.

"We've been ordered to attack the enemy, sir."

Reynolds blinked. "Isn't this a rescue? Haven't the Space Corps arrived with reinforcements?"

"Negative to both, sir. Lieutenant Cruz has ordered us into the Central Command Building to destroy the main Tillos data arrays."

"You'll get slaughtered! The place is crawling with these alien *things*."

"I'm told they are called Vraxar, sir. I was also told you were accompanied by civilians."

Reynolds looked shifty. "They didn't make it."

"But you did, sir."

"That's what military training does for you. I should probably lead this mission but I can see you are much better equipped than I am. I would like three of these men to escort me to the surface and then you can continue."

"I can't offer you an escort, Lieutenant Reynolds." McKinney thumbed over his shoulder. "Up these stairs, across two rooms until you get to 1415A. It's clear. I'm sure you can find your way out from there. Lieutenant Cruz is outside. Maybe you can help her get to the underground bunker. It'll be safe in there – as safe as anywhere else."

Reynolds narrowed his eyes. "Lieutenant Cruz is hurt?"

"Not badly."

"She'll appreciate my assistance."

With that, Reynolds turned towards the staircase. He was clearly a good enough judge of character to realise he wasn't getting an escort and he didn't ask again. McKinney watched Reynolds go and saw the man's hand touch the gauss pistol tucked into his belt, as if seeking reassurance it was still there.

McKinney put Reynolds from his mind, lowered his visor and set off in the direction of the CCB.

CHAPTER NINETEEN

THE INTERIOR of the Vraxar shuttle was spartan. Captain Charlie Blake took in the few details – he was in a long, narrow space with benches to either side. The floor was flat and covered in grating, whilst the roof curved overhead. Light came from a series of pinprick sources, casting a dirty yellow illumination onto the occupants.

The interior walls were a grey so dark it was easy to mistake for black. There was a mixture of smells – overwhelmingly metallic, but also other odours. Blake picked up the bitter scent of greasy liquids as well as something which he thought very similar to formaldehyde. It was unpleasant and clung to the insides of his nostrils.

From his position sitting on of one of the hard benches, he could see screens on the front bulkhead wall. Alien letters scrolled across, appearing and disappearing at irregular intervals. He lowered his suit visor, wondering if the built-in language modules could make anything of the script.

[Failure – language not recognized. Download additional language packs for interpretation. ERR CODE#932]

He lifted the visor again. Lieutenant Caz Pointer sat opposite him, her suit and face smeared in grime. She wore an expression of absolute misery. Lieutenant Gabriel Rivera sat a few feet away from her, his suited arms folded across his chest and his visor pulled down so he wouldn't have to meet Blake's eyes. The man was a disgrace and it was difficult to avoid the uncharitable thought that it would have been better for Commander Cain Brady to have survived instead of Rivera. Added to that were the deaths of every single one of the *Determinant*'s soldiers. Blake hadn't known them well, but the loss was difficult to bear. He grimaced.

"What's going to happen to us?" Pointer asked, not for the first time.

"I don't know, Lieutenant. They didn't kill us and that's a positive sign."

"How do they know our language when we don't know theirs?"

"They must have extracted and analysed enough examples from the Tillos base to piece together how we speak. Whatever they are, they're only partially biological – I'm sure they've got processing units to interface between the alloy part of their bodies and the flesh. Maybe they don't even have an organic brain."

"They look like Ghasts, sir."

"Yes. The flesh parts look like Ghasts."

He had an idea why that might be. It was only an educated guess and he didn't want to share it for the moment, since the ramifications weren't something he wanted the others to dwell on.

The shuttle ride was a short one. The craft's engines had a peculiar buzzing note to them, which Blake was curious about. The buzz increased in volume and they felt a gentle thump.

"Touch down," said Blake. He caught Pointer's eye. "Keep it steady, Lieutenant."

She attempted a smile and didn't answer.

The shuttle had a rear door. This door hissed to indicate its seal was broken and it fell smoothly away from the hull, revealing the light of early morning outside. Blake squinted – there were six Vraxar waiting, standing in pairs at the bottom of the exit ramp.

"Come," said one.

When the *Determinant* crashed, Blake and the other two had been able to don suits and grab themselves a rifle each. When they emerged from the wreckage and found themselves facing numerous armed opponents as well as the vicious-looking nose cannon of the shuttle, it hadn't been a difficult choice to throw their rifles down and surrender. Therefore, they had nothing with which to offer resistance.

"We're coming," said Blake.

He stood and walked towards the ramp, his footsteps making the grate thrum. Behind, Pointer and Rivera did likewise, following out through the rear exit of the shuttle.

At the bottom of the ramp, Blake took everything in. They were on the Tillos base. Mountains of heat-blackened ruins stretched as far as the eye could see, some still alight though the fires were dwindling. The shuttle was on what might have once been a parking area for the installation's pool of transport vehicles. There were craters here and there, the size of which suggested they were caused by something launched from orbit.

Nearby, untouched amongst the rubble was a near-intact building. This building was four stories tall and slab-sided. A wide flight of steps led upwards to the main doors, flanked by flags representing each of the different worlds in the Confederation. He couldn't help but notice the flags for Roban and Liventor still fluttering amongst the others. There was a sign at the bottom of the steps. *Central Command Building.*

The Vraxar had reinforced the building – dozens of them were standing motionless around the perimeter and Blake counted six weapons batteries of a type he was unfamiliar with. Their likely function could be gleaned from their features. Two had multiple, slowly-rotating barrels protruding, whilst others were launchers of some sort. They weren't enough to knock out a fleet warship, though they would bring down most shuttles easily enough.

"Follow," said the Vraxar soldier closest. The voice was flat and synthesised, the alien's lips not quite moving in synch with the word.

This was the closest Blake had been to one of the aliens. He allowed himself the briefest of moments to study this new enemy. It was seven feet tall and bipedal, walking on legs reinforced with implanted alloy bars. The pelvis on this Vraxar was largely metal, which made Blake wonder if the original flesh had been blown away by some kind of weapon and then patched up with armour plates. The alloy covering its shoulders was pitted and scraped, as though it had seen a thousand engagements and come through them all.

While the metal had suffered, the Vraxar's flesh had also deteriorated, becoming a pallid, sickly grey with hints of yellow. It made Blake think of science's imperfect efforts to sustain flesh long beyond the time the cells should have withered and died. He looked into the yellow eyes and saw nothing in there he could relate to. With the Ghasts, there was an appreciation of their own lives – different to how a human would perceive it but identifiable nonetheless. This alien knew nothing beyond existence, perhaps long after it should have rotted and crumbled into dust. Hints of the odours he'd noticed on the shuttle wafted from it and Blake wrinkled his nose.

"There aren't many of them when you think about it," whispered Pointer. "This is a big base."

Her voice wasn't low enough.

"Your forces are defeated," said one of the Vraxar without triumph. "Some of us have returned to the *Hannixar*. Others are elsewhere."

Blake wasn't sure he liked the sound of that. "Where elsewhere?"

The alien was either unaccustomed to the idea of secrecy or it simply didn't care. "We have discovered an additional area of the base which interests us."

"Where?" Blake persisted.

None of their escort provided an answer.

"Come," said one.

Four of the Vraxar moved off towards the Central Command Building. Blake was half-expecting them to be synchronised and move with perfect timing. They were close, but not perfect. Their gait was somehow ungainly, yet without the variation found in creatures made entirely of flesh. The final two Vraxar waited for their prisoners to follow and then came afterwards.

"What do you want here?" asked Blake, unsure to whom he should direct his question.

The Vraxar didn't answer.

"Why have you attacked our base?"

"Life brings us," said one of the soldiers.

"What do you mean?"

None of their escort would answer further questions and Blake gave up trying. He didn't particularly want to anger them. Without a point of reference, he had no idea if they would tolerate his curiosity or simply shoot him to stop him talking. One thing was certain – there was something distinctly menacing about the Vraxar's words.

They were led up the steps. The main doors had been

smashed open by something heavy and they lay twisted and broken in the foyer of the CCB. Blake hadn't been to this specific building before, but he'd seen plenty like it. There were rows of security desks at the front, whilst the inner part of the building was protected by thick doors – all open - which in normal circumstances would only allow personnel with the highest clearance to go through. Standard-issue Space Corps carpet tiles covered the floor, surprisingly unmarked by the Vraxar incursion.

The Vraxar knew exactly where they were going. They crossed the floor and went through one of the doorways, which led into what appeared to be a main corridor running through the centre of the CCB. There were others here. They didn't actively patrol and stood in groups of two or four, holding their hand cannons at the ready. At no point did the aliens exchange words with each other, nor in any way acknowledge the presence of their fellows – it was as though they had no empathy whatsoever and the existence of other beings was completely unimportant.

The smell was stronger in this corridor and Blake found that prolonged exposure did not result in him become accustomed to it. He looked sideways at Pointer and saw she was breathing through her mouth. Rivera padded along a few paces back and Blake couldn't bring himself to check on his lieutenant.

They came to a staircase, which led up and down. The Vraxar headed downwards and they descended to the first underground level. The steps continued deeper, though their destination apparently didn't lie that way.

It was poorly-lit here and the emergency lighting had partially malfunctioned, making alternate strips turn off and then on. The effect was disconcerting.

The temperature was also much colder than Blake had expected. His suit was proof against the harshest of conditions on the coldest of worlds. Even so, the chill air brushed against the skin of his face and he shivered.

The Vraxar stopped suddenly, next to an open doorway. Blake caught the words on a sign above. *Secondary Data Repository Access Area – Restricted Personnel Only.*

"You will go into this room," said one of the aliens, stepping aside and motioning with its gun.

Blake went first, followed by Pointer and Rivera. The Vraxar allowed them time to enter and then also entered the room.

The repository access area wasn't a huge room – ten or twelve metres to each side. A drab metal cylinder with a four-metre diameter ran from the centre of a complicated-looking, circular bank of consoles in the middle of the room. He'd seen the like before – this was the storage unit for the whole of the Tillos base. Except it wouldn't just contain data specific to the base, it might well contain vast amounts of information on almost anything to be found within the Confederation. The Space Corps liked the comfort of multi-layered redundancy and when storage space was abundant, information tended to be copied to wherever it would fit.

Before he could spend much time wondering about it, Blake saw something new. There was another group of Vraxar in the room, standing halfway around the central pillar and with a large cube on the tiled floor next to them. There were several display screens on the device, and they showed the alien script Blake had seen on the shuttle.

These new Vraxar were different – they were smaller than the soldiers and did not look like Ghasts. One of them approached the three captives.

This Vraxar was hardly six feet tall and spindly. Its legs were organic – with paper-thin and decaying yellow-brown flesh which was hardly enough to conceal the yellow bones underneath. These limbs were partially encased in metal and this seemed to be the only thing strong enough to keep the alien from toppling over. Its torso was long and it ribcage was narrow. Bands of metal wrapped around, climbing up and covering the creature's shoulders. Its skull was mostly of metal, though its face was not – it had sharp, cruel features, with a thin nose and lips. Whatever eyes had once been in the sockets were now prosthetic – copies poorly made to mimic the originals. It stank and Blake retched when it came close.

"You will be killed if you fight," said one of the Vraxar soldiers. "There will be no additional warning."

The smaller Vraxar stood in front of them for a moment, its glassy brown eyes studying them. Blake had no idea what it wanted and was absolutely sure he didn't want to find out. Pointer was next to him. She stared directly ahead as though her mind was hiding behind mental walls she'd created to block out everything around her.

The Vraxar came closer to Blake. Its mouth opened in something that may have been an attempt at a smile. The alien had yellow teeth, some of them blackened and decaying. There was a sense of age about it – even more so than from the Vraxar soldier he'd studied outside. Blake couldn't shake the feeling this one had lived a hundred times longer than he had.

"How do we access this cylinder?" asked the alien. Its voice had a sibilant edge to it, mixed with the same synthesised tones of the others.

"I don't know," said Blake. "I don't work here."

"You came down on a warship. That means you know."

Blake struggled to make the logical connection. It sounded like the Vraxar had pulled some details about humanity which made them believe officers on a spaceship had a way of accessing whatever they liked. In truth, he had the clearance to access most things, except he wasn't about to give that away.

"It's offline. There's no power."

"You have authorisation to bring it online."

"If it's offline, it's gone," said Blake. "You can't access it anymore, no matter what you do."

"I don't like that answer."

"It's the only answer I have."

The Vraxar smiled again and its stench reached into Blake's nose. He coughed.

"I am rotting and my power source is failing," said the Vraxar. "I have seen a thousand years and as each additional one passes, the decay of my flesh advances. Not all flesh is equal when it comes to the rate at which it deteriorates, though I do not expect you to encounter one of our elders. For us, conquest brings renewal. I might not live to witness the extinction of the race after yours, but humanity will join us before I perish."

"What happened to the Estral?" asked Blake, stalling for time by asking the first question that jumped into his head.

"Like those before them, the Estral succumbed. Their strength has become ours, along with their power. The same will happen to your race soon."

"Not if you're relying on data from that storage cylinder to find us," said Blake, wondering at the Vraxar's odd use of the words *strength* and *power* in the same sentence.

"It is no matter. If necessary, we will break the cylinder down and find what it contains. It would be preferable if we did not have to wait. It is a shame for us that the other installations on this planet all feed their data into this central array, otherwise we might already have what we need. You will tell me the location of your other worlds."

Blake forced himself to laugh. "I don't know the coordinates! They are strings containing many digits. We rely on our navigational computers to take us from place to place – there is no need for anyone to commit anything to memory."

The Vraxar nodded as if in acceptance. Then, before Blake

could react, a pair of hands grabbed his arms. The hands were strong and he was unable to break free.

"Stand still or be killed," said the smaller Vraxar, its voice still completely devoid of emotion. It lifted one of its arms and revealed a silver tube in one of its long-fingered hands. "The contents of this syringe will ensure you speak the truth."

With that it made a stabbing motion, aiming the needle end of the syringe at Blake's chest. The material of the spacesuit was exceptionally strong, but it wasn't designed to stop piercing weapons as sharp and hard as the needle. The cold metal crunched between Blake's ribs and entered his heart. The pain was excruciating and he shouted out with the agony of it.

CHAPTER TWENTY

"ARE we going to wait here for them to return, Lieutenant?" asked Larry Keller. "It sounds as if that underground bunker is going to be a lot safer than sitting around under this piece of concrete."

"I can't move very fast, Larry. I won't be able to shoot straight if I have to hop towards the enemy."

"Yeah, ha ha," he said. "Seriously, though – we're not exactly in the best place here, are we? What if this stuff above us comes crashing down?"

"Sergeant McKinney knows where we are. He'll come back for us. I can see it in his face – he's a good man."

They both heard the noise at the same time – the scuffing footsteps of someone coming from the entrance McKinney and his men had recently gone through. Cruz lifted her gauss pistol and aimed it at the opening, in case one of the Vraxar had found a way past the soldiers. It wasn't an alien, but the person who came through was almost as unwelcome.

"Lieutenant Reynolds," said Cruz. "You made it out."

Reynolds looked at her, his eyes gleaming in the faint light. "I got away. I lost Nelson and Akachi. Poor bastards got shot. There was nothing I could do for them."

Cruz couldn't bring herself to think about the dead civilians – not yet. "We pulled the last core. Larry and I found it – the Vraxar won't be able to get through our encryption now."

"That's excellent work, Lieutenant! If there was anyone who could get it done, I knew it would be you."

There were many unanswered questions, not least of which being Reynolds' decision to go in the wrong direction when they were looking for the processing room. It wasn't the time. "Thank you," she said.

"I met Sergeant McKinney. He said you got hurt."

"I broke an ankle on the way out."

"The sergeant said there was an underground bunker. He said I should help you get there."

"We'll be exposed if we try to make it with me limping."

"He told me he planned to meet you there instead of coming this way again."

Cruz was surprised. "Really? He must have changed his mind."

"Maybe we should give it a try, Lieutenant," said Keller. "The way I see it, there could be replicators running off the backup power. If Sergeant McKinney doesn't make it, we'll be stuck here without food or water. And when it comes to it, there's a big old warship under the ground. One way or another, the Space Corps is going to want it back. When they come, we'll be there waiting for them."

Cruz made her mind up. "Come on, then. Let's get moving," she said. "That painkiller is still working its magic, so I guess now is as good a time as any."

With Keller's assistance, she got to her feet and slung her gauss rifle over her back. The break in her ankle felt like a bad one and the bones grated together. The sensation was distant and remote – without the painkiller, she could only imagine how unpleasant it would be.

Soon, she was limping alongside the pile of rubble, with her arm around Keller's shoulder. Lieutenant Reynolds didn't offer to help and Cruz was happy he was so lazy – she couldn't stomach the thought of him touching her.

They kept vigilant, eyes scanning the skies for enemy shuttles and the ground for patrols. Cruz kept her gauss pistol ready and Reynolds did likewise. There was a wind blowing and it carried smoke in thick, unpredictable clouds across the ruins of the base. It clung to the insides of their lungs and left a layer of soot on whatever parts of their bodies it touched.

The broken buildings seemed to have a life of their own and they shifted constantly, huge chunks of concrete scraping and screeching as they settled. Smaller pieces clattered down from above, occasionally bouncing across their paths. The noises made them jumpy, in case they heralded the approach of Vraxar soldiers.

"Getting into a rhythm," said Keller as their speed increased.

"We're doing okay, Larry."

To Cruz's relief, they reached the ramp leading to the underground bunker without having to fire a shot. The slope cut out the wind and the effects of the smoke were lessened.

"There it is – Section D entrance," said Keller. "Right where Sergeant McKinney said it would be."

"Do either of you two know what's inside?" Cruz asked.

"Nope," said Keller.

"I've done a couple of stints down here," said Reynolds. "What's the plan, Lieutenant?"

"There's a weapons room at the bottom."

"I think I know the place," said Reynolds. "There used to be a replicator for the guards' station. I assume it's still there. Whether it's operational or not is another matter. Want to head that way?"

"Sounds like a good idea. There should be suits in the weapons room – I'm going to need painkillers again before this is over."

They made their way down the ramp. Reynolds brought up the rear, claiming he wanted to guard their backs. Neither Keller nor Cruz were fooled for a second – the only person Reynolds was looking out for was himself by allowing them into the bunker first.

Once inside and when it was obvious there were no Vraxar lying in wait, Reynolds got in front and led them across the guard room. "It's a long way to the bottom, Lieutenant Cruz. Down a lot of stairs."

"I'll manage," she said. "Larry's doing a great job."

"I hope you didn't forget about that date," Keller whispered. "After all this, I think I deserve one."

She grinned at him. "I didn't forget, Larry."

Cruz was aware of the tales about the extent of the Tillos underground bunker, but it was one of those things she needed to experience in order to fully appreciate the magnitude of what the Space Corps had achieved in excavating such a monumental hole in the earth and fitting it out to allow potentially thousands of people to work here. There weren't thousands working now – it was empty and the loudest sound was their feet on the floor.

They travelled a few hundred metres along a main corridor. The lighting functioned, though there was little to see. Once you'd experienced how the Space Corps did things, there was rarely anything left to surprise. Whatever they built and wherever they put it, everything looked the same as it did elsewhere in the Corps. In spite of the fact that personal music players were frowned upon and there were only a limited quantity of artificial plants to share around, serving personnel were almost invariably dedicated and professional.

"Are you two managing?" asked Reynolds when they reached

the top of the first stairwell. "I'd offer to help but you seem to be getting along nicely."

Reynolds had a way of being insolent, whilst not being quite insubordinate enough to allow Cruz to confidently call him out on it. She knew as soon as she reprimanded him, he'd play the victim and she'd end up looking like she couldn't control lower-ranked officers. Cruz cursed herself for having this problem. Against other officers, Reynolds was predictably obsequious and grovelled enough to make her cringe when she saw it. *He's just one of those people.* The thought wasn't a helpful one.

"Think you can manage if I go in front?" asked Keller. "These steps aren't too steep."

"Go on," she said. Her ankle was throbbing and she couldn't muster a smile.

They reached the bottom of the steps without incident and without assistance from Reynolds. Cruz found herself despising him and she was appalled he had so much power over her that he could elicit such an emotional response.

"How long until we get rescued?" Reynolds asked over his shoulder.

"If I had to guess, I'd say it'll be several days. Assuming rescue comes."

"You think these Vraxar are here to stay?"

"I think they'll stay on Tillos until they've got what they want."

"You shut the processing core down, right? That leaves them with the main array which the good Sergeant McKinney is going to destroy for us."

"What's your point, Lieutenant Reynolds?" Cruz asked.

"No point in particular. It strikes me they'll want to leave as quickly as they arrived. That data array has got to weigh a few thousand tonnes – it's too big for a shuttle to carry off-world, even a big shuttle equipped with a gravity winch. They'll need a lifter of some type. Whether or not Sergeant McKinney succeeds or fails it won't affect how long they'll stick around. If the data array is gone, they'll leave. If the data array survives, they'll lift it and vanish into lightspeed anyway."

"You believe they'll be gone in a few hours," said Keller.

"I reckon so. After that, the Space Corps will return and start digging through the rubble to see what remains of Tillos."

"There's not much left."

"It'll be impossible to put most of it together, I'm sure," said Reynolds. "Like a giant jigsaw with half of the pieces missing. Twenty thousand deaths to investigate, whilst the threat of a new alien menace looms above us."

"Best we hole up somewhere so we can help them out," said Keller.

"Which is exactly why we're here," Reynolds replied.

"He's a bit creepy," Keller whispered to Cruz. She could only nod in response.

They reached another set of steps and descended to another wide corridor. This led to another room, another corridor and yet more steps. More corridors and steps followed, each one increasingly difficult for Cruz to manage.

"We're most of the way down," said Reynolds. "A couple more of these long stairwells and we should be close to the guard station." He winked. "There might be some painkillers in there as well."

"Oh shut up, Tez," said Keller. "Can't you see she's had enough of your crap?"

Reynolds didn't respond. He led them into a long, wide passage, which curved slightly to the left. There were doorways at regular intervals in the right-hand wall and a series of huge windows in the left wall.

"One of the many viewing areas," said Reynolds, indicating the closest window with one hand. "To allow the technicians to see their work whilst remaining only a short distance from their comfortable offices."

Neither Cruz nor Keller had seen the working area of the bunker before and they moved past Reynolds in order to look at the *ES Lucid*. There were no seats here, so Cruz tucked her pistol into her belt and leaned forward with her hands on the sill. She peered into the vastness of the bunker, with Keller standing reassuringly close in case she needed support.

"That's one big spaceship," said Keller with a low whistle. "I wouldn't like to be the one responsible for flying it in and out of the bunker."

"I wonder why it's still running," said Cruz. "Sergeant McKinney seems to have more than a passing interest and he didn't have an idea."

"Obsidiar cored," said Keller promptly. "That's what it'll be."

"It's fairly important the Vraxar don't find it, then?"

"We don't know exactly what they want, Lieutenant," Keller replied. "We assume they're here to find out where the other Confederation worlds are, but what happens after that? Do they want resources? If so, I'm sure our Obsidiar will be high up on their wants list."

Cruz heard a noise, something out of place, followed by a high-pitched cracking. At first, she didn't recognize it and she turned, puzzled, towards Keller. He had a strange frown on his face. Then, Cruz saw the blood – a large, uneven circle of it spreading from the left-hand side of his chest. With a sigh, he toppled to one side.

Cruz tried to turn, doing her best to keep the weight off her broken ankle. Too late, she realised it would have been better to risk the additional injury in order to spin around as quickly as possible. She heard footsteps across the floor. A dark shape appeared in her periphery, coming down towards her. She was struck hard on the back of the neck. The single knee carrying her weight sagged and she reached out to grab the sill. She felt something hit her again, this time high on the cheekbone. A third strike knocked her to the ground.

Gasping and struggling to remain conscious Cruz fell forward, dazed. Her broken ankle twisted beneath her and the pain of it made her shout in agony. Coloured spots danced across her retinas and she landed hard on the floor. She put her arms out but found her brain unable to control them properly and the side of her head bounced off the hard floor tiles. Her vision swum.

A hand tugged at her belt and she heard her gauss pistol clatter away in the distance. There was more tugging and the gauss rifle followed.

"You won't be needing those, will you?" asked Reynolds.

Then, he grabbed her wrists and started dragging her across the floor. She tried to struggle and kick out, but nothing seemed to be working anymore.

"There's no one left, princess," he said. "No one to hear you and when the cavalry finally arrives they'll be too busy with all the other crap to care about one more dead body."

She tried to speak, to ask him why he was doing this. Talking was too much effort and the best she could manage was to mumble under her breath.

"If you're asking yourself why I'm doing this, well it's just because I can. I might as well take the chance while it's there to be taken, eh?"

She closed her eyes for a moment and when she opened them again, Cruz found herself somewhere new. She didn't know where she was at first and then her brain registered the sight of a desk and some shelves. Reynolds had taken her into one of the offices along the inner wall of the viewing area. Her eye socket hurt like hell and waves of nausea rolled through her stomach.

He didn't waste time and started pulling at her uniform. Cruz heard him swear when he figured out he was far too weak to rip the material. The fastenings were at the back and Reynolds pushed and pulled until she was lying on her side. From this angle, she could see through the open door. Larry Keller's body lay still – the gauss slug had caused too much damage for him to get up and rescue her.

"What the hell is that?" said Reynolds.

Cruz had no idea what he was talking about and tried feebly to strike him with a fist. He batted her arm away impatiently and strode through the door, his head tipped to one side as though he was listening to something.

Reynolds swore and ran back into the office. He took hold of Cruz's leg – luckily not the one with the broken ankle – and pulled her towards the desk.

"Sounds like the rescue team has come earlier than expected," he panted. "We're going to wait it out in here. If you're a good girl, I might let you go afterwards. However, if you make any noise at all, I'm just going to shoot you."

Reynolds hauled her behind the desk. Cruz hadn't yet come fully to her senses, but she was no fool. Whatever happened, Reynolds had given himself no choice other than to murder her. The only thing stopping him from killing her immediately was the fact he was still thinking with his trousers rather than his brain.

She heard the approaching footsteps. They were heavy and deliberate, metronomic almost. The footsteps were accompanied by the clunk of metal and a scraping sound she didn't recognize. Whoever had arrived, they'd done so in great numbers.

Once in while we're put in a situation where all roads lead to the same shitty destination, she thought.

Through one half-open eye she saw Lieutenant Reynolds, crouched over her legs and leaning to look through a gap in the side of the desk. His brash self-confidence was gone and his skin was pale. He exuded the odour of cold sweat and he rubbed at his beard.

Maria Cruz made her decision. It wasn't really a decision when she boiled it down. It took a few seconds to summon the energy and she waited until she was confident of success.

"Help!" she shouted. Her voice croaked and sounded pitifully quiet. "Help!" she repeated, louder this time.

"Shut up!" Reynolds hissed. He punched her in the face, and then pressed his open palm hard over her mouth and nose. She couldn't breathe and lacked the strength to struggle against him. He held her in place and she could see from his eyes he wasn't going to let up until she was dead.

As her vision faded, Cruz saw a shape looming over her and Reynolds. It was broad and tall, a fusion of grey flesh and alloy plates. She heard the crack of a weapon and felt liquid spill over her. Then, she knew no more.

CHAPTER TWENTY-ONE

SERGEANT ERIC MCKINNEY crouched behind a row of floor-standing metal cabinets, his shoulder tight up against the surface. Something hummed quietly in the room beyond, not loud enough to conceal the footsteps of the Vraxar walking across the floor on the other side. The humming was peculiar and at first sounded like it came from within the cabinets. He listened closely - it was coming from somewhere he couldn't quite pin down.

McKinney swore inwardly – progress had been easy so far, lulling him into a false sense of security. They'd encountered no hostiles and the routine of advance-secure-advance had taken them across a large section of the underground complex without firing a shot. The map on his HUD used a solid line to demark the comms hub/general area and the CCB prohibited zone. That line was mid-way along the corridor behind him, in which the remainder of the squad gathered.

"I've got movement," he said, the sound of his voice completely hidden behind his visor. "Sounds like four Vraxar –

they're on the other side of some cabinets in room 94CCB with me."

He checked the map overlay once more. There were four exits from this particular room. This row of cabinets ran from north to south near to one of the walls and there was another row at the opposite side of the room. The Vraxar couldn't see McKinney, nor could McKinney see enough to execute an effective surprise attack. When the stakes were so high, every choice became laden with meaning.

Then, the footsteps stopped. McKinney held his breath and listened. The visor sensor was more sensitive than his ears, but it didn't pick up anything he could use to his advantage. In a training exercise, he could have waited it out, or crept away to rejoin his men. It wasn't an option here.

"What going on, sir?" asked Corporal Li.

It was time to act. "Garcia, Roldan, McCall, Katz and Albers, move up," McKinney ordered. "If I hear a single sound, I'm going to shoot the man responsible."

From his periphery, McKinney saw shadows detach from the wall of the corridor fifteen or twenty metres away. The five men crept along in admirable silence until they reached the entrance to the room, where they paused a short distance across from McKinney, looking to him for guidance.

"What's that humming?" asked Roldan.

"Sounds familiar."

"I think some of the kit in the room is powered up again," said McKinney. "We're going to split – Garcia and Roldan with me. We'll go left, the others go right. On my command, we come around the cabinets and shoot anything that moves. Rifles only – we're going to be crowded up and I don't want any friendly fire deaths."

"Move and shoot - those are the plans I like," said Roldan – a stocky man broader and shorter than the others.

With his rifle at eye level and the stock held against his shoulder, McKinney crept sideways along the cabinets. He guessed the enemy to be somewhere in the centre of the room, which would make them an easy target unless there was plenty of cover. At the end of the row, he leaned carefully out, feeling Garcia and Roldan crowding in too close behind. He waved them back and withdrew his head before he'd been able to see the entirety of the room.

"Give me some room," he warned.

"Sorry, Sergeant."

Before McKinney could attempt another look into the room, he heard the footsteps again. This was followed by an unexpectedly loud crash.

"They're pulling over some of the cabinets on the other side of the room," said Albers.

"What are they playing at?"

There were other footsteps, this time coming closer to the west side of the room where the men were hiding. McKinney didn't know why the Vraxar were pulling the cabinets over and there was no more time to wait.

"Now. Shoot them."

With that, he took three quick steps to the side, taking him away from the cover of the dull grey cabinets. He saw the enemy – five of them rather than four. He took aim at the one furthest away as it pulled at the row of cabinets and knocked another one down. McKinney fired at it in controlled bursts, hitting it between the shoulder blades. It started to fall, blood and fluid ejecting from its chest in an arc. McKinney swung his rifle, seeking his next target.

Garcia and Roldan came, firing their rifles too. Coils whined and projectiles smashed into the enemy. McKinney was dimly aware of McCall, Katz and Albers a few metres away. McCall was in a crouch and the other two fired over his head.

The enemy fell quickly, given no time to raise their own weapons. Another sound rose to join the others – this one was a roaring staccato, out of place amongst the combined droning of the gauss rifles. McKinney didn't recognize the sound at once and he fired his third volley, striking the final Vraxar in the chest and stomach, punching it towards the floor. With the dead alien still in mid-fall, McKinney's brain registered the presence of an object in the middle of the floor. It was less than waist high and shaped like a truncated pyramid. *Looks like a turret* he belatedly realised.

McCall, Katz and Albers went down, their bodies torn to pieces by a hail of fire from the repeater turret the Vraxar had brought into the room. McKinney fired his rifle at the turret, knowing it was useless. Slugs pinged away from the armoured surface of the repeater.

"Back!" shouted Garcia, diving away into the cover of the cabinets.

McKinney followed. There was no time to turn, so all he could do was hurl his body to one side. He felt something scream by his neck, the proximity of the repeater slug making a noise like a mosquito as it went past.

He landed hard on the floor and his rifle was almost dashed from his hands.

"Down!" he screamed. "Stay the hell down! Repeater turret!"

The three surviving men hid out of sight, but the Vraxar repeater still fired, strafing left and right with incredible speed. Its projectiles clattered off the cabinets, pushing them slowly towards the wall and leaving a pattern of lumps on the metal where they'd failed to penetrate completely through.

McKinney huddled close to the ground, waiting for it to stop. "Garcia, Roldan, report."

He heard Garcia's familiar voice. "I'm okay, Sergeant."

"Looks like something got me in the arm. Hardly a nick." said Roldan. "My suit is holding me together."

"Are you able to fight?"

"I can still hold my gun, sir."

The rest of the men in the corridor were already in the process of withdrawing to a place further away and around a corner. If the repeater knocked over the cabinets, it would cut the unprotected men down easily. In the confusion, McKinney missed whoever it was gave the order and he was glad either Li or Evans was on the ball.

"We need to take that turret out," he said.

"There's no way to hit it with a plasma rocket from here, sir," said Webb. "Not unless you want to die in the blast."

"Grenades," grunted McKinney.

He twisted around and dragged himself past Roldan, trying to stay close to the floor. The enemy repeater didn't stop firing and holes began to appear in the cabinets.

"That's going to bring the Vraxar running, Sergeant," said Li.

"No shit."

McKinney slid a grenade out of his belt and left it on its default seven second timer. He didn't want to put his head into the line of fire, so he slid the grenade along the ground with an awkward side-on action, relying on his memory to get it into the right place.

The grenade exploded with a low, grumbling boom, filling the room with white light. The light faded and the noise from the repeater turret stopped. McKinney held his breath, counting slowly upwards from zero. At the count of three the repeater started again, producing the same insistent thunder as before.

"I think the grenade just shifted it across the room, sir," said Garcia. "The slugs are coming from a different angle now."

This wasn't the best time to congratulate Garcia on his perception. McKinney had no idea where the turret was, which made it much harder for him to aim his next grenade.

"Want me to move up?" asked Webb.

"Hold," said McKinney. There was a chance Webb would get himself shot trying to come along the corridor. The repeater would definitely kill him before he could fire the plasma tube.

Gritting his teeth, McKinney crawled a little further along the floor. Each additional inch he moved revealed a bit more of the room, but the repeater remained out of sight. Room 94CCB wasn't small, so a throw-and-hope approach with grenades would rely on luck rather than judgement.

One of the cabinets toppled backwards under the onslaught. Its top edge thudded off the wall and it threatened to fall onto Garcia. The man raised his hands defensively. The cabinet wobbled as more slugs pounded into it, but it didn't slide any further.

McKinney realised he was taking too long and wasting precious seconds trying to evaluate the risks of every action. He remembered something he was taught, a few years ago during training. *Sometimes you've just got to stop pissing about and start shooting.*

Lying on his side, he used his left hand to pull six grenades free, letting them drop onto the floor by his chest. One-by-one he picked them up, activated their timers and sent them skittering into the room. The first one exploded before he'd thrown the fifth and he continued until he'd thrown the last two grenades. They detonated in a slow chain, thumping and sending an expanding wave of hot air throughout the room. By the time the final grenade went off, the air was well over a hundred degrees. McKinney's suit was proof against much higher temperatures, but it chimed a warning into his ear to alert him. The repeater fire sputtered and then stopped.

The white fires died and the gloom of the emergency lightning reasserted itself. The repeater fire didn't resume. McKinney waited ten long seconds and then looked cautiously around the battered edge of the cabinet. A greasy smoke rose from the carpet tiles and his visor dutifully filtered out the stench. Most of the cabinets on the far side of the room were knocked over, some resting against each other precariously. They were scarred and buckled from the heat but otherwise surprisingly undamaged, with their doors mostly intact and still closed.

"They must have kept something important in these cabinets," said Garcia. "The metal is about two inches thick."

The repeater was amongst the cabinets, tipped onto one side, with a large chunk of its body melted to sludge and its twin gun barrels bent from the heat. In the comparative quiet, McKinney could hear the humming sound it made and he cursed himself for not realising what it was sooner. He'd lost three men who might have lived.

There was no time for further reflection. McKinney heard more repeater fire start up along the corridor where the rest of his men waited. A second repeater joined the first, clunking with the sharp sound of perfectly-engineered metal. It ended quickly.

"Got hostiles," said Evans. "Three down."

"Confirm no more are incoming, Corporal."

"I can confirm no more visible, sir."

"Move up on the double. It sounds like we've stirred the hornet's nest."

"Roger that."

The soldiers traded silence for speed and their boots pounded along the corridor. In the moments of waiting, McKinney, Garcia and Roldan did their best to get in positions that allowed them to cover each of the other three exit corridors.

"Keep your movement sensors active," he said. "They should give us a bit more warning."

The men arrived, fanning out and crouching where it was safe.

"Li, Evans, keep watch on the passages to the east and west," said McKinney. "I'll check out the north."

With his visor on full zoom, McKinney scanned the northern corridor. His HUD overlay told him it was less than sixty metres long, before opening out into one of the lower rooms directly beneath the CCB. There were doorways in both walls – offices which led nowhere, but which might provide cover if they needed it.

"We've got company," said Li. "Movement to the west."

"Movement east as well, Sergeant. Multiple hostiles."

McKinney opened his mouth to give the order to fire. Before the word had even left his mouth, he saw movement to the north as well. A fleeting shadow dashed across the end of the corridor. The shadow vanished, but it left something behind – an incandescent speck of something which became gradually larger as it raced along the corridor. It took McKinney a second to realise it was a rocket, fired towards them from the far room.

"Get down!" he shouted, knowing it was already far too late.

CHAPTER TWENTY-TWO

CAPTAIN CHARLIE BLAKE felt a burst of ice cold fluid enter his heart. The sensation faded rapidly as the heat of his blood warmed the drug and carried it through his body. The Vraxar watched him closely and made no effort to remove the needle, which remained protruding from Blake's chest.

Within five seconds of the needle piercing his heart, Blake felt four of his spacesuit's micro needles injecting him. He had no idea what remedy the suit decided to employ, but he was sure there'd be a best-guess antidote to the Vraxar truth drug and doubtless a high dose of battlefield adrenaline.

After a minute, the hands holding Blake in place lessened their grip and the Vraxar soldier stepped back. The smaller Vraxar, which clearly had authority, spoke again, its voice flat and lacking in inflection.

"Tell us where to find the remainder of the Confederation's planets."

Blake gave his best impression of a rebellious smile and tried to look as if he was fighting to remain awake. The Vraxar watched him without emotion.

"Tell us."

"I can't," said Blake. With a grunt of pain, he gripped the end of the syringe and slid the needle out of his chest. He opened his fingers and it dropped to the floor.

Whatever crap the Vraxar had injected him with it felt vile – designed to accomplish a single purpose without a care for the host body. If it wasn't for the synthetic adrenaline, he knew it would be a struggle to stop himself falling on the floor and retching his insides out. His suit injected him again and again as its tiny medical computer tried to figure out the best way to keep him within its programmed set of parameters.

"How many warships does the Confederation possess and what are their capabilities?" asked the Vraxar insistently.

"What do you care?" asked Pointer hotly. "You have shields and the ability to shut down our power sources."

The Vraxar ignored her. It poked Blake hard in the shoulder with a finger. "What is your name and rank?"

"I am Captain Charlie Blake."

The alien showed its rotting teeth and something in its manner suggested it was satisfied. "What is the nearest planet to here?"

"Overtide," said Blake. "Two days' high lightspeed."

"And where would we find this planet?"

Blake gritted his teeth and swayed. "1276.281.34," he began.

"Sir, you can't tell them!" said Pointer.

The Vraxar soldier standing closest struck her in the base of the skull with one end of its hand cannon. The attack came so suddenly that Pointer had no chance to move and she crumpled to the floor without a sound. Lieutenant Rivera didn't react and he continued to look ahead, doing his best to ignore everything around him.

"Where is Overtide?" asked the Vraxar.

"923.4.992.11.6456.9AAW," Blake continued.

In spite of the battlefield adrenaline, he was suddenly feeling enormously ill and though he was trying his best to lie convincingly, he wasn't sure how good an act it was. The suit injected him with another high-strength stimulant and a variety of antitoxins. It wasn't enough and he dropped to his hands and knees, vomiting. The sickly odour from the Vraxar didn't help and he threw up for a second time.

The alien didn't give him an opportunity to recover, nor to stand up. "I don't believe you have provided accurate information," it said simply.

Blake didn't say anything, since he was unable to marshal his thoughts to produce a coherent response. A pair of strong hands lifted him from the floor and held him in an upright position. The ancient Vraxar stepped in close, enveloping him with its stench.

"Sometimes the conversion to Vraxar destroys the mind of the subject. On occasions, enough is left after the process for us to extract a few memories from the biological matter which remains."

Blake wasn't so incapacitated that the words didn't register. It didn't take a genius to figure out that he needed to avoid this conversion process, whatever the cost. "Piss off," he replied.

"On this occasion we did not come seeking conversions," continued the Vraxar, ignoring the insult. "There will be an additional mission sent for that purpose. However, there are laboratories on the *Hannixar* which can attach the necessary implants. I will have you taken there to find out if there is anything we can make use of. They have a wider variety of truth drugs available, since you appear to be resistant to the one I injected you with."

"What purpose does all this have?" asked Blake, speaking through the fog in his mind. "Why the need to kill?"

"We cannot reproduce through other means," said the Vraxar. "We grow and we expand through the races we defeat. It is a journey that for us can never end. As soon as we stop, the

Vraxar will become extinct. Ours is an eternal war and our motivation can never diminish. There will be no cessation until the universe has run out of hosts."

"What then?" coughed Blake.

"Then we too will die. Until that time, the Vraxar will continue. The Estral were a powerful foe and would have defeated us if they had focused all their efforts on that task alone. Alas for them, they were distracted by many wars of their own making and now their flesh is ours. The walls of the universe are far apart. It may well be that we never encounter its extents, nor exhaust its supply of life."

"If all Vraxar smell as bad as you, death will come as a relief," said Blake.

"It is not death you will find, Captain Charlie Blake, but a period of subservience until the putrefaction of your body renders you incapable of action. At which point, you will be left where you fall, only to experience another hundred years of slow, conscious decay, until eventually awareness fades and you become nothing."

"An existence to be proud of."

The Vraxar was finished with the conversation. "The *Hannixar*'s lifter is on its way," it said, addressing the soldiers. "Once it has collected this installation's data array, put these three subjects onto the vessel. I will send instructions for their conversion."

Through the haze in his mind, Blake noted how the Vraxar continued talking in the Confederation's common language, as though it wanted him to know exactly what was planned. He looked desperately around the room for a way out and found nothing to give him hope.

One of the Vraxar stooped to pick up Lieutenant Pointer. To Blake's relief, she groaned as she was slung unceremoniously over its metal-covered shoulder. Relief was soon replaced by a sense of helplessness when the Vraxar soldiers directed him and Lieutenant Rivera towards the door. Without an acceptable choice they followed the soldier carrying Pointer, while the others acted as escort.

———

LIEUTENANT MARIA CRUZ felt something pressing on her face. At first, she didn't know what it was – it was soft and it moved in a rubbing motion over her cheeks and forehead.

A voice asked, "Are you awake?"

"Larry? Is that you?"

It wasn't Larry. Larry was dead and this wasn't a man's voice.

"I don't think Larry made it," said the owner of the voice in clipped tones. "You need to wake up, Lieutenant. It's not safe to stay here."

Larry's dead she thought. Cruz had worked with Larry for a long time and it had taken an attack by aliens to make her realise she might have just been a little bit attracted to him. *Gone now*, she thought sadly. *I can't let myself think about it yet.*

It took a monumental effort, but Cruz forced one eye open. Even the dim emergency lighting was enough to send crashing waves of pain through her skull. The rest of her body caught up and soon Cruz was fighting to stop herself crying out. A smell cut through it all – blood and raw meat. Cruz guessed she was wearing a significant part of whatever used to be in Lieutenant Reynold's skull

There was a figure crouched over her – not Larry and definitely not Lieutenant Reynolds. The new arrival was a woman, perhaps in her late forties with greying blonde hair and dressed in the uniform of one of the base technicians.

"Is Larry dead?" Cruz asked, not daring to wish he'd somehow survived.

"That man outside? I'm afraid so. This other one here isn't any better." The woman attempted a smile. "I've wiped most of this gunk off. We need to get out of here. If you can't get up, I'm afraid I'll have to leave you."

"I'm not sure if you're joking," Cruz said. She raised her head a fraction. "The Vraxar came. Where are they?"

"If that's what you're calling those invaders, I believe they're trying to get inside the ES *Lucid*. They did a sweep of the bunker on their way down, but it's the spaceship they're interested in. Most of them are there now, I suspect."

"Who are you? How did you make it?"

"I'm Technical Officer Kari Gibbs. On another day I might give you a little while longer to recover and gather your wits. Today, I'm going to tell you to get a bloody move on!"

With the assistance of Gibbs, Cruz struggled upright and sat on the edge of the desk, out of direct sight of the doorway. There might be a million Vraxar soldiers heading this way, but she needed a moment to gather herself. "My ankle's broken," she said.

"I can see that. Who was this man?"

Lieutenant Reynolds' body wasn't a pretty sight and appeared to be missing much of its head. He'd fallen in such a way that the worst was hidden from view, though there was plenty of blood.

"He attacked me and the Vraxar shot him." She put the matter aside. "I don't suppose you have any painkillers?"

"Not with me."

"I'm Lieutenant Maria Cruz, by the way."

"Great. Now that we're acquainted you can stop by my house for lunch whenever you please."

Cruz wasn't sure if she'd been revived by the most acerbic tech officer in the bunker, or if Gibbs simply had an exceptionally dry sense of humour. "Why were you in the bunker?"

"I was hiding until this blows over. You're lucky I found you."

"How *did* you find me?"

"The Vraxar came down to the floor directly below here. In the meantime, I ran to the next stairwell and came up. I thought it best to be on a different floor to them."

"Sergeant McKinney's coming back here. After he's destroyed the central data array."

"So, there's some resistance left, is there? This Sergeant McKinney is going to run into quite a lot of trouble when he arrives."

"We should go back and warn him," said Cruz.

"It's a long way to the nearest exit."

"The Vraxar have murdered enough of us for one day. We owe it to our guys to try and help them."

"By getting ourselves killed in some vainglorious effort to forge a way through elite alien soldiers and get a message to the brave soldiers of the Space Corps?"

Gibbs smiled and Cruz could tell the technician was trying to be funny.

A lightning bolt of an idea sparked into Cruz's mind. "How do you speak to the ship when it's in here for repairs or upgrade?" she asked.

Gibbs narrowed her eyes. "The diagnostic tablets, mostly. They're authenticated by a spaceship's AI and after that, a properly-trained technician can access more or less anything – propulsion, life support, you name it."

"Weapons?"

"Yes, weapons. And comms too."

Gibbs pulled a flat, square object from a tailored pocket on the upper leg of her uniform. "These tablets." She looked at the screen and gave it a shake. "The battery is dying on this one. Feels like I have to recharge it every few days now." She squinted at it. "See this?"

Cruz stared at the tablet. It was a sea of numbers and colours, many of which were so small she couldn't read from the short distance of a few feet. One area of the screen stood out.

"The Vraxar are trying to burn out the processing cores."

"Looks like it. I have no idea what they hope to achieve by doing that," Gibbs replied.

Neither did Cruz.

"They're not in this bunker for the good of their health," she said. "Whatever it is they're up to, they have the expectation it'll produce results." Then she realised. "The *Lucid*'s data arrays will hold plenty of useful information."

"They can't have that ship," said Gibbs with surprising fervour. "It's already a shame the Space Corps has decided to hobble it by taking away the Obsidiar. That ship is a marvel – an absolute marvel."

"If your tablet has an interface with the *Lucid*'s AI, could you activate the automatic weapons systems? That would give the Vraxar something to worry about."

Gibbs laughed bitterly. "I work on life support, Lieutenant. I certainly don't have clearance to start the weapons. Can you imagine if they allowed everyone working on the ship into every single system? The *Lucid* is carrying twelve thousand Lambda X missiles! What if someone accidentally triggered a launch?"

"I assume there'd be fail safes in place," said Cruz drily.

"Yes, one might think. Anyway, you'd need the codes from an active duty warship captain in order to trigger a weapons launch. Or Colonel Tenney, though I expect he's no longer with us. As for my own capabilities? I can perform any number of functions relating to the life support. Not much use against rampaging aliens, I shouldn't imagine."

"I work in the comms hub. I might have clearance to use the *Lucid*'s comms systems – if I could get a message to Sergeant

McKinney he'll know what to do. Can I have a look at your diagnostics tablet?"

"Here you go. I believe each tablet requires specialist setup," Gibbs warned.

Cruz took the tablet and entered her biological data. The screen didn't quite go blank, but it showed only a top-level overview of the *Lucid*'s comms system. Gibbs leaned over to look.

"That's all I would see as well – the bare minimum required in case I needed to check if two systems are speaking to each other. This tablet isn't set up for comms."

Another bright idea. "Larry was carrying a tablet and he worked in comms. I don't want to look at him."

Gibbs' expression softened. "I'll get it."

The technician walked quietly towards the doorway and looked furtively outside. Then, she dashed out of sight, returning a few seconds later with a second tablet and a gauss pistol.

Gibbs handed over the tablet and Cruz signed into it, trying to ignore the misting of her eyes and the physical pain hammering through much of her body.

"I'm getting the same on this tablet."

"Trust the bloody Space Corps," said Gibbs. "Each man or woman given only one specific task and not trusted with the access to do anything else."

"Where are the offices for the comms team working on the *Lucid*?"

"I thought you might ask that," Gibbs replied. "They are on the bottom floor, not too far from the guard's station."

"There might be a comms-enabled tablet in one of those offices."

"Almost certainly. Equally, there are likely to be many of these Vraxar on the lookout for survivors."

Cruz smiled tiredly. "I've come this far, I'm not going to stop now. Will you help me?"

"I'm not convinced this is the best plan to ensure our personal survival. I'll come."

"I'll need to lean on you. And I don't know the way."

"I was aware of the ramifications when I agreed to help," said Gibbs primly.

"You'll need Lieutenant Reynolds' pistol. Was there a rifle outside this office?"

Gibbs reluctantly picked up the second gauss pistol between her forefinger and thumb. "I didn't see a rifle. Maybe the Vraxar took it."

After a minute's preparation, during which Cruz tucked the gauss pistol into her belt and Technician Gibbs listened out for approaching enemies, the pair of them set off. Cruz was in great pain, particularly her eye where Reynolds had struck her, and also her broken ankle. She was pleased to note the fog had lifted from her brain and she could think clearly. There was no doubting her need for medical attention, but she pretended to herself it wasn't urgent.

"We'll need to move faster than this," said Gibbs, looking over her shoulder.

"I'll give it my best shot."

With her teeth clenched, Cruz dug deep and the two of them headed towards the underground bunker's comms offices.

CHAPTER TWENTY-THREE

THE VRAXAR ROCKET flashed across the room with a shriek, missed an overturned cabinet by inches and entered the south corridor leading from the room. It struck the wall a dozen metres along at a shallow angle and exploded in a thunderous roar, discharging plasma in a blossoming cloud of sickly green. It washed along the corridor, much of it roiling away from McKinney and his squad. The heat came after, sending a wave of scalding air over the closest of the men. Their spacesuits blackened and charred, but the material held up and didn't break.

McKinney didn't have time to offer thanks for the lucky escape. His brain took over his mouth and he started barking orders.

"Squad C, into position east. Squad B cover west. Not you Alvey. Grover, watch south. Shout if you see movement. The rest of you, keep your heads down. Repeaters, not rifles – spray those alien shitheads with everything you've got. Squad A, we're north. Webb, Alvey, plasma tubes with us. Two rounds of two. Take out that bastard firing at us. I don't want to see any more rockets coming this way."

The men scrambled into position, doing their best to keep out of the firing arc of the Vraxar along the corridors. Webb was quickest with his plasma tube – with impressive timing and dexterity, he charged the weapon, leaned sideways and launched a rocket along the north corridor.

"Yee-har!" he shouted in exhilaration. "Charging for the next shot."

Repeater fire started up from the men hiding behind the toppled cabinets. The ching-ching-ching sound of two or three weapons combined with that of another three, the sound building up to a roaring clatter of dense metal punching through the air at unimaginable velocity. There was something primal about the sound that made a soldier feel simultaneously unafraid and invulnerable, as if there was nothing which could withstand the onslaught and the grit behind it.

McKinney felt it too – the bloodlust coursed through his veins, urging him to throw caution to the wind and advance upon the Vraxar with his repeater cutting down everything which tried to stop him. With an effort he suppressed the desire and tried his best to do his duty as the commanding officer of these men.

More plasma rockets screamed away, fired by Alvey and Webb. The explosives detonated to the north in ferocious light, heat and sound.

"Webb – east. Alvey – west. Two shots."

The enemy responded. Their slugs poured into the room, pinging off the walls and the solid sides of the cabinets. McKinney's squad returned fire, whilst others threw primed grenades along the corridors, hoping to catch the Vraxar in the blasts.

"Got one!" shouted Musser.

"More coming north!"

"I'm out of grenades!"

Doing his best to keep a level head amongst the chaos, McKinney crouched behind cover to one side of the north corridor and evaluated their position. He checked his HUD map overlay to get an idea how easy it would be for the enemy to reinforce their positions and what scope they had to move from one cardinal point to the next. He listened to the reports from his troops and did what he could to ensure each of the corridors was defended. His movement sensor picked up shapes of orange. They came in and out of sight, never showing themselves completely. He put the barrel of his repeater through a gap between two cabinets and held down the activation trigger. The sound and recoil were brutal, and the muscles in his arms and shoulders fought to keep the weapon steady.

Brogan went down, his head shattered by a gauss slug ricocheting from the sloped edge of the cabinet in front of him. Roldan took a round in the shoulder and screamed in pain. Armand Grover was the only one who had any training with a med-box and he came around the edge of the room, half-crawling and half-running.

The clatter of metal grew in volume and intensity, until it was a constant droning thrum.

"They got a heavy repeater turret somewhere down here!" said Evans across the open channel. "Shit, that's the west. We need a launcher west!"

"Alvey get there," shouted McKinney.

"I've got this, Sergeant!"

The figure of Alvey rose up a few feet from where McKinney was positioned, the plasma launcher over his right shoulder. The coils whined and the projectile vanished along the corridor. Before he could get back into a crouch, bullets smashed into the soldier's body. A dozen high-velocity slugs meant for use against lightly armoured vehicles hurled him away as if he'd been picked up and thrown by an invisible giant. McKinney heard the soft impacts and he saw the blossoming cloud of red droplets scattering in the air.

"Shit, he missed," said Musser.

The heavy repeater turret continued firing, its slugs pummelling an ever-changing tapestry of dents and gouges into the metal wall.

Anger came upon McKinney, gripping his body and challenging him to defy it. He didn't try. The fallen soldier's plasma tube lay on the floor next to his mangled body. In four quick crouch-steps McKinney covered the distance and scooped up the launcher, clutching the heavy tube to his chest like it was an infant.

There was an art to the plasma tube. Men like Dexter Webb could spin the tube onto their shoulder at the same time as it was charging to fire. They could launch the rocket and be back into cover within a second. McKinney didn't have the knack and in the face of a devastating hail of gauss fire he'd usually have perished.

Something happened to him – the anger sharpened his senses and his brain began to detect patterns amongst the irregularities of the fighting. The shouts of his squad faded into the background and their movements slowed. His eyes recognized the swaying pulsation in the incoming gauss fire – how it moved this way and that, leaving streaks across his vision.

McKinney rose to his feet outside the arc of repeater fire. His hands swung the tube upwards even as his fingers pressed firmly on the activation trigger. His feet took him a step to the side, the movement perfectly in time with the dance of the Vraxar repeater. The orange shapes were still there – large shapes moving through clouds of smoke - not as quick as a human but stronger and tougher. They clustered around the mobile turret, using it as cover.

The rocket shot from the end of the tube, curving gently through the air. McKinney didn't need to watch it.

"Boom!" shouted Mills.

"Good shot, Sergeant!"

More smoke poured into the room and the heavy repeater stopped firing. The enemy fire was sporadic from every direction.

"Looking clear to the north," said Elder.

"Not much return fire to the west."

"It's time to move," said McKinney loudly enough to cut across the comms chatter. "We're going north before a thousand of these bastards arrive to reinforce their friends. Webb, send them a friendly warning that we're coming."

"You got it, Sergeant."

Webb fired his tube and ducked into cover, waiting while the others crawled amongst the wrecked cabinets to gather against the wall to either side of the north corridor.

"Musser, take this plasma tube off me," McKinney continued. "I could never aim them straight."

"Don't stand too close to him, that's all I can say, sir," warned Elder. "He's been known to point them the wrong way."

"This isn't the time - shut up."

McKinney checked to see if Roldan was able to continue. The material of the soldier's spacesuit had sealed over his wound and his face had the pale, frozen expression of a man pumped full of adrenaline and whatever other crap the suit and Grover's med-box had chosen to ensure his wellbeing.

"Squad A – it's your lucky day. We're going first. B and C follow when we're clear."

"Aw, shit," said Elder without noticeable rancour. "We get all the best ones."

"Webb, fire another one."

"There are only got three more rockets left in this tube, Sergeant. Just so you know."

Webb fired again. McKinney didn't wait to see the result; he gripped the barrel of his repeater and sprinted around the corner. The plasma rocket detonated with a thump, flooding his visor sensor with information. In the split second it took to adjust, he was at a full run, his repeater swaying from side to side in his grip. Smoke and heat came, producing alarms on his HUD. He ignored them and kept on running, the others from Squad A visible at the extremes of his periphery.

His movement detector highlighted an enemy soldier stumbling across the room ahead. McKinney shot from the waist, sending a spray of slugs into the Vraxar. It went down and another appeared. He realised he still had the trigger held and it was the easiest thing in the world to alter his aim a fraction to the left. The second fell, torn to pieces, and a third followed. The others of his squad dropped behind, unable to keep up with his pace even over this short distance.

Before he knew it, he was in the room. His eyes swept from corner to corner – the place was a mess of burning, twisted technology. Melted consoles and instrument panels glowed with heat, many of them torn from their fixings by the force of multiple grenade and rocket blasts. There were bodies amongst the wreckage, their flesh blackened and split, metal augmentations ripped away. Smoke rose, greasy and thick.

"Clear!" he shouted. "B and C move up on the double!"

The others of Squad A entered the room and instantly moved to positions of cover. McKinney felt his chest swell with pride – these men hadn't seen real action, but here and now when it counted, their training and instinct was taking over. *Let's show these Vraxar we're not so easily beaten.*

McKinney used the moments it took for Squads B and C to arrive to check his HUD map overlay. There were two additional exits from this room – one north and another to the west. Both passages led to the same place and were more or less the same length.

"Which way, Sergeant?" asked Bannerman.

"We're going west," McKinney replied. "One guess is as good as another."

"I see movement both ways," said Garcia.

He and Clifton fired their rifles, aiming to the west. Return fire pinged off the far wall of the room behind them.

"Crap," said Garcia, trying to shuffle to one side while firing again.

"I hit something."

"Clear."

"Sure?"

"Definitely clear, Sergeant."

"Squad A on point again," said McKinney. "Let's move!"

This time there was no grumbling. They ran along the corridor to the west. Aside from the sound of boots thudding against the floor, it was eerily quiet. It seemed to McKinney as though this engagement with the enemy had paused only long enough for a deep intake of breath, after which it would surely resume with a much greater intensity than it had before.

The west corridor wasn't long. It continued for twenty-five metres, past a series of deserted offices and then it turned north. McKinney paused only briefly to check for movement.

"Clear," he called, aware the rest of Squad A were crowded at his back. Now they'd had their first experience of combat the men had the rookie's eagerness for more. It was best to lose the taste quickly, McKinney knew – the first into battle was the first to be ripped to shreds by repeater fire.

He became aware of gauss fire behind him – his sensor picked up a short volley of it.

"I've got a group of them coming from the north," said Corporal Li.

"Where's Musser?"

"With me, sir. He just took them out."

McKinney made a decision. "Squad C, hold that room. We're

close to our target and I don't want to be cut off when we come back this way. Where's Clifton?"

"With me, sir."

"We'll need his explosives. Send him up. Mills, you drop back and reinforce Squad C."

"Roger that."

"Move," said McKinney, stepping around the corner and breaking into a run.

There was a stairwell near here which led up to the ground floor, as well as to the levels below this one. It was the likely direction from which reinforcements would come and McKinney didn't want to stumble into hundreds of the enemy if he could avoid it. Although it felt as if they'd been fighting for hours, in reality it was only minutes. He didn't know how long it would take the Vraxar to muster a full response, but his squad's advantage of surprise was definitely running out.

The corridor executed an inexplicable dog-leg left-right at the end. McKinney stopped again and looked around. The corridor stretched on for another seventy or eighty metres.

"Movement," he said, ducking out of sight.

He found himself in a situation where his eyes absorbed the scene, but it took his brain a few moments to interpret the details. By the time he realised something was amiss, the finer edges of the memory had begun to blur.

"What is it, Sergeant?" asked Webb.

"Wait," he snapped. "There are Vraxar coming towards us – six, maybe seven. I think there's someone with them."

"Like a *person* type of someone?" asked Webb.

"More than one. I don't know."

Webb wasn't the quickest thinker. "We've got to do something," he said.

"That's right, soldier, we're going to do something."

The sound of a woman's voice reached them. The voice was

raised in anger and it didn't care who heard. "Put me down you stinking shitbag!"

"Whoever that was, she doesn't sound happy," said Garcia.

McKinney looked at the soldiers with him, deciding who he trusted most. "We're going to use rifles. Garcia, Elder, Causey – come up here. The targets are coming our way. We're going to step out and shoot them, taking great care we don't hit anyone human."

It wasn't the most elaborate plan ever conceived. There was no choice – the corridor branched off midway along, leading towards one of the main stairwells. He had no idea if the Vraxar were heading that way but it seemed a logical enough destination for them.

"On my command...now!"

McKinney was determined to be a man who led by example. He walked three quick sideways steps until he was against the far wall and looking along the corridor. He crouched, keeping his gauss rifle at eye level and looked along the barrel. There were six Vraxar and they had humans with them. In the confines of the corridor it was hard to select a target at speed whilst also being absolutely certain it wasn't a friendly one.

McKinney squeezed the activation switch. The gauss rifles were the finest, most expertly-crafted examples of metalworking this side of a fleet warship. They were perfectly calibrated in the factory and if you aimed straight with one, you could rely on hitting whatever you pointed them at. Every ranker in the Space Corps was extensively drilled in their use, until most soldiers could put a slug through a tin can a thousand metres away.

The Vraxar fell, mowed down by several expertly-placed volleys of gauss projectiles. McKinney didn't wait – when the last alien toppled he was up and running towards them. The short time it took him to cover the distance was enough to tell him what he needed to know. There were three humans amongst the Vraxar. They wore spacesuits and looked badly used.

Two of the three were men, both of whom looked dazed. They stared at McKinney as if hardly believing he existed. The woman was struggling to pull herself from beneath the body of a Vraxar soldier. McKinney reached out a hand and hauled her free.

"We need to get out of here," he said.

Lieutenant Caz Pointer groaned and pressed a hand to the back of her neck. "No shit?" she said.

"However, there's some unfinished business to deal with first, ma'am."

McKinney pointed along the corridor. There was an open doorway there, with a sign on the wall above. He read the words on the sign: *Secondary Data Repository Access Area – Restricted Personnel Only.*

CHAPTER TWENTY-FOUR

THE CORRIDORS OF THE BUNKER, which had seemed far too long when Maria Cruz only had a broken ankle to contend with, now appeared to stretch on forever. The emergency lighting was slowly fading and distant noises echoed strangely, making it hard to pinpoint exactly where they came from. Technical Officer Gibbs was becoming increasingly jumpy and on one occasion she nearly dumped Cruz to the ground by spinning to check an empty room they passed.

"I'm not trained for this," Gibbs said in a hoarse whisper. "I studied life support systems, not warfare."

It's all part of the same thing when you work on fleet warships, thought Cruz. "How much further is it?"

"One set of steps, a corridor and then another set of steps. After that, a short walk and then we reach the offices. By that stage we may want to keep fingers and toes crossed that someone left a tablet on their desk for us to pick up. After that, we should continue to keep everything crossed and hope the comms tablet will allow you to interface with the *ES Lucid*."

"I like hopes and maybes," said Cruz.

They reached the steps and paused to listen. There were sounds, but it was impossible to be sure where they came from. The bunker was huge and Cruz was relying on it being too large for even an entire division of Vraxar to keep adequately locked down. Not that she thought there were thousands of the aliens here – a couple of hundred seemed a more likely number and that was way too few to patrol everywhere.

"Come on," said Gibbs. "Hold onto the rail."

The steps were concrete and solid, carved through solid rock, though you wouldn't know it simply by looking. It wasn't easy to descend without producing a quantity of noise and Cruz found it hard to keep her damaged leg from scraping on the edge of each step as she hopped down.

They went down one flight of twenty steps, reached a landing and then started on the next set of steps. At the bottom, a square doorway led into the next passage. Cruz didn't know what made her stop. She gripped the railing tightly and pulled Gibbs to a halt.

"What...?"

"Shhh."

There was something at the bottom, Cruz was sure of it. The two of them waited on the stairs, trying to make as little noise as possible while listening for whatever might be in the room below. Gibbs was beginning to look wild-eyed with fear.

"I can't..." she began.

"You can," Cruz interrupted, barely mouthing the words.

Other memories from her training returned. Sometimes the waiting played more on a combatant's fears than the action itself. Once you were committed, there was no choice other than to give it your best shot.

Cruz hopped down another step. Gibbs tried to resist and

Cruz pulled hard until the technician followed. She hopped again, bringing the reluctant Gibbs after.

"Stop. Please."

"No. We're going down there."

There was another landing at the bottom of the steps. There was a metre or so between the last step and then there was the doorway on the left. They huddled in this space, Cruz leaning against the wall while Gibbs did her best to look into the room beyond. She stepped back, her face pale and with a sheen of sweat across her forehead and cheeks.

"I think there are three of them," she mouthed.

"Where?"

A wave of the hand. "Over that way. Maybe fifteen metres from here and looking out of the window."

"We are going to shoot them."

A single nod.

"I will lie down and shoot from the floor. You will lean out and shoot."

"Which one do I aim for?"

"The closest one. Keep firing until I say otherwise."

Another nod.

With a grimace, Cruz lowered herself to the floor and shuffled along. There wasn't lots of space to pull this off and she was sure the training officers would be able to suggest a dozen better ways. The grenades she still carried dug into her chest, mocking her inability to use them without alerting every Vraxar within five hundred metres.

She poked her head around at floor level. This was another one of the viewing rooms – she could see the window, though the extents of the room itself were hidden by the sides of the doorway. The assessment that the aliens were looking out of the window was inaccurate – in fact, they had their backs to the window and were standing stock still, three pairs of eyes staring in three different directions. *I should have realised they wouldn't be interested in anything as mundane as looking at a warship.*

Realising she'd be dead already if they'd spotted her, Cruz studied the Vraxar for a long moment. There was something absolutely vile about them – it wasn't an emotional response to see them as an abomination and an affront to nature. Whatever they wanted from the Confederation, it would be worse than anything the military's projections teams could ever imagine.

There was a row of chairs between the doorway and the window, but not enough to stop her getting a chest or headshot. Cruz made a mental decision on her targets and dragged her pistol from her belt. A foot nudged her in the hip.

"Well?" asked Gibbs.

There was no easy way to coordinate. "You start shooting and then I'll go."

"I can't hear you."

Gibbs stooped lower and Cruz repeated the words.

Having been primed, Gibbs was suddenly eager to get on with it. She gave no further warning, took one sideways step and started firing wildly.

Taken by surprise, Cruz rolled into position, holding her own pistol a few inches above the floor. In the viewing room the Vraxar hadn't moved from their original positions, nor attempted to take cover behind the chairs. The closest was mid-stumble, while the other two fired their wide-bore cannons.

Cruz responded with her gauss pistol. It had minimal recoil, but from her position on the floor it was enough to make it harder to aim straight. The Vraxar slugs pinged and ricocheted away from the doorframe. One of them toppled. She changed target and shot at her second target. Bullets punched through the back of one chair, tearing razor-sharp chunks of the metal free.

"Oh," said Gibbs.

After another exchange of fire, the third Vraxar went down in a shower of clear fluid. Cruz caught it with a shot to the head on the way and felt a surge of satisfaction at the finality of it. The shooting stopped.

A weight came down onto Cruz's back and then slipped off to one side. She twisted around and saw Kari Gibbs, lifeless and covered in blood, the gauss pistol still clutched in her hand as though it was the single possession she wished to carry with her into death.

"Shit." Cruz struggled into a sitting position.

There was a lot of blood – it covered the floor, reflecting her face in accusation. She gave Gibbs a shake. The technician was dead, gone in the same way as Larry and thousands of others on the Tillos base. Cruz felt anger rise anew and she snarled, not only at the Vraxar, but at the damage to her own body which slowed her down. She took strength from the anger and before she knew it, she was on her feet, her injured leg raised from the ground.

There was no movement from the room and she hopped through the doorway, pistol still in hand. The first Vraxar was slumped across three of the straight-edged metal chairs. She put a couple of slugs into it and hopped closer. The second was also dead. Again, she fired into its prone form.

The third was not dead, though she didn't know why she was so sure since its chest didn't move. It lay on its side, eyes open and unblinking. She came closer and saw the bullet holes in a diagonal line across its chest. Blood oozed from one, clear fluid from another and from the third there was nothing, as though the final bullet had punched into a part of the alien with no organs or blood vessels. *Or whatever the hell it has inside.*

It didn't react when she lifted the gauss pistol and took aim.

She fired twice into its face and lowered the pistol. This time, it was definitely dead.

"You smell terrible," she told it in one final show of hatred.

She crossed to the nearest viewing window and propped herself at one side. This level was so low she could see the underside of the *ES Lucid*. The emergency lighting wasn't good enough to illuminate everything, though it was sufficient for her to see groups of hulking shapes standing amongst the landing legs.

She had no idea what they were using to interface with the warship's main AI cores – there was no sign of a physical connection. Everything she'd experienced so far suggested this was the kind of warfare the Vraxar were good at. There was no doubt they'd have the technology – it was simply a matter of how long it would take them to shut down the cores. *Maybe they can take over the ship,* came the unbidden thought. *Squirt in their own code or something.*

There was no time to stare. The engagement with the three Vraxar soldiers hadn't lasted long, nor had it produced a lot of noise. There had been *some* noise and she was fairly certain any organised group of soldiers, anywhere in the universe, would have some way of finding out when a few of their number had been killed.

She pulled at her belt and stuck the pistol behind it. Ideally, she wanted it in her hand – the problem was, she needed both hands free to help her move. Kari Gibbs had provided adequate directions to the comms offices and Cruz did her best to make haste. With one hand against the side wall, she hopped along the passage towards what she hoped would be the final set of stairs.

It was tiring and put a lot of strain on her good leg. In addition, each hop produced waves of pain from her broken ankle. If there was any positive to take from it, the pain of her ankle stopped her thinking about her cheekbone and eye socket, both of which were probably broken.

The worst part was the knowledge that the painkiller Sergeant McKinney gave her had definitely *not* worn completely off and was in the process of doing so as the minutes went by. Cruz had no idea how bad the pain would end up and she didn't want to think about it.

To her dismay, the steps weren't quite so close as Gibbs had described and it took Cruz a number of minutes to reach them. This was meant to be the final stairwell and then it would hopefully be a short distance further to the comms area.

The Space Corps put safety above everything and there was a standard high-grip railing on both sides of the stairwell, combined with signage to let personnel know which side they should walk on. Trained to perfection, Cruz made three excruciatingly painful additional hops to reach the prescribed side of the stairwell and struggled downwards.

She paused at the first landing and listened carefully. The loudest sound was her own blood rushing through her ears, which didn't prevent her from also hearing the ephemerally distant sounds of enemy activity. She drew the pistol again, its cool handle comforting and smooth.

It didn't take long to reach the end of the second flight of steps. There was another landing, identical to the one on which Kari Gibbs died and Cruz hopped to the doorway. Another passage lay beyond. It curved noticeably to both left and right – this was the narrowest end of the bunker and she was at the nose end of the *ES Lucid*.

To the left, a considerable number of hops away, she could just make out three doorways in the metal wall of the passage. Her heart beat a little quicker and she emerged into the passage, conscious she was an easy target if anything happened to come from either direction. At the moment, the coast was clear.

"I can do this," she muttered.

With one steadying hand pressed to the wall, she pushed her damaged body towards the first doorway a hundred metres or so ahead. It didn't take long to comprehend exactly how drained she was – she required food, water, sleep and medical attention. It was a wonder she'd made it this far, she thought, fully aware it would all be in vain if she was spotted and killed at the last second.

With sixty metres to go she heard the sounds of heavy footfall, coming from somewhere behind and carried to her ears by a funnel effect from the passage. She chanced a look over her shoulder and nearly fell. The glimpse was enough to tell her there was nothing in sight. The footsteps continued and to her perception they became neither louder nor quieter, as if the Vraxar patrol was marching on the spot. It didn't seem likely they would be doing so and she drove herself to one final effort.

At forty metres, she looked again.

"Crap."

Shadows, elongated and warped by the overlapping emergency lighting, loomed over the floor and walls, just out of sight around the curvature of the passage.

She turned her head forward. *Thirty-five metres to go.*

The sound of the footsteps remained at a constant volume, while the shadows of the Vraxar grew ever larger. She tried desperately to figure out if she'd reach the closest office in time before the enemy saw or heard her attempted escape.

Even if Cruz wasn't pessimistic by nature, she was rapidly learning. Her brain added everything up and informed her she was travelling too slowly to make it to the office. There was no fuel left in the tank to give herself that one final burst – her body's reserves were spent. Her anger, however, was not.

"I'm damn well not going to fail."

Maria Cruz ran for it. She put weight on her damaged ankle

– only just enough to use it as a pivot for her good leg. The pain was like nothing she'd ever felt, nor imagined was possible. Her resolve was stronger and she used the leg again. She wanted to scream and clenched her teeth so hard they screeched against each other.

After three steps, she found a rhythm of sorts, which allowed her to put just enough weight down at just the right angle to keep the pain below the threshold above which she wouldn't be able to continue. She ignored the sounds of the footsteps and didn't attempt to look for the chasing shadows.

It was the longest twenty-five metres she'd ever run and when she made it to the office, Maria Cruz hurled herself inside, away from the sight of the Vraxar. The pain didn't go away. In fact, it hardly lessened and pulsed away from the snapped bone and filled her senses with an unbearable white noise of agony.

She scrambled across the floor. There was a desk, a chair and a shelf unit holding a couple of textbooks. Behind the desk she huddled, curled up in misery. *It's my birthday,* she thought, unsure who she was accusing and of what. Except it wasn't her birthday any longer and the aliens walking along the corridor outside didn't care.

They walked by the office without so much as a break in stride. Cruz waited a moment longer to see if the pain would subside. It did, if only slightly. She raised her eyes over the edge of the desk.

"No tablet."

There were drawers in the desk. They weren't locked – nobody in the Space Corps stole anything. In the case of this particular desk, any hypothetical thief would have been as disappointed as Maria Cruz at the lack of diagnostic hardware within.

There was no reason to stick around. The Vraxar patrol was gone and the adjacent office was no more than twenty big hops away. She reached it without incident. Her first reaction was one of disappointment – the desk was clear.

She rattled at the top drawer in the desk and pulled it open with a scrape. There was an unopened bottle of water, a bar of chocolate and some over-the-counter painkillers. She washed down a handful of the tablets with deep gulps from the bottle. It was empty before she knew it. For some reason, she didn't feel enormously hungry and shoved the chocolate into one of her pockets along with the rest of the painkillers.

Cruz checked the second drawer and closed her eyes when she saw the diagnostic tablet, its screen facing upwards. The previous user had locked it against unauthorised use. She snatched it from the drawer and sank onto the floor out of sight, in order to take a look.

With a press of her thumb, she provided her biological data to the tablet. In less than a second, the lock on the tablet opened and showed her the top-level data relating to the *ES Lucid*'s comms systems. Not daring to hope, she attempted to open up a sub-menu. For a split second, her pain was forgotten and Maria Cruz could have cried in relief.

It took a few minutes to figure out. Cruz wasn't trained for warship duty, but she certainly knew how to work the Tillos comms hub. The hardware on the *Lucid* was practically identical, barring a few modifications necessary to keep the array operational in a combat situation. The main comms were online and functioning at one hundred percent.

The underground bunker was heavily shielded. However, the *Lucid*'s comms system was powerful enough to cut straight through and when Cruz checked out the list of available receptors, she was given an insight of exactly how well-connected a fleet warship was. There was an option to force open a top-level channel to the *Juniper*, as well as to Fleet Admiral Duggan's sentry – Cerys - in the New Earth Central Command Station.

Aside from that were hundreds, perhaps thousands of different connection options.

Here and now, Lieutenant Maria Cruz didn't care for any of the others. She found what she was looking for.

[Field Comms Pack – Bannerman, Nitro. Loc Tillos Base, Atlantis. Receptor: Open [More]]

She connected to it and waited for a response.

CHAPTER TWENTY-FIVE

THE CENTRAL DATA array didn't look like much to Sergeant Eric McKinney's eyes - a big cylinder of metal that could have been anything, except it was a bit colder than most metal he was used to. There was a group of dead Vraxar around one side, killed by the substantial quantity of gauss rounds which had penetrated their flesh. These Vraxar were different to the others and didn't look anything like a Ghast, nor indeed anything else McKinney had set eyes on.

A repeater roared somewhere close by, followed by the distinctive whump of grenade explosions deeper in the CCB complex. The enemy were beginning to rally and McKinney kept his fingers crossed their confusion would last a short while longer. The mission was so close to success.

"How're those charges coming along, Clifton?"

The soldier darted around the base of the array pillar, planting pale blue cubes in an apparently random fashion.

"Nearly done, Sergeant."

"Will it be enough?" asked Lieutenant Pointer.

"You better believe it'll be enough. It's going to bring the

Colonel's emperor-sized bed crashing down four stories and into this room. Anything on this array will be melted into something you could spread on your toast."

"Soldier," McKinney warned.

"Very descriptive," said Pointer. It hadn't taken her long to recover from the effects of captivity and she was taking an active interest in what the squad were doing. So far, she hadn't interfered.

Captain Blake was nearby, carrying a gauss rifle one of the squad had donated. The distant expression on his face was gone and he looked alert. McKinney was relieved – he didn't want any dead wood coming on the way back. Lieutenant Rivera already seemed like a lost cause – sullen and uncooperative, even though his own life was in danger. The man did the bare minimum and he looked remote from the events around him. Still, he was one of the Corps and he was coming with them, whatever it took.

"Can you definitely fly the *ES Lucid*, sir?" asked McKinney for the second time.

"If it's online like you say, I can fly it, Sergeant. I'll need that field comms pack to transmit my access codes before it'll open the boarding ramps."

"I'll make sure Bannerman doesn't lose it." He was desperate to ask if Blake thought he could destroy the Vraxar ships. Blake was approachable enough, but McKinney had a respect for authority and didn't want to pester with questions to which there might be no easy answer.

Blake saw the turmoil. "If the *Lucid*'s Obsidiar core is active, it'll pack a real punch. It's a valuable asset – as soon as we're onboard, I might be ordered to take it elsewhere. I'm lacking a full crew as well – Commander Brady is dead and Lieutenant Rivera is relieved of duty."

"I understand, sir," McKinney replied, not really sure why the Space Corps would order the *Lucid* to withdraw.

"We're good to go, Sergeant," said Clifton. "These explosives are on a synchronised timer – as soon as I activate it, we'll have five minutes to get out of here."

"The Vraxar won't be able to interfere with the charges?"

"No, sir. They're like limpets these things. Once they're stuck, they aren't going anywhere."

McKinney joined Captain Blake at the doorway and leaned out to listen. He couldn't be certain, but he got the impression the intensity was building.

"Squads B and C, please report."

"We're holding them here," said Evans.

"The action is picking up at our position, sir," said Corporal Li. "These Vraxar don't seem to have much of a survival instinct."

"Keep shooting them." In the grand history of motivational of speeches this was a poor example, but McKinney didn't care. "Clifton, activate the explosives."

"That's done, sir."

"There's going to be a big blast in five minutes," said McKinney on the open channel. "I'm leading Squad A back towards the location of Squad C. Squad B, break off when we come past and follow us. No pissing around."

McKinney left the room first. Blake appeared keen to test himself and he followed at once, his rifle held with the easy grace of a man born to it. Pointer came after and then the rest of Squad A.

"Garcia, Elder, watch our backs."

"On it."

The voice of Clifton urged them on. "We need to get moving, Sergeant. Perhaps I didn't sufficiently emphasize the size of the blast when those charges go off."

"Sufficiently emphasise?" asked Garcia. "We've just left the room and you can already tell we're not going to make it?"

"Yeah. I have this affinity with explosives. If we keep going at this speed, we'll be incinerated."

McKinney walked faster, unwilling to break into an outright run that might lead them into trouble. Darell Causey was ahead in the corridor, in a crouch and with his repeater aimed around the corner. As they approached he fired the weapon. It kicked in his hands and its slugs clanked out in their hundreds.

"Clear!" he shouted.

McKinney and the others sprinted past the opening and Causey stood up to follow.

Clifton spoke again, his voice tinged with excitement and edged with fear. "Sir, we need to move."

"Why the hell didn't you set the charges for six minutes?"

"I thought you'd prefer the certainty of a five-minute timer."

"There's something wrong with you, Clifton," said Garcia.

"Hey, man, I passed my psych evaluation with flying colours."

"Must have got the sympathy vote."

"Do you always talk this much during the fighting?" asked Pointer, having joined the squad's comms channel.

"It focuses the mind, ma'am," said Garcia. "Two behind." He fired a burst from his repeater. "Clear."

Fearing they wouldn't make it far enough away, McKinney increased the pace until he was jogging. The men of Squad B joined up as they ran and it was noticeable how few of the original twenty-two remained. Someone fired three quick shots from a gauss rifle – it was Captain Blake.

"Clear," he said.

They reached the room in which Squad C was under pressure from a Vraxar counterattack coming from both the north and south. Bullets came and went, creating an irregular beat of metal on metal.

"We're running low on grenades and repeater ammo, sir," said Li. "Musser's out of rockets."

"Webb," said McKinney, pointing to the south exit.

"Sir."

Moments later, Webb fired a plasma rocket expertly into the room filled with broken cabinets. Shots came from the north and he dived quickly to one side to get out of the enemy's firing arc.

"Fire another one to the north. Everyone else, throw whatever grenades you have left and fall back on my command. We're making a run to the south."

As soon as Webb fired another plasma rocket, the men holding the north corridor sprinted away towards the south wall of the room. There wasn't a lot of time to act – any delay would see the soldiers trapped in a crossfire from north and south.

"I can hear something behind us," said Garcia.

"We have to go," said Clifton, shifting from one foot to the next.

"What the hell have you stuck to that data array?"

"The good stuff, Sergeant. It wouldn't matter so much if we were on the surface. In tunnels, the explosive energy tends to form..."

"Enough," McKinney tried to cut him off.

"...a powerful blast wave," Clifton finished.

"We'd better hope we stay ahead of it."

McKinney listened – there was little in the way of gunfire to be heard. "Move," he ordered, sprinting away along the south corridor.

"Boom," said Clifton.

Halfway along the corridor, McKinney found himself punched off his feet. He fell forward and a force behind threw him onwards. The blast wave passed as quickly as it came, but not before it finished throwing McKinney, the remains of his squad and the crew of the *Determinant* into the room of metal cabinets. The Vraxar had moved the cabinets into a defensive wall, which the squad crashed into at speed.

The blast wave travelled faster than sound and a moment after it went by, the rumbling of the explosion reverberated through the walls, building to a crescendo.

McKinney coughed as he struggled to recover – his spacesuit had protected his ears and kept him insulated against much of the shock, but he was winded. Before he could regain his feet, his eyes registered the presence of Vraxar in the room. There were seven or eight of them in one corner - he guessed they'd been taking cover there and then been stunned by the blast wave. They were big, solid bastards and they recovered quickly. The first one was already on its feet.

With a twist of his shoulder, McKinney brought his repeater to bear and held down the trigger. It fired two or three shots towards the Vraxar and then stopped. The alien soldier flinched and started to lift its hand cannon.

It took McKinney a moment to figure out what was wrong. There was a message on his HUD which he'd neglected to watch closely enough.

[Repeater Ammunition: 0%]

Into the briefest moments of silence, the sound of a plasma tube coil intruded.

"Oh shit, no," said one of the men.

"Get down," said Webb.

He fired the last of his rockets at the Vraxar. The room was large enough for McKinney's brain to register the streak of movement. The rocket detonated in the far corner at ceiling height, directly above the Vraxar and twenty metres or so from the squad.

Before he knew it, McKinney found himself engulfed in fire. It came, embraced him and then dispersed within the blinking of an eye. In its wake, it left half of his visor HUD covered in critical failure alerts. The other half of his HUD no longer showed any data at all.

"We need to get out of here," said Blake.

The comms on McKinney's suit wasn't working. He raised his visor. "On your feet!" he barked. "Now!"

Miraculously, no one apart from the Vraxar had died in the plasma blast. Not one of the squad was untouched by it – the material of their suits was blackened and cracked. A few of the men groaned in pain and McKinney saw breaches in the material, which allowed the plasma to char the skin beneath.

"You're hurt," said Blake.

McKinney looked about, before realising it was him Blake was concerned for. He felt pain and when he checked, a piece of his suit was burned away, revealing a hand-sized patch of red and weeping skin on the side of his ribcage. McKinney ordered his suit to inject him with something. He wasn't surprised to find it was too damaged to comply.

"Damnit."

"Here," said Pointer.

Without ceremony, she jabbed a needle from her emergency belt pack into the burned skin. McKinney yelled out.

"Thanks," he growled, feeling cold, numbing relief spread from the area of the injection.

The rest of the squad were on their feet and the most alert were already covering the exits from the room. Without his HUD overlay, McKinney took a moment to figure out which way to go. He remembered and urged the men onwards.

"Be prepared," he said, pushing forward. "Squad A on point."

"As usual," grumbled Garcia.

Wincing as his burned flesh stretched and split, McKinney dropped his useless repeater and broke into a trot, keeping his rifle in hand. A man he recognized came alongside, no longer carrying the spent plasma launcher. With a grunt, McKinney clapped him on the shoulder.

"Thanks."

"No problem, Sergeant."

"Promise me you'll never do that again?"

Webb laughed. "No promises. My grandma told me never to make them."

The squad encountered no further resistance in the CCB complex and they entered the main comms hub area of the base. McKinney's memory didn't fail him and he led the others exactly the route they'd come. It seemed shorter on the way back and it wasn't long until they reached the entrance leading to the place underneath the rubble. McKinney was out first, relieved the slabs above hadn't settled or collapsed enough to force them to seek another way. He felt a momentary disappointment when he realised Lieutenant Cruz was no longer waiting.

"The Lieutenant must have gone to the bunker," said Huey Roldan, pressing a hand against his wounded shoulder.

"Oh crap," said Blake.

"Sir?"

"I just remembered something one of the Vraxar said when they took us prisoner. He told us they've discovered an additional area of the base which interests them."

"That's got to be the bunker. Did you learn how many troops they've sent?"

"They didn't give anything else away. I got the impression it was a significant number."

"That's what I thought too," said Pointer.

"There are only fifteen of us left," said McKinney. "Our kit is damaged, we're almost out of explosives and our repeaters are low on ammo. We can't take on half the Vraxar assault force and expect to win."

There was a flurry of movement to one side – it was

Bannerman dropping his pack and crouching next to it. "Someone's opened a comms channel," he said in puzzlement. "There shouldn't be anyone able to do that." He opened the flap, plugged in his earphone and then looked up in excitement. "It's the *Lucid*, sir!"

"How?" said Blake.

"One moment," said Bannerman with a faraway stare of concentration. "It's Lieutenant Cruz, sir. She's linked to the *Lucid* using a diagnostic tablet and using its onboard comms to reach us. I'm getting a text-to-speak interpretation of what she's typing."

McKinney dropped to his haunches next to the comms pack. "What's her status?"

Bannerman provided the details in a series of short sentences. "Lots of Vraxar. Trying to burn out ship's core. Too many to fight."

"How is she?"

"She says she's fine. Holed up."

"She isn't fine," said McKinney with a frown. "She was hurt."

"She had that Larry guy with her and maybe Lieutenant Reynolds. It could be they've found somewhere safe," said Bannerman.

"Are the Vraxar near the ship?" asked Blake.

"She can't be sure. It's her belief that many of them are in the main hangar bay area, though she's seen others on patrol. She asks if we found the captain from the warship which crashed."

"Happy to make her acquaintance," said Blake. "I think I know what she's going to ask."

Bannerman listened intently to his earpiece and relayed the next question. "Can you activate the automatic countermeasures on the *Lucid*?"

Blake rubbed his chin. "I can send my codes through this field comms pack and it'll start the fireworks. My concern is what the

Vraxar warships in space will do when the *Lucid* starts shooting. They might decide to destroy it before we can get onboard."

"They have their own troops in the bunker," said McKinney. "They'd be wiped out."

"Would you bet on them acting with humanity, Sergeant?"

"Not for a second."

"The bunker is massive," said Corporal Evans. "The enemy would need thousands of troops to keep it secure. What if we fought our way to the lower levels before they realised what was up? Then you could activate the countermeasures and we could get onto the warship before the Vraxar in space were able to respond."

"It would give us a chance to rescue Lieutenant Cruz and Keller," said McKinney.

"What about Lieutenant Reynolds?" asked Webb.

McKinney laughed. "He can come too. Captain Blake, will the plan work?"

"In the absence of a better one, we'll make it work."

"Bannerman, let Lieutenant Cruz know we're coming. Tell her to keep her head down."

"Preferably with at least a hundred metres of metal or rock between her and the *Lucid*," said Blake. "The automated defences aren't gentle."

It was settled. The remainder of the squad formed up and left the illusory safety of the rubble. It was a warm morning and the sun was shining.

"We're going through the Section D entrance, sir," said McKinney. "It's this way."

"What the hell is that?" asked Causey, looking upwards.

There was a large dot far above them, the only blemish in an otherwise perfect sky. The dot grew bigger and bigger, until those watching could identify a shape and features. It was an ugly spaceship, with a cuboid shape, covered in angular outcroppings which served no apparent purpose. Flat bay doors, currently closed, ran along almost its entire length.

"Lifter," said Blake, one hand shielding his eyes. "Three klicks in length – a small one."

"It's too late to get the data array," Clifton laughed. "Maybe they've come to recover their dead."

Blake wasn't so sure. "It could pick up the *Determinant*," he said. "Not all of its memory banks were fried by particle beams."

"There were several intact," said Pointer.

"Come on," said Blake, urging McKinney to set off. "The *Determinant* could well be a consolation prize they'll be very interested in. We need to destroy that lifter."

McKinney didn't wait to be asked twice. He set off in the lead, and the others followed. Every minor success, every hurdle jumped led to another and he wondered when it would end.

CHAPTER TWENTY-SIX

THIRTY MINUTES LATER, the squad were deep into the underground bunker, several levels down and advancing with a mixture of speed and caution along one of the countless wide corridors. Corporal Evans' assessment was correct – there were too few Vraxar to provide an adequate defence of the many kilometres of tunnels and the hundreds of rooms and offices.

Blake was near to the front. It was apparent that the injections from his spacesuit were finally overcoming the Vraxar truth drug and his nausea was gone. He was vastly relieved, having begun to fear there'd be permanent, irreparable damage from whatever crap they'd filled him up with.

"Three engagements and no additional casualties so far," he said. "We're doing well."

"The guys have learned fast, sir," said McKinney.

"You're probably the last ones alive, so you've done something right."

"How long until we can activate the countermeasures, do you think?"

"Corporal Evans said this passage will eventually take us to the front storage and maintenance area. From there, we should be within shouting distance of the *Lucid*'s forward boarding ramp and also close enough to pick up Lieutenant Cruz."

"We'll be *really* close by then," said McKinney. "In the thick of it."

Blake caught the meaning. "The enemy warships can travel at a speed in excess of eighteen hundred klicks per second, Sergeant. Once they've made the decision to launch missiles at this bunker it won't take them long to get into position. We're relying on them being slow to make a decision."

"Lieutenant Cruz reckons things are stirring on the bottom floor," said Bannerman. He had the field comms pack over one shoulder and the remote earpiece in place.

"We need to get moving," said Blake.

They reached the final set of steps. McKinney and Blake took them two at a time, keeping their rifles ready. There was a landing at the bottom, which emerged at the mid-point of a long, straight passage. They stopped and checked both ways.

"Clear," whispered McKinney.

Corporal Evans joined them, doing his best to keep out of sight.

"That big doorway along there goes directly into the storage area. Once we're inside, we'll be able to see the *Lucid* through the main doors to the right. There should be another exit to the left which leads back to the guard station, near to where Lieutenant Cruz is hiding."

"Something's coming out of the storage area," said Blake. "Four Vraxar."

Evans raised his rifle.

"Wait!" hissed McKinney.

"Sir?"

"Give them a chance to get clear of the doorway."

Evans held fire. Several of the squad crouched at the landing, doing their best to find a position that would allow a clear line of sight to the approaching enemy soldiers.

"Rifles only," said McKinney. He released his breath slowly. "Fire."

Five gauss rifles hummed once, twice and then a third time. The Vraxar soldiers crumpled to the ground.

"Hold."

"Shit there's more!" said Garcia.

There was movement in the doorway and two more Vraxar stepped into view, with others behind. The men fired, but not quickly enough. The front two went down, while those coming after realised there'd been an ambush. They vanished from sight, taking refuge in the storage area.

"There goes the element of surprise," said Blake.

"What now?" asked McKinney.

"We try and stop them. Cover me."

Blake sprinted out from the stairwell and made for the doorway, with McKinney and Garcia following. He held his rifle at chest height while he ran. It wasn't the ideal position from which to fire and he hoped no more Vraxar soldiers would come into sight. He vaulted over the dead aliens and reached the doorway a few paces ahead of the others.

"Clear," he whispered.

McKinney brought his arm around in a wide, exaggerated arc. *Move up!* the gesture said.

There was a clatter of activity and the rest of the squad detached from the landing and advanced at the run, spreading themselves in a line against the wall. Blake looked into the storage area and then darted through the doorway into the massive space on the other side.

The closest object offering cover was a Lambda IX missile, lying horizontally on a steel rack. Beyond that was a stack of solid Gallenium blocks intended for use in a fission drive. They were piled halfway to the ceiling and likely weighed a few million tonnes.

Keeping low, Blake reached the missile and crouched with only his head and his gauss rifle showing over the top. With his motion sensor, he scanned for the enemy soldiers.

Blake wasn't familiar with this particular storage and maintenance area. On the other hand, he'd seen plenty of similar ones and this place was only different in the details. There were cargo lifts, cranes and several flatbed lifters. Racks of missiles and various containers were scattered across the floor – all the signs of a maintenance operation interrupted midway through. Two hundred metres away was the huge opening that led into the hangar area.

Sergeant McKinney arrived and crouched next to him. "Sir? This is a live missile we're hiding behind!"

Blake's rifle whined twice. "It won't go off by accident. Got one of them," he said. "Can't see the others from that patrol. I think it's likely they've made it into the hangar."

"Can you see the Vraxar, sir? My HUD is broken so there's no feed from the movement sensor."

"Crap – there might be more than a hundred of them. They're taking cover, so it's about to get messy."

"For them or us?"

Blake laughed. "Let's say for them, shall we? Do you know which way you're going, Sergeant?"

"To find Lieutenant Cruz? Over that way."

"You'd better decide who you're taking and start running. I can't activate the *Lucid*'s defences if you're anywhere in line of sight."

"There's a nuke in here, sir. Will it go off?"

It wasn't news Blake wanted to hear. "No, but the radiation might kill us now that our protective suits are damaged from that plasma rocket. We've got no choice other than to see where this road takes us."

"Squad A, you're coming with me," said McKinney. "Squads B and C, follow Captain Blake's orders."

Blake reached out a hand towards Bannerman. "Give me that pack before you go."

"All yours, sir."

The five men of Squad A headed off across the floor of the storage area. There was plenty of cover for them and they wended their way around the side of a flatbed lifter. In moments, they were lost from sight.

A shot pinged away from the edge of the Lambda IX casing. Blake dropped quickly out of sight and warned the men of Squads B and C to remain in the doorway. He pulled the field comms pack towards him and lifted the flap which covered the main panel. These packs were versatile kit and it was easy enough to send his command codes to the *ES Lucid*. The warship's AI responded sluggishly and he guessed the Vraxar's attempts to burn it out were the cause.

"We've got movement from both directions in this passage out here," said Corporal Li through the doorway.

Blake heard the sound of three or four gauss rifles firing.

"Hold them off."

It was easier said than done. Blake knew he needed to move fast, else the soldiers risked being caught in a crossfire. His concern was for McKinney and the others in Squad A. They needed to be away before he activated the *Lucid*'s defences. He squinted at the stack of Gallenium blocks between him and the warship. They'd be enough, he was sure.

More shots pinged against the Lambda. A figure crawled through the doorway and made its way towards him. It was Lieutenant Pointer and she'd got hold of a gauss rifle from somewhere.

"Thought you might want some company."

She looked over the tube and fired, before dropping flat to the floor. "There's quite a lot of Vraxar coming into the storage area, sir."

"I know! Keep your head down!"

More shots came. They whined through the air and ricocheted from the walls next to the doorway.

"Sir, we can't stay here much longer!" said Corporal Li.

"Send the men in. Stay low and keep these blocks between yourselves and the *Lucid*. Leave two to cover the passage."

The soldiers came in hastily. It was a nasty position for them to be in, with attacks coming from three directions. There was plenty of room behind the Lambda, but the necessity to keep the Gallenium blocks between the men and the hangar bay opening made things cramped.

Something exploded on the other side of the missile, the force of the blast pushing it a few inches along the floor. With the enemy using explosives, there was no more time to delay. Blake made a decision and sent a command to the *ES Lucid*, activating its automatic defence systems. *Maximum response,* he told it, an order to keep firing until every target was neutralised.

When the ship's core sent its acknowledgement, Blake ducked a little lower. Against anything other than the Vraxar he may have felt sympathy for what they were about to endure. When it came to this new enemy, he felt only satisfaction.

The *ES Lucid* was the newest model in the Galactic class and an evolution of older ships such as the *New Beginning*. It was equipped with eighty-four Bulwark cannons, distributed more or less evenly across its hull. The warship's battle systems detected the presence of hostile life forms underneath the ship, as well as five more behind a window three hundred metres from the ground.

Within a tenth of second, twenty-four lower Bulwarks and

one upper cannon emerged from their places in the hull and began firing.

The noise was terrifying. Tens of thousands of Gallenium slugs punched out in all directions. Those Vraxar still beneath the *Lucid* were killed instantly, their bodies crushed to unrecognizable smears of bloody paste, while the Bulwark projectiles smashed countless pits and craters into the hardened floor.

The five Vraxar behind the viewing window had no time to react. A single, short burst from the lone upper cannon crashed through the window and the metal holding it in place, killing the aliens and leaving deep holes in the wall and ceiling behind them. The upper cannon withdrew and an armoured hatch slid across to cover it.

Within the storage area, it was a little different. The Vraxar were spread out through the heavy machinery as they sought to locate the squad. Since the aliens weren't all in direct sight of its sensors, the *Lucid*'s AI decided to saturate the entire area with projectiles.

The devastation was incredible. Sitting with his back to the Lambda propulsion section, Charlie Blake watched in awe as a massive flatbed lifter was flipped onto its edge and then punched at tremendous speed for several hundred metres across the floor, the punishment of the Bulwark knocking it into a new, unrecognizable shape.

Pointer said something, the words lost in the storm of noise. Blake tried to smile and wasn't sure exactly which expression came to his face.

Elsewhere within the storage area a torrent of bullets tore through a row of gravity cranes, ruining them utterly. Gantries crashed down and Blake saw another truck sail through the air, heading towards where he and the men were hiding. Mouths opened in horror – the looks of those who saw unavoidable death coming.

The truck collided with the stack of Gallenium blocks. It was deflected and crashed down upon the live warhead of the Lambda IX. Everything Blake had been taught told him it couldn't go off, but he didn't want to be the man to test it. There was no explosion – the weight of the truck caused the end of the missile to lift off the ground. It hung in the air, teetering, whilst those below could only stare as it threatened to crush them. Then, the truck slid away from the crumpled warhead and the propulsion tube thumped down onto its rack.

The cannon fire stopped, taking the shrieking of tortured metal with it. Most of the emergency lighting was out, and much of what remained operational flickered on and off randomly. Blake lifted his head cautiously. Noise returned – the creaking of torn and overstressed metal toppling over or succumbing to its weakened state and tearing along joints not designed to handle such an onslaught.

"Is it done?" asked Corporal Li, eyes wide.

Blake checked the display on the comms pack.

[No Threats Detected. Scanning Mode 18 Active. Awaiting Input.]

"It's done," Blake confirmed.

"I think we've got more trouble," said Grover. "My HUD is showing potentially fatal levels of radiation coming from over on that side of the storage bay."

Twelve pairs of eyes searched. The opposite wall was a long distance away and bathed in darkness. There were shapes, barely distinguishable, their true forms indistinct. At that moment, a section of the emergency lighting came back, giving them a glimpse of a broken missile, bent and propped at an angle against the shattered parts of a gravity crane. Compared to the Lambda IX, this missile was technologically crude, though it carried a much heavier payload. The lights went out once more and darkness hid the nuclear missile within its shroud.

"We've got to go," said Blake.

"What about Sergeant McKinney?" asked Corporal Li.

"We can't wait around in this crap," said Pointer.

"She's right," said Blake. "We need to secure the ES *Lucid* while we have the chance." He saw their faces. "No one gets left behind, but we must get to the spaceship."

The men believed him and followed Blake onto the floor of the storage area. There was nothing untouched by the Bulwark cannons and there was no way any of the equipment could ever be salvaged. It would have to be broken down and re-forged in a foundry somewhere off-world.

It was a short distance to the main hangar, though there were places the men were required to clamber across jagged, twisted fragments of metal, split from whatever they'd originally been part of. Most of the equipment in the storage area had been thrown against the side and back walls, so there was no significant impediment to progress.

"We're going to need treatment once we get onboard," said Grover. "Otherwise, we're all going to start vomiting up our insides in the near future."

They crossed into the main hangar, where the floor was even more cracked and broken than it was in the storage area. Objects on the ground caught Blake's eye - here and there he noticed a limb or piece of bloodied metal. He felt no sorrow over the deaths.

Any vestigial doubts over the operational state of the *Lucid* were dispelled – the spaceship was definitely running. Its engines hummed and sent a vibration through its landing legs and into the ground. Blake hurried on, excitement building within.

"The forward boarding ramp should descend any moment," he said.

With a thump, a section of the *Lucid*'s hull detached a short distance ahead of them. The ramp dropped towards the ground rapidly and with utter smoothness. It touched the ground softly, making no sound.

"This is it," said Pointer, her gaze fixed on the red-lit airlock above. "We made it."

"Ready to see what a real warship can do, Lieutenant?"

"Yes, sir."

The sound of a raised voice came to them.

"Here's the sergeant," said Mills. "Looks like he's got Lieutenant Cruz with him as well."

"Bring him onboard," said Blake. "Have Lieutenant Rivera held in the troops' quarters. I'll be on the bridge. We'll need treatment for this radiation."

"I'll see to it, sir," said Grover. "I might need to grab something from the medical bay first."

Blake breathed in, filling his lungs with the scents of Gallenium and electricity which wafted out from the *ES Lucid*'s interior.

"Go on, sir," whispered Pointer. "The Vraxar might have warships on the way."

The sudden roar of a Bulwark jarred him into motion. There were still Vraxar in the bunker and it didn't make sense to hang about here in the open. Realising he was standing at the threshold like a shy child waiting for an invitation to a party, he set foot on the ramp, climbed rapidly and entered the airlock.

CHAPTER TWENTY-SEVEN

THE BRIDGE WASN'T FAR from the forward ramp airlock. Blake sprinted through a series of wide, cold corridors, lit in Space Corps blue-white, with Lieutenant Pointer following him. He reached a thick blast door which opened automatically, allowing him onto the bridge. It wasn't much different to what he expected – a compact, tapering room with three console sections for the crew and a fourth for the captain to sit at. The dozens of screens glowed soothingly, awaiting input.

Blake leapt into the main seat. "Powering everything up," he said. "The gravity engines are warm. We'll have sufficient thrust to lift off shortly."

He ran through a well-rehearsed series of pre-flight checks. Every system and subsystem were showing green lights, except those relating to the main source of the warship's power. The output from the Gallenium, of which most of the *Lucid* was comprised, showed zeroes across the board.

There was an additional screen in the centre of his console, which wasn't installed on most fleet warships. It was the status display for the Obsidiar core. He studied the readings – the gauges indicated that the single, comparatively tiny core was providing power for everything on the *Lucid*. Those few thousand tonnes of Obsidiar were able to generate enough raw muscle to replace approximately eighteen billion tonnes of Gallenium and it was the only substance capable of sustaining an energy shield large and powerful enough to block incoming attacks.

It wasn't perfect, of course. The Obsidiar's output drained away rapidly when it was put under strain. Expecting to fly at maximum thrust for long periods while under the protection of an energy shield would dry up the core's reserves quickly and it required twenty minutes to recharge from empty to full.

Pointer was on the ball. "Internal life support readings show we have everyone onboard. I'm sealing the forward ramp."

"This isn't going to be easy," said Blake. "I don't know how I'm going to manage the weapons as well as piloting this thing. I've never been in charge of a Galactic before, let alone an Obsidiar-cored one."

Neither of them suggested bringing Lieutenant Rivera back. There was no telling what he'd do.

"I'm sure you'll manage, sir," said Pointer.

He looked at her, expecting to see the usual calculating expression on her face. For once, there was only sincerity. *She's changed.*

The warm-up gauge on the gravity engines climbed steadily. The *Lucid* wasn't quite ready for take-off and Blake wanted the engines to be as close to maximum as possible. If it responded sluggishly, the warship would be an easier target.

He checked the upper sensor feed. The bunker doors were closed above them and with the Tillos Gallenium generators offline, there was no way to open them. It was the unspoken question he'd seen on the lips of every one of the soldiers. To Blake, it wasn't something to worry about.

"Use the comms," he said. "Find Sergeant McKinney and tell

him to get Lieutenant Cruz up here to the bridge. If she knows how to work the main comms hub on Tillos, she can help out up here."

While Pointer did her stuff, Blake did his best to bring himself up to speed with the operation of an Obsidiar-cored ship. He'd been to classes and sat in a simulator, but there were always slight differences when it came to the real thing, which introduced an undesirable element of delay into a combat situation.

His main concern was knowing how far he could push matters once the firing started. If he went too hard against the Vraxar, he might drain the Obsidiar core too soon. If there was a way to stop the Vraxar neutralising the ship's Gallenium power source, he would simply leave the Obsidiar to maintain the energy shield. At which point, the ES *Lucid* would become something of a juggernaut.

"Lieutenant Cruz is on her way, sir."

"Good. Next step is for you to contact Fleet Admiral Duggan. Use override code 23Blake-162C. Let him know our situation and ask what his orders are."

A few seconds later: "Fleet Admiral Duggan wants to speak to you."

"Don't keep him waiting."

The Admiral's voice reached the bridge, projected through a series of speakers so that it seemed to float in the midpoint of the bridge, just in front of the captain's console. Duggan didn't waste time on niceties or pointless details. His voice was strong and clear.

"Captain Edwards. How confident are you?"

"I'm not familiar with the *Lucid*, sir and I'm lacking a full crew. I will be able to achieve lightspeed once we break out of the Tillos bunker. If ordered to, I will engage the enemy."

"You have avoided answering my question. How confident are *you*?"

Blake cursed his mistake. With men like Duggan, you responded to exactly what they'd asked, not the question you thought they'd asked.

"Sir, I'm very confident. Some have told me I am too confident."

"Captain Kang was scathing of your efforts."

Blake sensed a test in the words. Everyone knew tales about Admiral Duggan's exploits in the Ghast and Estral wars. He was a fighter, not a diplomat.

"Captain Kang fled the scene, ensuring our defeat and the deaths of many of our personnel. If I see him, I will punch his teeth out."

"What do the Vraxar want?"

"They need us, sir. They do something to the bodies of the races they conquer to make new Vraxar. It's their only way to survive."

"Then we face all-out war."

"Victory or extinction, sir. There will be no inbetween."

"Atlantis is already doomed, but I will not abandon the people. Destroy the Vraxar, Captain Blake. Free Atlantis and buy us some time."

"Yes, sir."

The connection ended. Blake turned at the beeping sound of the bridge door activating. Lieutenant Cruz arrived, supported by Sergeant McKinney on one side and the squad's stand-in medic Armand Grover on the other.

"How are you feeling, Lieutenant Cruz?"

"Absolutely outstanding, sir!"

"That'll wear off in a few hours," said Grover. He lifted up a portable med-box. "It's given her something of everything, I reckon. On top of that it filled her with her so much battlefield adrenaline, she could probably carry the *Lucid* home on her shoulders."

"Don't exaggerate," said Cruz.

"Take a seat, Lieutenant. You're on the comms."

"Sir?"

"Sit." He checked the status of the engines. "You've got approximately two minutes to familiarise yourself with our comms and sensor arrays. It shouldn't hold any surprises."

Cruz hopped over and sat.

"I can help you out," said Pointer. "Look at this screen here, this is where you..."

"You did a year as weapons ensign, didn't you, Lieutenant?" said Blake, cutting in.

"Yes, sir." She hesitated, struggling with pride. "I failed and got shifted to comms. There're a lot more openings in comms than weapons."

"Now's your chance to prove how wrong they were to fail you. I need you to take some of the load, so get onto the weapons console."

She blinked.

"Do it now!"

Pointer did as she was asked and her eyes darted this way and that over the different screens, while Blake reminded her of the important details.

"Remember the Lambdas and Shatterers failed to target reliably during our previous engagement, so you'll need to instruct the Bulwark tracking system to aim at anything hostile, rather than just missiles."

"Yes, sir."

Grover appeared at Blake's shoulder, holding a flexible tube with a fat needle at one end. The man raised an eyebrow in question. Blake nodded and the medic shoved the needle into his thigh.

"This will act as a temporary flush for that radiation, sir," he whispered.

Blake felt a large quantity of fluid enter his blood. He tried to ignore it and continued addressing Lieutenant Pointer. "The *Lucid* has two first-gen Shimmer launchers, which the *New Beginning* lacked. Keep your fingers crossed they target more reliably than the other missile systems."

"Yes, sir."

"We have four particle beams. The front and rear ones will overcharge. Don't fire the overcharge unless I tell you – it'll likely knock off a chunk of our power reserves. We've got an eight-bank disruptor chain with a two hundred thousand klick range. That's going to do the same thing to our power gauge as the particle beams."

"Yes, sir."

Pointer looked dazed. It wasn't an ideal situation and the Space Corps didn't normally let semi-trained officers loose on their newest heavy cruisers and particularly not the ones with New Earth's GDP worth of Obsidiar in the hold. Blake couldn't handle everything himself and he hoped Pointer and Cruz would rise to the occasion.

"Lieutenant Cruz, how are you doing?"

"I'm good, sir! Most of this onboard kit is familiar, with a few boosters and extra top-secret options."

"What exactly did that med-box give her?" he asked Grover quietly.

"It judged her in need of some mood-enhancers as well as everything else, sir," he replied, equally quietly. "She could be the most miserable bastard in the fleet and you'd never know it."

Wondering what he was getting himself into, Blake waved Grover away to perform a radiation flush on Pointer and Cruz. He was beginning to feel light-headed himself and considered asking if the med-box had decided Captain Blake was also in need of some mood-enhancers.

"Better to die happy," he muttered.

The gravity engines finished their warm-up procedures and just in time.

"The ship's sensors are reporting a series of explosions on the surface above us," said Cruz. "I'm certain that's what these codes are telling me."

Blake cursed. "They're looking for the *Lucid*. The Vraxar warships must have got the message there's something down here and they've decided to blow us up."

"They've missed," said Pointer.

"The bunker is shielded. I imagine there's some trial and error involved in locating us."

"There's a lot going on," said Cruz. "Hundreds of explosions."

"We're going, before they get lucky," said Blake. "Sergeant McKinney, Medic Grover, I suggest you get to quarters."

The two men hurried off, while Blake cobbled together his thoughts. "Lieutenant Pointer, please target the bay doors above us with a grid pattern of thirty Lambda missiles. Don't question it and launch at once. The explosion won't significantly harm the *Lucid* from this distance."

Pointer responded with impressive speed. "They've fired."

"Upper sensor feed shows the bunker doors are still intact, sir. There was no explosion."

It took Blake a moment to understand. "We're too close, The Lambda warheads don't activate for a short time after they exit the launch cluster. To prevent accidents."

"The Vraxar missile strikes are coming closer, sir," said Cruz. "I wouldn't like to be on the surface."

"What do we do?" asked Pointer.

"We'll have to break out through the roof," said Blake.

The ship's autopilot wouldn't countenance what he planned without going through numerous overrides. With time running out, Blake took hold of the *Lucid*'s manual control rods. There wasn't much of a gap between the spaceship and the walls, but in theory it should lift off at an exact vertical if the pilot used the control bars correctly.

"Here goes nothing."

The *ES Lucid*'s engines vibrated as power flowed through them. The sound reverberated within the hangar, setting furniture throughout the complex buzzing in sympathy. A gap appeared between the ground and the landing feet – first a few inches, then several metres. The warship's wedge-shaped nose crunched partway through the opening into the storage area, smashing away several hundred tonnes of metal and wall. A contact warning bleeped on Blake's console.

There was no point in trying to fine-tune the spaceship's position. Instead, Blake went for broke. He hauled on the control stick, feeling it glide through its slot with the perfect amount of resistance. The *ES Lucid* climbed, creating a wide, rough gouge in the hangar bay wall as it went. It struck the underside of the bunker doors, pushing them outwards and buckling the alloy. The *Lucid* had a tremendous amount of inertia, but the bay doors were thick, solid and designed to soak up repeated missile strikes.

In the cockpit, the crew felt little more than a slight shaking though the floor – the life support systems on a fleet warship could shield the occupants from more or less anything this side of a hull breach.

"They're holding," said Blake. "I'm being too damned cautious."

He tried again and power coursed through the gravity engines. This time, the *Lucid* accelerated upwards at a tremendous rate. It crashed through the doors, bending them upwards and ripping one of them completely free of it gears. A series of sonic booms followed, their sound joining with the storm of plasma outside.

"Oh, shit," said Cruz.

The already-damaged Tillos airfield was no longer an expanse of torn and cratered concrete. Now it was a furious sea of plasma fires, from which tendrils of white flame reached into the sky. In the briefest of instants during which Blake was able to look at the external sensor feeds, he saw a thousand additional explosions adding their own unquenchable anger to the tempest.

The onslaught was greater than Blake was expecting. The *Lucid*'s energy shield was turned off in an attempt to conserve the Obsidiar core's energy until it was needed most. Consequently, there was nothing to stop two of the Vraxar missiles striking the warship's rear section as it rose at immense speed from the flames. The missiles detonated, tearing deep holes into the heavy cruiser's armour plating.

"We're meant to soak," Blake muttered.

He threw the control bars forward and the *ES Lucid*'s gargantuan engines threw it away from the surface. The planet Atlantis fell rapidly behind as the spaceship reached maximum gravity drive velocity. *Two-thousand one hundred klicks per second,* Blake saw on the gauge. *Obsidiar power already down to ninety-five percent.*

"I can see some Vraxar ships," said Cruz.

Under her guidance, the *Lucid*'s sensors detected the enemy and sent the data to Blake's tactical screen. "Three of their mid-sized ships," he said. "Where are the others?"

"And most importantly, where's the Neutraliser?" asked Pointer.

"Three will do for the moment, Lieutenant."

"Are you going to activate the stealth modules, sir?"

"There's no point. They know we're coming."

Rather than seeking to escape, Captain Charlie Blake aimed the *ES Lucid* directly towards the enemy warships. He felt no fear, only an all-consuming desire to destroy everything they sent at him. In his head were the beginnings of a plan – something he hoped might turn the tables as long as he could pull it off.

CHAPTER TWENTY-EIGHT

THE THREE VRAXAR warships made no attempt to get away. Originally stationary above the Tillos base, now they accelerated rapidly towards the *ES Lucid*. The odds weren't great, but with the energy shield available, Blake had hopes the heavy cruiser would do more than bloody the Vraxar noses.

"Give it your best, folks. I can't ask for anything more. Don't spread our firepower. I've assigned a target already - we hit it until it breaks up."

"Yes, sir."

"Target Shimmer missiles and fire."

There was no launch and he heard Pointer banging her fist angrily onto her console. "They're locked down," she said. "The battle computer tells me I don't have the required authority to commit this resource."

"Shit," said Blake. "I was relying on giving them a trial run."

He'd only read the spec sheets on the Shimmer missiles and never flown on a ship which had them equipped. The warheads were fitted with an Obsidiar guidance chip and carried a monumentally high payload. Each missile was so expensive it was rumoured Fleet Admiral Duggan had to personally sign approval for them - one at a time.

There was a good chance Blake could override the lock on the Shimmers. In other circumstances, he would have been delighted to attempt it. However, with the Vraxar ships closing fast, his efforts were needed elsewhere. Putting his irritation to one side, he checked the range between the *Lucid* and the Vraxar. It wouldn't be long until they could target and fire the rest of the cruiser's arsenal.

"The Bulwarks are activating," said Pointer.

With those words, it started. Fifty-two of the *Lucid*'s Bulwarks had line of sight and they emerged through the armour and began firing at once, sending a high-velocity stream of slugs towards the target Vraxar warship. The enemy craft began evasive manoeuvres, twisting and rotating, while the *Lucid*'s battle computer tried to predict and adjust.

"Fire whatever Shatterers and Lambdas will target."

"I'm trying, sir. There – sixty Lambdas away and seven Shatterers."

"I'm loading up for a short-range transit. Holding on three of our cores. Ready in less than twenty seconds."

Blake was already struggling with the amount of incoming data and again he cursed Lieutenant Rivera for his actions on the *Determinant*. That fourth officer would make all the difference. In the absence, Blake had to keep an eye on damage reports as well as manage the SRTs and attempt the rerouting if any major system failed.

"There's the enemy," said Cruz, locking the sensors onto it at last. "It's jumping about like crazy."

It was another of the tapered cylinders. With faint satisfaction, Blake noticed the Bulwark scars across its hull from the earlier confrontation with Response Fleet Alpha.

"This time you're not getting away to lightspeed."

He activated the *Lucid*'s energy shield in anticipation of what was to come. An invisible barrier sprung into existence, encompassing the entire ship and coming no closer than a few hundred metres from the hull.

The Vraxar ship had no intention of breaking off. High-intensity particle beams jumped out from its batteries. They struck the *Lucid*'s energy shield, which dissipated the attacks, keeping the warship unharmed.

"Obsidiar core down to eighty percent already."

"We've had five confirmed Shatterer impacts on the enemy's shield," said Pointer. "Plus a further sixteen Lambda hits and approximately eighteen thousand Bulwark strikes."

A good engine tech officer would likely be able to predict how close to failure the Vraxar shield was. *Stop it,* Blake told himself.

"There's something coming from the third Vraxar ship," said Cruz. "This one looks different to the others. Missiles! It's missiles! Four hundred!"

This Vraxar ship hadn't been in the previous engagement. Blake guessed its main use was surface bombardment and the missiles it launched travelled comparatively slowly. It seemed the Vraxar weren't ahead in every field.

"Splinter countermeasures away," said Pointer.

Splinter interceptors raced away at forty thousand kilometres per second, seeking to collide with whatever their guidance systems identified as a threat.

"Divert Bulwarks to the incoming missiles," ordered Blake. "Drop shock drones."

"Done."

At Lieutenant Pointer's command, shock drones spilled out in their thousands. The drones spewed forth an ever-changing stream of signals and white noise, intended to confuse or jam enemy weapons systems. Meanwhile, their circular, reflective bodies flashed with lights along every wavelength.

The wave of enemy missiles closed on the *Lucid*. Dozens of them were intercepted by the Splinter countermeasures, whilst dozens more were punched from the sky by the Bulwark cannons. Many of the remaining missiles detonated fruitlessly into the shock drone cloud. A few came through and they exploded against the *Lucid*'s energy shield, depleting the gauge further.

"Eight missiles got through," said Pointer.

"I have detected two more enemy warships coming around the edge of Atlantis," said Cruz. "Heading towards us. Where else would they be headed, I suppose?"

"Keep focus, Lieutenant. I don't need the fluff."

"Sorry, sir."

"More Lambdas on their way," said Pointer.

Blake spent precious seconds studying his tactical screen. The two new Vraxar arrivals were approaching from a clockwise direction, pursuing the *Lucid* as it travelled anti-clockwise around Atlantis. It was a pincer movement, albeit a clumsy one. As he watched, one of the new Vraxar warships vanished into a short lightspeed jump and reappeared less than twenty thousand kilometres from the *Lucid*. It fired immediately.

"That's a big chunk out of our shield," said Blake.

Mindful of his instruction to focus on a single target, Blake ignored this new, closer threat. Instead, he moved the control bars, bringing the *Lucid* sharply away from Atlantis. The Vraxar immediately changed course to follow. The extra strain on the engines caused the Obsidiar reserves to trickle steadily downwards. The power core could maintain the ship at idle for a lifetime. Once the fighting started, every single action drew a little more from the source.

Wherever the Neutraliser was hiding, they needed to get far enough away for the Gallenium engines to fire up again.

"Overcharge the front particle beam and fire."

"Firing."

The overcharge capability was tech stolen from the Estral decades past. It was slow-firing and with a low range. It was also devastating. In the blinking of an eye, the target Vraxar ship became white hot and exploded, sending huge pieces of metal spinning away from the centre at an enormous speed.

Blake growled in triumph and activated one of the three short-range transits. The *ES Lucid* entered high lightspeed for somewhat less than one hundredth of a second and then emerged, with Atlantis far behind.

"Far enough for them to see us, not so far the Neutraliser can keep us offline."

"Shouldn't we be targeting the big one first?" asked Cruz.

"I need sensor reports, Lieutenant! Not questions!" He saw Cruz flinch and realised he was being too hard on her. "You're doing great," he said without the edge to his voice. "You just need to keep razor-sharp on those comms and sensors."

"Yes, sir."

While Cruz got on with it, Blake took stock. His heart leapt.

"I'm getting a power feed from the Gallenium," he said. As if glad to be free of the suppression, the available power climbed rapidly. An automatic switchover process diverted the Obsidiar core away from the engines, life support and targeting systems, until it only maintained the energy shields and the overcharge units on the particle beam. It gave them a chance.

Cruz didn't take long. It seemed she had talent and training, only lacking in experience. "All four Vraxar warships are back where we left them. Approximate range: seven million klicks."

"As soon as they find us, they'll do a synchronised lightspeed jump towards us and do their best to blow us to pieces."

"We're not going to let them," said Pointer.

"Not if we play our cards right."

The Vraxar came suddenly. They disappeared from high Atlantis orbit and reappeared within a hundred thousand kilometres of the *ES Lucid* before Lieutenant Cruz could do so much as open her mouth again. The Vraxar were evidently familiar with overcharged particle beams and they kept at a distance – close enough to fire their own weapons, but too far for Lieutenant Pointer to activate the weapon a second time.

The onslaught against the *ES Lucid*'s energy shield began immediately. Vraxar particle beams and missiles were joined by bolts of dark energy. Each strike wore down the *Lucid*'s energy shield, hacking chunks away.

In return, the heavy cruiser launched its own missiles in sporadic waves. Bulwark projectiles flew across the intervening space, striking at the shield of Blake's second designated target. Countermeasures spilled out as quickly as they could reload, tracking and destroying the Vraxar missiles.

With the main power source back online, there was less need to worry about running out of power for the many onboard systems. It wasn't enough - the *ES Lucid* was one of the most advanced, powerful warships in the Space Corps and it was being gradually overwhelmed.

"Our energy shield is almost gone," said Blake. "Give our target an eight-chain disruptor strike."

"Firing."

A disruptor was an old weapon, first used by the Ghasts long ago. When directed against a vessel with a single, slow core, a disruptor could shut the whole spaceship down for many seconds. Gradually, newer, faster and multiple-cored spaceships made the weapon nearly obsolete since the effects could be shrugged off almost at once. A disruptor chain relied on firing a perfectly-timed series of attacks to keep the enemy locked down for longer and was designed to be effective against all but the most advanced processing cores. If it worked, the Vraxar ship would be without its shield.

A critical alert flashed across his console. Firing the disruptor chain had overloaded one of the cores already primed for an SRT and it was shutting down. *Seven additional cores still operational.*

The disruptor chain worked. The Vraxar's energy shield went offline at the precise moment three high-impact Shatterer missiles arrived. The warheads buried through several metres of armour and exploded, creating a line of deep, overlapping craters. Bulwark fire pummelled into the softer engine matter beneath.

"Firing the front two particle beams – normal discharge," said Pointer, her voice admirably calm.

As soon as he heard those words, Blake hauled the ES *Lucid* around in a tight arc. The gravity drives rumbled as almost four thousand metres of solid Gallenium spaceship twisted through an impossibly sharp turn. Blake's head thumped with pain.

"Firing the rear two particle beams – normal discharge."

The sensor feed showed extensive damage to the Vraxar ship. Patches of orange encircled the missile craters in its hull, becoming blue-white deeper inside its hull. It was certainly out of commission and thirty Bulwark cannons continued their bombardment. A second later, the enemy warship broke into two pieces. A dozen Lambda X missiles plunged into the widening gap, their explosions covering the irregular surfaces with plasma. All the while, thousands of Gallenium slugs drilled into the Vraxar hull.

"Upper Bulwarks sixteen and nineteen have overheated and shut down," said Pointer. "Twelve more have exceeded their design tolerances."

"We have no option other than to keep them active," said Blake. "Switching target to the next enemy warship."

Two more dark energy beams hit the *Lucid*. The Obsidiar power gauge fell to zero and flashed red.

"I think we're out of tricks," he said.

This was the point at which a wise captain would cut and run – activate the final pre-loaded lightspeed jump and break off the engagement, taking two confirmed kills and a mostly-intact heavy cruiser back to the shipyard for repairs.

Captain Charlie Blake and his stand-in crew didn't have that choice. They were the only ones in a position to do anything for the billions of people still on Atlantis and the only ones able to stop the Vraxar making off with the wreck of the *ES Determinant*.

The engagement became a messy punchout with no finesse. The *ES Lucid* continued to spit out Lambda X missiles – sometimes twenty at once, occasionally more than a hundred. The Shatterers targeted marginally better and they flew out in fours or sixes from the heavy cruiser's eight launch tubes. Their reload was slow and it was frustrating to wait.

Meanwhile, Vraxar particle beams and waves of dark energy washed across the *ES Lucid*'s hull. This generation of Galactic was designed for precisely this kind of warfare. The heat from the particle beams was carried away and dispersed. Where an older ship would have been quickly reduced to a molten sludge the *Lucid* kept going, refusing to accept defeat.

The dark energy was a different problem. There was no way to analyse it during the battle, but the damage it wrought wasn't caused by heat. This was something new and even the *Lucid*'s AI couldn't offer up an exact answer as to what it was. The weapon was as filthy as the Vraxar themselves and where it struck, millions of tonnes of alloy and Gallenium simply crumbled away, scattering into clouds of abrasive dust.

As the battle went on, it occurred to Blake that he'd unwittingly tricked the Vraxar into fighting to the *ES Lucid*'s strengths.

They were smaller ships and evidently accustomed to seeing their enemies succumb to beam weapons, whilst the Vraxar hid behind their energy shields. When it came to it, the *Lucid* carried a little bit of everything – missiles, high-velocity cannons, energy weapons and countermeasures, so it had an answer to most situations. On top of this, it was designed to absorb as much damage as a full battleship. Bit-by-bit, Space Corps brute force was starting to turn the tide away from defeat.

"Yes!" shouted Pointer.

The third Vraxar ship broke apart, its energy shield spent and its hull riven with Bulwark fire and plasma craters.

"Come on!" roared Blake.

The *ES Lucid* was battered and two-thirds of its hull was burning, leaving a trail of orange and sparkling flashes of crumbled Gallenium as it sped through space.

There were still two opponents and they must have sensed victory simply by the appearance of the *Lucid*'s hull. Two more particle beam strikes hit the mid-section of the heavy cruiser.

"It's going to get hot in here soon," said Blake. "That's right above us."

"I've detected something big way back near Atlantis," said Cruz. "It's accompanied by a single smaller vessel."

"The mothership, come to rescue her babies," said Blake.

"Disruptor chain fired."

The disruptors were becoming less effective with each use – it was expected. The Space Corps built special routines into their warship cores to combat just such attacks, so it was logical the Vraxar – a species much more practised in war – would do likewise.

"Got one particle beam through before their shield came back online," said Pointer.

Blake looked at the Obsidiar power gauge. It had climbed to three percent – not enough for an overcharged particle beam strike. On the adjacent tactical screen, the Neutraliser glowed a dangerous red, assigned a threat level of ninety-nine by the battle computer. It was eighteen thousand metres of unknown alien tech that could shut down an entire planet. *We can't beat it. Not a hope in hell.*

His finger hovered over the activation for the last available short-range transit. The Neutraliser disappeared from Atlantis orbit and reappeared close to the scene of the *ES Lucid*'s engagement. With a sense of anticipation and reflexes far beyond the human norm, Blake used the SRT.

"Where are we?" asked Pointer.

"Back at Atlantis," said Cruz. "At an altitude of ten thousand kilometres."

"We were told to fight," said Blake. "I'm buying us some time."

"The Neutraliser is still back where it jumped," said Cruz. "Along with three other Vraxar vessels."

"It won't be long until they come for us," said Blake. "We need to locate the *Determinant*."

There was a part of him knew it was already far too late – that the Vraxar lifter had taken the wreckage away and up to the mothership. Seeing the truth on the sensor feed didn't make him feel any better.

"Gone."

"Most of its arrays were burned out," said Pointer.

"You know how they work these things, Lieutenant. Ten copies of everything."

"Yeah."

"There'll be plenty of stuff on the *Determinant* that we don't want them to see."

"We did our best. Like you wanted."

"That we did. Where's the Neutraliser?"

"Same place, sir."

"Are you ready to go down fighting?"

"Is there a choice?"

"No."

The Neutraliser disappeared from the tactical screen, along with the three remaining escorts. Blake waited for it to reappear and crush them with whatever incredibly powerful weapons he was sure it was packing. He counted five seconds before he allowed himself to accept the truth.

"They've gone," he said.

"Where?"

"Who knows? They came for intel and they got plenty of it. They'll dig through the *Determinant*'s arrays and pull out whatever takes their fancy. Then, they'll come back, except this time it won't be with a handful of ships. They'll come with hundreds – a Neutraliser for each of our planets."

"And they'll turn us into Vraxar," said Pointer.

"Unless we can stop them."

"Sir?" said Cruz. "I've got Fleet Admiral Duggan on the comms."

"Bring him through," sighed Blake. "Someone's got to tell him the bad news."

CHAPTER TWENTY-NINE

WHEN HIS CONVERSATION with Admiral Duggan was finished, Blake spent a short time in thought, whilst trying to ignore the insistent chiming of a dozen separate damage alerts on his console. The results of the previous day were catching up, leaving him hungry, thirsty and tired. On top of that, he was starting to feel wretched and weak, something he attributed to either the onset of radiation sickness or the aftereffects of the Vraxar truth drug.

"I think I should get Grover back up here," he said. "And where's the closest food replicator?"

"I've got Sergeant McKinney asking for you on the internal comms," said Pointer.

"Is it important?"

"He thinks it might be."

"Where is he?"

"Waiting outside the bridge."

Blake smiled and ordered the bridge door to open. "Sergeant McKinney. We have driven the Vraxar away, yet on balance we have suffered a defeat."

McKinney was clearly agitated. "Sir, you need to hear this."

There was another of the squad with him.

"Comms Trooper Bannerman," said Blake.

Bannerman came forward, carrying his field pack with reverence.

"I've received a comms message from a civilian on Atlantis, sir – just a few minutes ago. A man called Jerry Greiner – he used to be in the Corps, so I guess that's how he managed to connect to a military field pack. It's the second time he got through – the first time we were still on Tillos."

The soldier was dithering, but Blake could see there was something important coming. "What did Mr. Greiner want?"

"He's stranded out on the Plangaean Sea. On a boat."

Blake wasn't unsympathetic to the plight of an old man lost at sea. "We can't rescue him. The *Lucid*'s hull is far too hot to launch a shuttle. The power is returning on Atlantis. If his boat won't start I can request someone on the surface goes looking for him as soon as they are able."

"No, sir. He says the Vraxar dropped something in the water. Something really big. He sent me the coordinates of it."

Blake felt a chill run up his spine. "Did he say exactly what it looked like?"

"A big metal cube a few hundred metres along each side, carried by a larger vessel."

"I need those coordinates. Transmit them to the *Lucid* immediately."

"I sent them while I was waiting for the bridge door to open."

With a sense of impending dread, Blake turned in his seat and accessed the list of recently-received coordinate data. The location was a third of the way around the planet, seventy or eighty kilometres offshore.

"Lieutenant Pointer, target those coordinates and launch clusters 1F and 2F."

"Missiles locked on. Launched."

The *Lucid* was at an altitude of twenty thousand kilometres. Forty Lambda X missiles exited the frontmost batteries, accelerating rapidly to their maximum speed of three-thousand five hundred kilometres per second. The crew and soldiers watched a sensor feed on the front bulkhead screen, which showed the faint trails of the missiles as they sped off around the curvature of Atlantis.

The heavy cruiser wasn't nearly so fast, but Blake followed the path of the Lambdas. The *Lucid* groaned as its overstressed hull took the load of another bout of high acceleration.

Far ahead, the missiles plunged into the Plangaean Sea, their armour-piercing warheads designed to survive such an impact. At a depth of eighteen hundred metres they struck the Vraxar object and exploded, tearing it to pieces and destroying the unusual array of components held within. The surface of the Plangaean ruptured outwards and upwards in a spray of scalding steam, water and dead fish.

A few kilometres away, the still-drifting Jerry Greiner caught sight of the fountaining water and nodded to himself.

DECISIONS

Fleet Admiral Duggan faced the gathered members of the Confederation Council through his wall-mounted viewscreen. Unused to scrutiny they averted their eyes, as though they could feel the waves of his fury buffeting them.

"I will have what I need," he stated simply.

"Yes, Admiral. You will have what you need," said Councillor Stahl. "We are fully aware of your plans to utilise the Obsidiar reserves anyway."

"They were needed for our defence!"

"Indeed," said Councillor Newport. "We had hoped the Space Corps would be able to face the Vraxar without Obsidiar. It is apparent we were mistaken." He made it sound like the failing was Duggan's.

Perhaps it is, he thought. "The funding must continue. The research labs in particular must have no constraints. We cannot be so vulnerable to these Neutraliser vessels."

"You will have the funding you require," said Councillor Dawson. The next words were a struggle for him, even in the circumstances. "Unlimited funding. With the usual oversight, of course."

"How long will it take the Vraxar to analyse the *ES Determinant*'s data arrays?" asked Stahl.

"I have teams figuring it out. The early best guesses range from a month to five years."

"Somewhere in between, then?"

"It won't be five years," said Duggan with certainty. "It won't even be two."

"We have new hulls in the shipyards?" asked Dawson. "Even during peacetime there is an ongoing programme?"

"You are correct. We are switching every yard to an around-the-clock shift."

"There's something you are not telling us, Fleet Admiral."

"I won't pull my punches, Councillor Watanabe. The Vraxar defeated the Estral, whom we know conquered thousands of worlds. The Confederation does not have the resources of fifty worlds, let alone thousands. It may be that the Vraxar deem us a minor prize – unimportant to their wider goals. Even if we assume that to be the case, we can be sure when they come next it will be with a crushing, overwhelming force."

There were grimaces and looks of discomfort at this highly unpleasant truth.

"What do you suggest, Admiral?"

"And what of Atlantis?"

"We need to convince the Ghasts. This is their fight as well as ours. As for Atlantis? The only solution I can think of is evacuation. We have sufficient capacity on our Interstellars."

"Evacuation is something we cannot agree to with a click of the fingers," said Kemp. "You can understand this?"

"I can understand," said Duggan truthfully.

"We will provide you with our decision shortly. As for the

Ghasts – you may approach your opposite number once again and inform him there may be some flexibility in our position."

"In the meantime, please begin the process of bringing the Interstellars back online. I'm sure it won't be so easy to enact as it is for me to speak the words," said Watanabe.

"Indeed it won't be easy," said Duggan. "Most of the carriers are still on the rebel planets Roban and Liventor from the time they were first populated. There is much for me to do, gentlemen. The rebellion on our frontier has not gone away and we have a new, proven enemy seeking mankind's annihilation. Perhaps we could reconvene twelve hours from now?"

The agreement was made and the viewscreen went blank. For the first time he could remember, Duggan was hopeful the Confederation Council would be able to put their squabbling to one side and provide their full backing and support to the military.

There was a report on his desk – printed out in hard copy the way he liked it. He opened it and checked the summary from the *ES Lucid*'s in-depth scan of the wrecked Vraxar object. The mysterious cube wasn't intended to explode and fracture the core of Atlantis in order to facilitate the formation of Obsidiar, that much was certain.

The current best guess was more unpleasant if that were possible. The Vraxar object was some kind of reactor with its own advanced power source. Some of the tech was similar to that found within the Confederation and long-since banned. The Space Corps' best scientists believed the intention was to turn the Plangaean Sea into a gas of some type. It was certainly intended to kill everyone on Atlantis and it was this which had finally shocked the Confederation Council into full cooperation. Other than that, many questions remained unanswered.

Fleet Admiral Duggan put the report to one side. The events on Atlantis had decided his future for the next several years or more. He sighed and ran fingers through his short-cropped hair. A time of turmoil had come and he was starting to feel he might not be the man to handle it.

———

Follow Anthony James on Facebook at
facebook.com/AnthonyJamesAuthor

ALSO BY ANTHONY JAMES

The Survival Wars series

1. Crimson Tempest

2. Bane of Worlds

3. Chains of Duty

4. Fires of Oblivion

5. Terminus Gate

6. Guns of the Valpian

7. Mission: Nemesis

Printed in Great Britain
by Amazon